The Porcelain Fish Mystery

A
Detective Simon Brade Mystery

By Harriette R. Campbell

Originally published in 1937

The Porcelain Fish Mystery

Published by Resurrected Press

This classic book was handcrafted by Resurrected Press. Resurrected Press is dedicated to bringing high quality classic books back to the readers who enjoy them. These are not scanned versions of the originals, but, rather, quality checked and edited books meant to be enjoyed!

Please visit ResurrectedPress.com to view our entire catalogue!

For updates on future releases, LIKE us on Facebook:
http://www.Facebook.com/ResurrectedPress

ISBN 13: 978-1-943403-22-6

Printed in the United States of America

Resurrected Press books in A. E. Fielding's
The Chief Inspector Pointer Mystery **Series**

RESURRECTED PRESS BOOKS IN ELAINE
HAMILTON'S *INSPECTOR REYNOLDS OF
SCOTLAND YARD* SERIES

Peril at Midnight (1934)
Tragedy in the Dark (1935)
The Casino Mystery (1936)
Murder Before Tuesday (1937)

MYSTERIES FROM THE JAMES "BONNIE" DUNDEE
MYSTERY SERIES BY ANNE AUSTIN

The Black Pigeon
The Avenging Parrot
Murder Backstairs
Murder at Bridge
One Drop of Blood
Murdered, But Not Dead

AVAILABLE FROM RESURRECTED PRESS!

BRITISH WOMEN OF MYSTERY
Three Novels Penned by
Women of the Golden Age of Mysteries

Three Full Length Novels in One!

- **Whose Body by Dorothy L. Sayers**
- **The Westminster Mystery by Elaine Hamilton**
- **The Clifford Affair by A. E. Fielding**

Prior to World War I, detective fiction in Britain was largely a male preserve, but in the period between the wars—an era that has been called the Golden Age of British Mysteries—women authors in Britain not only embraced the genre, but came to dominate it. Authors such as Sayers, Allingham, Marsh not to mention the great Agatha Christie topped the best sellers lists, but there were numerous other women writers working to satisfy the public's demand for mystery fiction. Unfortunately, many of these authors are virtually unknown today. This volume brings together the first mystery novel of one of the best known of these writers, Dorothy L. Sayers' Whose Body?, along with novels by two of the lesser known women of the period, Elaine Hamilton's The Westminster Mystery and A. E. Fielding's The Clifford Affair, in the hopes that it will serve as an introduction to the British Women of Mystery.

RESURRECTED PRESS CLASSIC MYSTERY CATALOGUE

Journeys into Mystery
Travel and Mystery in a More Elegant Time

The Edwardian Detectives
Literary Sleuths of the Edwardian Era

Gems of Mystery
Lost Jewels from a More Elegant Age

Anne Austin
One Drop of Blood
The Black Pigeon
Murder at Bridge

E. C. Bentley
Trent's Last Case: The Woman in Black

Ernest Bramah
Max Carrados Resurrected:
The Detective Stories of Max Carrados

Agatha Christie
The Secret Adversary
The Mysterious Affair at Styles

Octavus Roy Cohen
Midnight

Freeman Wills Croft
The Ponson Case
The Pit Prop Syndicate

J. S. Fletcher
The Herapath Property
The Rayner-Slade Amalgamation
The Chestermarke Instinct
The Paradise Mystery
Dead Men's Money
The Middle of Things
Ravensdene Court
Scarhaven Keep
The Orange-Yellow Diamond
The Middle Temple Murder
The Tallyrand Maxim
The Borough Treasurer
In the Mayor's Parlour
The Saftey Pin

R. Austin Freeman
*The Mystery of 31 New Inn from the Dr. Thorndyke
Series*
*John Thorndyke's Cases from the Dr. Thorndyke
Series*
The Red Thumb Mark from The Dr. Thorndyke Series
The Eye of Osiris from The Dr. Thorndyke Series
A Silent Witness from the Dr. John Thorndyke Series
The Cat's Eye from the Dr. John Thorndyke Series
*Helen Vardon's Confession: A Dr. John Thorndyke
Story*
As a Thief in the Night: A Dr. John Thorndyke Story
*Mr. Pottermack's Oversight: A Dr. John Thorndyke
Story*
*Dr. Thorndyke Intervenes: A Dr. John Thorndyke
Story*
The Singing Bone: The Adventures of Dr. Thorndyke
The Stoneware Monkey: A Dr. John Thorndyke Story
*The Great Portrait Mystery, and Other Stories: A
Collection of Dr. John Thorndyke and Other Stories*
The Penrose Mystery: A Dr. John Thorndyke Story

The Uttermost Farthing: A Savant's Vendetta

Arthur Griffiths
The Passenger From Calais
The Rome Express

Fergus Hume
The Mystery of a Hansom Cab
The Green Mummy
The Silent House
The Secret Passage

Edgar Jepson
The Loudwater Mystery

A. E. W. Mason
At the Villa Rose

A. A. Milne
The Red House Mystery

Baroness Emma Orczy
The Old Man in the Corner

Edgar Allan Poe
The Detective Stories of Edgar Allan Poe

Arthur J. Rees
The Hampstead Mystery
The Shrieking Pit
The Hand In The Dark
The Moon Rock
The Mystery of the Downs

Mary Roberts Rinehart
Sight Unseen and The Confession

Dorothy L. Sayers

Whose Body?

Sir William Magnay
The Hunt Ball Mystery

Mabel and Paul Thorne
The Sheridan Road Mystery

Louis Tracy
The Strange Case of Mortimer Fenley
The Albert Gate Mystery
The Bartlett Mystery
The Postmaster's Daughter
The House of Peril
The Sandling Case: What Would You Have Done?

Charles Edmonds Walk
The Paternoster Ruby

John R. Watson
The Mystery of the Downs
The Hampstead Mystery

Edgar Wallace
The Daffodil Mystery
The Crimson Circle

Carolyn Wells
Vicky Van
The Man Who Fell Through the Earth
In the Onyx Lobby
Raspberry Jam
The Clue
The Room with the Tassels
The Vanishing of Betty Varian
The Mystery Girl
The White Alley
The Curved Blades

Anybody but Anne
The Bride of a Moment
Faulkner's Folly
The Diamond Pin
The Gold Bag
The Mystery of the Sycamore
The Come Back

Raoul Whitfield
Death in a Bowl

And much more!
Visit ResurrectedPress.com
for our complete catalogue

FOREWORD

Though an American, Harriette R. Campbell set the
series of novels featuring her reluctant detective Simon
Brade and his friend the psychiatrist Dr. "Jerry" Jerrold
in Britain. The novels are prime examples of the
mysteries that were written in the period between the
World Wars, a era that has been called "The Golden Age
of British Mysteries." The mysteries of this period relied
more on wit than violence, and usually involved a strong
puzzle element meant to challenge the reader as much as
the detective.

Simon Brade is an amateur detective whose is much
more interested in Chinese porcelain than crime,
especially murder. In *The Porcelain Fish Mystery*, he is
down at Medbury Grange, ostensibly to examine a rather
ugly example of San Ts'ai porcelain made in the image of
a fish, but really to consult on a matter with Selford
Prentice, the owner of the Grange. However, when
Selford is found murdered in his sitting room, the local
police ask Brade to investigate.

Though in many ways a typical British "country
house" mystery, with the usual cast of family members,
employers and domestic staff, the story is set against a
backdrop of politics, as the murdered man and several of
his family members are involved in socialist politics,
including his son, Maurice, who is running for parliament
and seems destined for higher office. His nephew, Tom
Prentice, on the other hand, is mainly concerned with
country matters, namely horses, hounds, and the hunt.

The investigation reveals that a number of those
present at the time of the murder had a motive as well as
a number of them who had the opportunity.
Unfortunately, to the consternation of the police, none of
the suspects had both motive *and* opportunity. It also
becomes evident that more than one member of the
household is hiding a secret that may be pertinent to the

case. In the end, the best witness to the crime may be Chen, the murdered man's Cairn Terrier.

As with a number of mysteries from the era, international politics plays a role in *The Porcelain Fish Mystery*. Europe was in a particularly unsettled state, with the Communists taking brutal control in Russia, Fascists coming to power in Italy, Nazis in Germany, and civil war is Spain. Order over democracy was on many peoples mind, even in Britain, particularly amongst the upper classes, who were seeing their old lives of privilege and status fade away under the pressures of the modern world. The author has reflected that angst, and showed, perhaps, how close Britain was to becoming to becoming a totalitarian state.

Harriette Campbell isn't well known today, but *The Porcelain Fish Mystery* is a fine example of the British "Golden Age" mystery, even if it was written by an America. Resurrected Press is pleased to offer this new edition of this 1937 novel.

About the Author

Harriette Russell Campbell (1883-1950) was an American author who married a Scot and eventually settled in the U.K.. She wrote a series of novels featuring the detective Simon Brade. Later novels incorporated supernatural elements.

Mystery of Saint's Island (1927)
The String Glove Mystery (1936)
The Porcelain Fish Mystery (1937)
The Moor Fires Mystery (1938)
Three Names for Murder (1940)
Magic Makes Murder (1943)
Crime in Crystal (1946)
Murder Set to Music (1941)

Greg Fowlkes
Editor-In-Chief
Resurrected Press
www.ResurrectedPress.com
www.Facebook.com/ResurrectedPress

SELFORD PRENTICE'S SITTING-ROOM

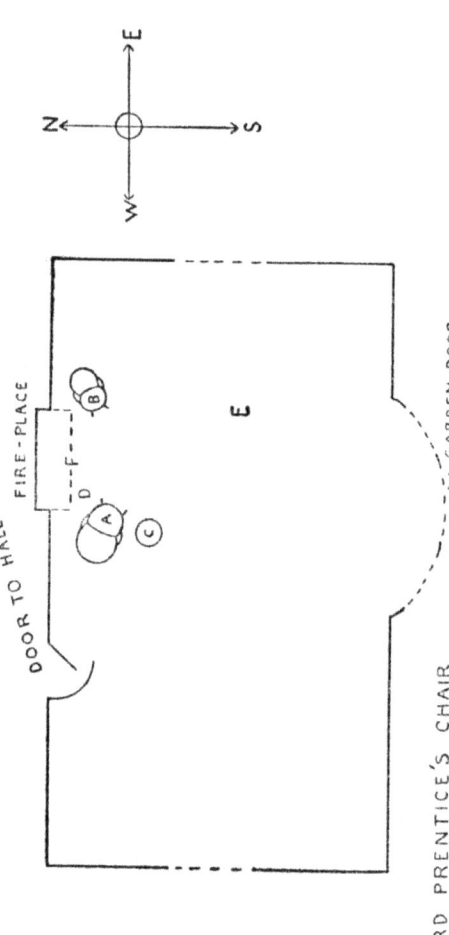

DOOR TO HALL

FIRE-PLACE

GARDEN DOOR

E

A SELFORD PRENTICE'S CHAIR

B CHAIR

C SMALL TABLE with MANUSCRIPT

D FILES of NEWSPAPERS

E POSITION of HANDKERCHIEF

F BRASS FENDER

N
W → E
S

CHAPTER 1

A HAND-CARVED crucifix from Bavaria hung on the wall above two men who looked at each other in helpless rage. The wood fire burned white and weak under the onslaught of November sunlight sweeping through the south window straight upon it.

A squarish young man, in hunting pink, straddled the hearth, his broad face as colourless as it could be under its tan. The older man leaned back in an armchair, his fine head raised, his eyes brilliant, studying his nephew's face. His shabby black silk dressing-gown, his white linen, and the spiritual cast of his thin cheek and brow gave him a priestly look. A rug lay over his crippled legs, and a cairn terrier like a fox-cub stood, alert, inside his arm.

Selford Prentice, as efficient in speech as his nephew was efficient in action, said quietly: "I wish you would try to see my point of view, Tom."

And Tom, no more able to be silent in his wrath than equipped to explain it, answered: "Good Lord! I do see it. You've got the whip hand and you mean to use it. You'd think I was a bloody rotter to hear you talk. I'm just as fit to handle my father's money as Maurice is fit to handle yours. It's not your business how I want to spend it. When my father died and left you in control I was ten. Now I'm thirty and I have to ask you for every farthing. I won't stand it another day and that's flat, Uncle Selford. I'll jolly well—" What he would jolly well do was left in doubt, for he found that he was shouting, and it is somehow humiliating to find yourself shouting at a man who can't get up and kick you out of the room!

"You've said all that before. And I've said before what I will repeat. Your father was a Socialist, like myself. His money, like mine, was handed on to him by our mother, a follower of Godwin, and a Socialist too. He left me in control because he knew your own mother's people and was afraid you would be like them and spend your inheritance on horses and gambling on horses. I make you a fair allowance and never interfere with your sport, within reason. Please remember that I raised no objection when you took over the hounds and increased the stables. But when you ask for four thousand pounds to pay your racing debts, I'm bound to refuse."

"Then I'll have to sell Parasina. Can't you see that?" Tom looked down at his uncle hopefully. Almost anyone would understand how impossible it was for him to sell the mare who had so nearly won the Oaks. He had bred her himself and trained her, and but for the worst of luck she would have repaid his outlay before this. To sell her now, at a quarter of her value, would be dead loss and break his heart.

This was an argument that must convince his uncle. He was so hopeful that his face changed to something like its habitual cheerfulness.

"I'm sorry. I really am sorry, Tom. But I can't justify racing and hunting except as diversions and I'm allowing you more to spend on them already than I think right."

"Then there's only one thing I can do—raise the money on my prospects. You know what that means."

"You won't do that."

"By God, I will." Tom beat one fist on another and his face flushed scarlet.

"You forget that I can prevent any such step. I shall alter my will. I have power to leave your share of the money in trust and I see the time has come to do it. Your trustees will control your income when I'm gone."

For a moment Tom did not understand. For another moment he would not.

"I shall appoint Maurice and Rachel Norbury and my solicitor," Selford Prentice added.

"Maurice—and Rachel—Socialists! Cranks! You can't do that."

"Rachel understands my mind better than anyone. They'll be fair to you, and to their trust. Try to be reasonable, Tom. Can't you understand that the world isn't a playground any more—if it ever was? You put energies into your hunting and your horse-racing that could be used to better purpose. You'll see that yourself some day."

Prentice had said the wrong thing. He had passed from the personal to the general and from attacking Tom himself to attacking his faith. The young man might defend himself half-heartedly, aware of errors of judgment and impulsive extravagance, but to dismiss the job he was made for as a mere pastime, an occupation unworthy of a man's whole devotion, was to free Tom from any misgivings at all. His conviction gave dignity to his manner, and lucidness to his speech.

"All right. You've said your say, sir. Now I'll say mine. You're so used to impressing everyone, you don't know when you've overshot the mark. You sit here and plan great schemes to make the world into a sugary heaven, and you jolly well forget the kind of men and women who've got to live in it. A man, like that friend of Rachel's, that paints a picture of a telegraph pole and a coal truck and gets paid well for it and never gives a penny of it away either—he's a hero, but a man that breeds and trains a grand horse, and the man that rides him to victory, are just fooling about and wasting time! And it's your working man in millions you love so much who watches the horse and it's a handful of silly geese that pose and gabble in front of the telegraph pole. And as for you, you sit and scribble all day and think how you're making the world over, and people come and say how wonderful you are and you like it. You get a kick out of it, and whenever you want to do a mean thing you say it's for the cause and so it's right of course. You like having us all in your power. It bucks you up. Make your will however you want to. I can go to Canada and farm, I suppose, or join the Mounties. I'm damned if I'll stay in this house another week to be bullied by you and sneered at by Maurice. So now you know!"

The cairn stood stiff and expectant on his master's knee. Selford Prentice stroked the tawny coat, slowly, as Tom went out, and the door slammed.

It was opened again, almost at once, by another young man, also dressed for the hunt. He came around to the hearth, walking slowly, for he was awkwardly built, long from the hips upward and short of limb, but this defect was used as part of a personality notable and instantly felt. He had a long, distinguished face, long, clumsy hands, and when he spoke, a magnetic voice under admirable control.

"Tom seems to be in a passion. What have you been saying to him, Father?"

"The usual things. Why do you suppose Tony and I had to marry the last women on earth we should have, Maurice?"

"What's wrong with Aunt Charlie? She's a harmless old dear. And she makes her garden grow." Maurice glanced around the bright room, where bowls of gladioli and chrysanthemums reached up to the sunlight.

"She's a carrier of the Weleven germ and Tom's caught it. If his father had meant all the money to go to the turf and the hunting field he'd never have left me with power to stop it. Is that reasonable or not?"

"Of course it's reasonable."

Maurice struck a match and lit a cigarette, slowly and carefully. The tiny match in his long fingers might so easily drop or go out, and he hated such trivial accidents, aware of his own clumsiness. There was no feel for things in his finger-ends.

Prentice left it at that. But in a moment he added: "Tom made some remarks before he left. I'm not sure that they weren't to the point, though he's not exactly an articulate person. Do you think I am too fond of power?"

"You?" Maurice looked down at his father. "I should say you avoided it. No one could accuse you of abusing it."

"Yet it has come my way." He fingered the manuscript lying on the table beside him.

"Yes, it's come your way; and you use it too little."

"I know you think so. I'm sorry for that. Have you seen the attack on me in this morning's *Sentinel*? That paper seems to have sprung up in the night and has already done harm. Who is behind it, Maurice? The writer of this article is well informed. I've been watching the leaders. So far your inquiries seem to have got us nowhere. There's always someone behind the man who seems to be responsible. They're far keener to defeat the Sanctionists than to strengthen labour. Directly or indirectly, I believe there's Italian money oiling the machine. It's doing us harm with the voters. Make no mistake, Maurice, I mean to get to the bottom of this mystery."

"I've carried out your instructions, sir."

"Maurice—well, we'll talk this out tonight."

"If you want to talk to me I'll give up the hunt."

"No, I must work this morning. Go and have your ride."

When Maurice had gone, Prentice sat inactive. The sun shone in at the semicircle of windows on the south. The garden door in the centre was shut against the wind. A high window on the east and another on the west framed a pattern of cherry-tree branches against a clear sky, but out of sight black clouds were gathering and mounting. The cairn jumped down and scratched at the hearth-rug, making an imaginary bed in an illusory thicket. Satisfied, he fitted his rounded body into it and slept.

Prentice rang a bell that stood on the table on his right. A manservant answered it promptly.

"Give me a piece of notepaper, Braythorpe. Wait." H wrote a few lines, enclosed them, sealed the envelope an addressed it. "I want this note to catch Mrs. Norbury before she starts for the meet. Telephone and ask her to wait for it. And I expect a letter in a green envelope by the midday post. If it comes, bring it straight to me as usual."

"Yes, sir."

He gave the note to the servant. "And tell Phelps to take Chen for his walk. Don't go yourself. I want you here today. You can send Mr. Litton to me. I have some letters to write."

In the library, where Stephen Litton worked, he and Maurice Prentice stopped talking when the servant came with the message. As soon as he had gone, Maurice said: "I hope you'll reconsider your decision, Stephen."

"Probably I will. If he tries to persuade me to stay, I'm sure to. Your father is a marvellous man."

"I still don't understand why you are leaving us. You say you've no post in view."

Stephen, a young man with an agreeable face, was too tactful to have the habit of candour, but now he spoke out.

"I said your father was a marvellous man. He's too marvellous. If I stay any longer he'll make me his slave, like the rest of you."

"Absurd!"

"Well, is it? Maurice, it's no use pretending that you aren't ambitious. You want power. He likes being invisible and anonymous, swaying the men who act, by sheer force of his intelligence. That's not your line. You want to be in the limelight. Yet you play second fiddle to him. He keeps the whip hand of Tom through the cash-box, my sister Rachel worships him, all the young people come here to listen to him as if he were an oracle. And look at the way he treats your mother. He hasn't seen her for thirty years, but he won't free her, and he pays her brothers to guard her as if she were dangerous. She's a magnificent woman—so everyone says—still beautiful and brilliant. I don't know why you don't do something about it."

"Because I know my father's reasons and you don't."

"I want to leave while I can call my soul my own. I'm no a Socialist. I'm a diplomat by trade and temperament and want to get back to my job. I was a fool to risk it for a woman. If I stay here much longer I'll be thinking Selfdor Prentice's way and only be fit for Russia."

Maurice said: "Don't tell him today, anyway. He's worried about Tom and other things. Wait till tomorrow."

Stephen took up his note-book and pencil. "I only hope tomorrow won't be too late," he said.

CHAPTER 2

IT HAD been a grand day, and it was not over yet.

Along the ride cut straight through Franklin's wood, horses, sobered by the last hard gallop, stood easily, one alert, ready to be off again at a gathering up of the slack reins and pressure of his rider's knee, another showing his fatigue, boring at the bit, slacking, or standing with drooping head. Here and there a horseman had dismounted. Tassy was one of these, but she stood close to the bright chestnut flank of her thoroughbred, prepared to be in the saddle at the least warning.

It was after three o'clock on a November afternoon, and the hunted fox was nearly done. With a little luck they would have him yet. Tom Prentice, the master and huntsman, was moving along the far side of the covert, and the field had been marshalled down-wind along the ride.

The tops of the trees were bare, but a russet garment still hung over the ride, and the earth and air were rich with the colour of falling leaves. The rank, warm smell of autumn blew away on the rising wind. There had been a heavy fall of rain earlier, and Tassy, who had not stopped to unstrap and put on her mackintosh, was cold now in her damp coat but she did not think of that. She was listening, trying to follow Tom's progress, knowing how he would hate to finish the day like this.

That was Mendleson's voice! She swung herself into her saddle. Others heard the challenge too. Reins were shortened, the horses raised their heads, there was a stir of expectancy. Everyone stopped talking.

"Better mount," said Tassy to Maurice, who was leaning against a fine black gelding and smoking a cigarette. Maurice, a busy politician, was not a regular member of the field. In short, he did not take his hunting seriously. He was ways leisurely in his movements, partly because of the defect in his build.

He smiled at Tassy, but was in no hurry to take her advice. "Just like Maurice, to think the fox will wait till he's quite ready!" thought Tassy.

His hands blundered over his reins. "I'd never let him ride a horse of mine," Tassy thought. "Lucky the Pirate got the mouth of a mule, or he'd never stand for it." Her fingers itched to sort the curb from the snaffle reins while Maurice fumbled with them.

Before he could settle himself in the saddle a horn sounded and Tom Prentice came galloping down the ride, followed by hounds. Horses were hastily backed away, heads turned to face the huntsman. But Maurice's black gelding, swerving as his rider mounted, stood across the ride, and before Maurice could pull him round and back, Tom was on them.

The master's face was red and hot. Mendleson's signal been taken up by Anarchy and they were out of the cover heading toward the valley. Tom had no eyes or ears for anything but his hounds, when suddenly his horse stuck his hooves in to avoid the black, his stable-mate.

Curses rolled from Tom's lips, and he struck out at the black haunches in his way with his crop, but as he did so the black wheeled around and Maurice took the blow on his hand. For a second the cousins glared at each other. Then Tassy leaned over and dragged at the snaffle rein of the black, and Tom galloped on, while Maurice, white with pain, tried to quiet his mount.

"Served you right, Maurice," Tassy reproached him. "Are you hurt?"

Maurice did not speak, and in the scamper to get clear of the wood there was no time to question him again.

An hour later, when the fox had gone to ground in a chalky hillside and the horn had sounded the "Home—going home," Tassy, riding along the wet tarmac, thought resentfully of the incident. She looked ahead, blinking in the fan-shaped glare of passing motor lights, at Tom, who rode with the three hunt servants and the hounds, a blurred and patchy mass of rocking bodies, lowered muzzles, drooping sterns. Tassy's heart went out to him. She had worshipped Tom Prentice ever since he, a boy of nineteen, and she, a reckless morsel of eight and a half, coloured in various shades of brown, with a pair of intelligent hands, had fallen into the same brook and he had fished her out. It was Tom who told the master to give her the brush that day. Tom had taught her to ride, Tom had shown her the points of a horse, Tom had selected her first real hunter, Tom had opened up to her the mind of that peerless animal the fox.

Tom's world was her world, and she would have followed him over barbed wire itself if he had taken it into his obstinate head to risk it. And Tom, who saw the least wrinkle of flesh under a too tight girth, who knew to the smallest fraction of an inch the right adjustment of a bit and was the best judge in Bramshire of the points of a young horse, had never guessed the truth about Tassy Litton.

They were passing through the town of Medbury, where shopping women, carrying bags and parcels, moved to and fro under the lights, and men lingered in groups outside the inn doors. Tom called the hounds close to his horse's heels. As they drew near to the swinging sign of the Duke's Head Inn they had to pull up to avoid twenty or thirty persons who came out of the door in disorder and pushed each other into the road. Their leader, a little man, with reddened eyes and waving arms, was shouting: "The red flame beckons. Who'll follow?"

A policeman stepped up and said something, laying a hand on the arm of the agitator, who swung round, cringed and whined some voluble apology. The policeman laughed and turned to Maurice Prentice, who had leaned from his saddle to ask a question.

"Just Langrove, sir. We have to keep an eye on him. It's that new paper that's doing the mischief. *The Active Sentinel.* Thank you, sir; good night."

The riders went on.

At last they turned off the tarmac into a stony lane leading uphill, and Maurice Prentice moved up to Tassy's side. Tassy could see his face turned toward her in the gloom. She was a little afraid of Maurice. He was brilliantly clever, for one thing, and a Socialist, like his father, for another.

"Did you see Tom hit me, Tassy?" asked Maurice.

"What rot! All he did was to send the Pirate off the ride. You were in the way."

"I was!" Maurice's voice was grim. He lifted his right hand and held it out. It was gloveless, swollen and bruised.

"He got me fairly with that murderous crop of his. Aches like hell!" He nursed the injured member tenderly. "It's lucky it was all in the family and not a stranger. I heard Tom cursing old Braithwaite too. He was positively savage."

"He was, and I don't blame him. That old man ought to be painlessly removed. He can't ride straight, and, what's worse, he stops other people doing it, and he nearly as anything headed the fox today taking one of his short cuts, and that brute he rides kicks like hell. The Angel Gabriel would have sworn at him."

"Well, I don't like it. Tom's temper is worse than ever. People are talking about it. He'll have to pull up."

"You don't know anything about it, Maurice. Tom's the best amateur huntsman in the provinces, and as for you, you're too busy with your horrid politics to hunt more than once in a blue moon, and I don't know why you do that. I thought Socialists didn't approve of hunting. Look out for Jennifer J. She hates that black gelding."

"What a little spitfire you are, Tassy!"

"I'm going into the Grange," called Rachel, as they turned out of the lane on to a high plateau where the flat earth shouldered a starry sky, and the wind beat them back. "Can you lead my mount home, Tassy, and send the car for me?"

Tassy supposed she could. It was another two and a half miles to Hartover House and there was the Agminton-Medbury road to cross and the town of Hartover to ride through. Her hands were cold, and Jennifer J. resented contact with a lead horse, even Big Ben, her stable-mate, was a stolid slacker outside the hunting field and slouched along at half the speed of Jenn's springy walk.

"Well, you can jolly well get down here, then," Tassy crossly, as they stopped at the gate of the Grange where Tom and Maurice lived.

"Sorry, Tassy, but Selford wants to see me. He asked me to come on my way home. Take care in Hartover Street, won't you, and don't forget the car," said Rachel as she slipped from the saddle.

"You'd much better come home yourself," grunted Tassy, deftly slipping Big Ben's reins through the near of his bridle and gathering the double lot up in her hands. "You must be soaked. I know I am. You've got a meeting tonight, too."

"I'm all right—my skirt's wet, that's all. I must see what Selford wants. Aunt Charlie will give me some tea."

Maurice dismounted and handed his reins to a groom, and he and Rachel turned in at the gate and walked toward house. Tom rode on with his hounds, and Tassy moved beside him. The kennels were a mile farther on, half-way to Hartover, where she and Rachel lived in an agreeable Georgian house with a garden and paddock running down to the river and big old-fashioned stables with a farm beyond.

"A good day, Tom," Tassy sighed, sorry it was over. Tom grunted.

"That cast you made in the plough was all right."

"Changed foxes in Franklin's," grumbled Tom. "That's why we missed seeing a kill. Fresh fox."

"Well, you showed us good sport anyway, and Jennifer J. never put a foot wrong. I heard Colonel Ridyard say he'd ridden with the Medbury Vale off and on for twenty years and he'd never seen a finer pack nor better handled than since you took over."

"I must say nobody gives me much help. The way the range field behaved today you'd think none of 'em had ever heard that fox-huntin' ain't a paper-chase, nor point-to-point neither."

This was all wrong. There was a lingering streak of angry red in the sky, the bared branches of a cherry orchard chattered, and the wind shouted down the lane. Tassy was cold and uncomfortable. "Why didn't I stop to put on that mackintosh?" she thought. Though her clothes had dried outside in the gale that followed the rain, they clung damply to her skin. But the after-the-hunt mood should have warmed her soul and Tom's in unison. Instead of that, he was cross and she was disturbed and unhappy.

"I think I'll resign in May," Tom threatened sullenly. "Don't see why I should carry on. I pinch and scrape and work like a nigger, and no thanks for it."

"Tom, you can't!" Tassy's eyes stung. He had made this to threat before, but now he spoke as if he meant it.

"You could take on the hounds yourself if you were five years older."

Tassy, who sat a saddle with more confidence than a drawing-room chair, nearly fell off. The suggestion that she would make a suitable bride for the King, or a successful advertisement for a beauty cream, would not have sounded more fantastic.

"Tom, you must be mad."

"You're not far off, I think I am. Good night."

She drew back to let the procession trail by on heavy feet, toward warmth, rest, and food.

"Good night, Vick. Night, Fred—good night," she called clearly.

"Night, miss."

The red glow had vanished. Her hands were stiff and she could hardly feel the reins. Big Ben dragged back sluggishly, half asleep already. Jennifer J., annoyed, sidled off and presented her flank to an approaching car. Tassy sorted out the tangle, gave Big Ben a cut over his withers, and scrambled past.

"I know what's the matter with Tom," she told Jennifer J. "It isn't the money. It's that red-headed cat! Blast and damn! Will you come up, Ben? Jenn, keep over, I say. Glory, what a night!"

CHAPTER 3

"WHAT a night!"

Upstairs at Medbury Grange the pretty Irish housemaid said it as she shut up the bedrooms, remembering to leave her ladyship's casement half open in spite of the gale. For Lady Charlotte Prentice, the widow of Selford Prentice's brother, and Tom's mother, had a phobia against rooms with shut windows.

"What a night!" Braythorpe the butler-valet said it as he drew heavy curtains across the windows downstairs.

"What a night!" Mrs. Myster, the cook, came down the stairs carefully, for she was a ponderous creature, only half awake after her afternoon nap. "Time to get the scones in the oven," she told the kitchen girl, "and it'll be seven eggs wanted. They'll be starvin' after their hunt, and Mrs. Norbury'll be with them, I shouldn't wonder, if not Miss Tassy. Now look sharp or Mr. Braythorpe'll want to know why not.

"Leave the south door open, Braythorpe, the wind's blowing that way," said Lady Charlotte Prentice, look anxiously out into the dusky garden. "What a good thing I saw that clematis trained yesterday! She's safe, I should think, but I'm not so certain about the new standards. We will have our tea now; there's no telling when the others will get in. What a night!"

"The rain has stopped, my lady."

"And in time it did, Braythorpe, with the last chrysanthemums spilled all over the garden, and the ground too heavy for planting for days to come!"

Lady Charlotte was a gardener and she looked like one. She had a thick active figure, a broad reddened face, and fine small hands with blunt finger-nails. Out of doors she was silent, efficient, and happy. Inside of four walls she was easy to ignore in spite of her incessant chatter. Such casual thoughts as scrape the surface of the mind and usually remain unspoken pattered from Lady Charlotte's lips steadily as she sat knitting beside the great stone chimney of the old studio, now the family sitting-room. Even when she alone, her lips would form words, which became vocal soon as a listener appeared.

Medbury Grange had begun as a modest farmhouse tucked into a cherry orchard. An artist had added an enormous studio and a bedroom or two. Fifteen years before, Selford Prentice, attracted by its position on a windy plateau, bought it and built on all the rooms he required for himself and his son, his widowed sister-in-law, and her Tom. It jutted out, roughly, in three arms from the central nucleus of the old farmhouse. The north arm was taken up by the studio, converted into a living-room by cutting windows in the west and east walls. The south arm became a hall and Selford Prentice's sitting-room, built to his own plan, with high windows looking east and west and a huge bay on the south with a garden door in the centre. He could be pushed in his wheeled chair out of this door in fine weather. He had his bedroom and a room for his nurse in the old house on the other side of the hall. To the west went the kitchen and offices, and the space above just accommodated the family, with a couple of spare bedrooms for guests. It was an incoherent but an amazingly sunny house, at the mercy of the wind and the rain in storms, little more than a shelter in the always spreading garden in bright weather. Paved paths had been laid all around it to accommodate Prentice's chair, and he could wheel himself between borders and even dig out weeds with the aid of a long-handled fork.

"A wild night, Braythorpe," he said. "Mr. Brade and Dr. Jerrold will have tea here with me. Mrs. Norbury is coming with Mr. Tom. I want to see her before she goes. Remember that. It is important."

"Yes, sir."

In the light springing up from the single lamp on the table beside his chair, the big bones of his face cast sharp shadows. The cairn terrier lay curled up, a tawny ball, on a fold of his dressing-gown at his feet.

"You might tell Mr. Brade when you've brought in the tea, Braythorpe. I suppose he's still upstairs looking at the Chinese jug."

"Yes, sir."

Dr. Jerrold, who was sitting opposite Prentice, looked after the servant as he went out.

"He looks like Charlie Chaplin with the fun left out," Jerrold remarked. "And tidied up, of course," he added, smiling, "severely pressed and laundered."

Prentice laughed a pleased laugh. "Very good," he admitted; "Braythorpe hasn't a spark of humour. Perhaps that's why he's so reliable. He knows what I want before I do. He knows what Chen wants too." His hand went out to the cairn, who opened one eye and closed it again.

Jerrold looked at the dog.

"Why a Chinese name for a Scotch dog?" he asked.

Prentice smiled. "There's a legend someone told me about a fox who won immortality. Chen was so like a fox-cub that I had a fancy to give him the name of that fabulous beast."

"He must be getting on. It's five years since I met you, and I've never seen you without him, I think."

"Oh, but he leaves me sometimes. Two walks a day, rain or shine, in winter and one in summer. And one hour in the evening for his supper and a run in the garden. You can set the clock by his habits, except in the early spring, when he goes in search of adventure."

"He adores you."

"He prefers me to other people, but he's a self-centred little beast, with a dog-fox somewhere in his family tree. The servants are afraid of him. He sits and stares at them till they give him what he wants, and he barks at things no one else can see. I'd find another dog a tame companion after Chen. Here's our tea. Put the table in front of Dr. Jerrold, Braythorpe. I don't want my work moved." He laid a hand on the table beside him, where sheets of foolscap paper, covered with his fine writing, lay in a heap.

"Do you write your books in longhand?" asked Jerrold, interested.

"Yes, but I dictate all my letters. I learned my writing in the days when no one thought of dictating original work and I think more clearly with my pen in my hand."

There was a pause. Then Prentice said: "I'm very grateful to you, Jerrold. You've helped me with a serious problem. To tell you the truth, when I asked you to bring your friend Brade to see that piece of porcelain it was just an excuse to get you here. I didn't want anyone to know that I was so anxious to see you. As a matter of fact, it is very important that no one in the house should guess it. You won't forget your promise?"

"No, my dear man. I'm trained to disregard information pick up from patients, and this has been filed away in that special corner of my head and locked up. You can trust not only my will but my habit. For all ordinary purposes I know no more about the matter than I did an hour ago."

"Even if I died—"

"Even then."

"And yet—if I should die and if what I have told you should in some unimaginable way become known to others, then, Jerrold, I'd like you to act for me. Then, and then alone."

"I understand. Here's Brade."

Braythorpe opened the door.

"Mr. Simon Brade," he announced.

A little man hurried in, his colourless person enlivened by a porcelain fish clasped to his bosom. He stood there a second and then danced around the back of Prentice's chair to face him from the hearth-rug. The fish leered, its stiff lips opened in a spout, its gorgeous scales of yellow, green, and brownish purple lit by the fire and the lamplight. It was ugly and arresting and had a life of its own utterly separate from the life of the bookish, many-windowed room or anything in it.

Chen woke up. He looked once at that fish, and then he began to bark, in shrill, outraged spasms. He stiffened till he stood braced on all four feet, every tawny hair on end, his sharp nose and earthy eyes pointing at the leering, multicoloured effigy of the fish. Then he made a spring straight for this inimical creature. If Brade had not lifted it high over his head, the force and agility of Chen's leap might have reached its aim. The little dog fell back, furious, watching for another chance. Prentice leaned over with some difficulty and picked him up. He stood on his master's knee, stiff and observant, his slanting eyes awake to suspicious hate.

"Sorry, Mr. Brade. Do sit down. Dr. Jerrold will give you tea. Chen gets these ideas sometimes. He never did like that fish. That's why my sister-in-law tucked it away upstairs. Someone said it was valuable and I thought, as no one appreciates it here, we might as well sell it if we can."

"Sell it!" Brade set the fish on the mantelpiece, where it stood, leering timelessly, like some embittered sceptic's idea of life itself. A severe modern clock beside it ticked away the minutes it seemed to mock. "Sell it! My dear man, you don't understand. You can't sell a thing like that. I can write you a cheque, to be sure, and take it home with me, but you and I have nothing to do with it. There's more vitality in that clay than in yours or mine. Heaven help you, do you know what it is? A perfect specimen of the San Ts'ai, the one perfect example of multi-coloured glaze, produced in the supreme period directly after the downfall of the Ming dynasty, under K'ang Hsi. I should place this work about the middle of the reign, not earlier than 1690, perhaps a little later." Brade looked from Selford Prentice's face to Jerrold's and threw up his hands in a gesture of despair. "You don't understand," he cried. "Even Jerry doesn't understand. I've tried to explain to him. It's useless. Look at him. He's being patient with me. Why, the ignorant workmen that dug the sacred earth for the clay to bring to the Imperial factory knew more than Jerry here even guesses. He knew that his very thoughts must be guarded when he handled the stuff. And every finger that touched it was a consecrated finger. And the master mind of the century— perhaps you've heard of Ts'ang Ying-Hsuan, Mr. Prentice"—Brade's tone implied that no one would dare admit ignorance of that name—"aren't you swept into his thought-stream when you react to that shape and colour?" He stepped back, worshipping. Chen indulged in a snappish bark, and apologized to his master, when reproved, with a twist of his ears and a glance that said plainly: "I know your objection to noise, and that it is part of our bargain that I shouldn't bark like common dogs, but this is too much to bear." Prentice watched Brade, amused, and Jerrold drank his tea in patient silence.

"The fish is, of course, used as a symbol in many philosophies—" Prentice encouraged the little man.

"Even I do not understand. 'The Water Shuttle Flower'—that is the name of the fish there. That tells you something about the Chinese."

Brade babbled on, and as Prentice seemed amused, Dr. Jerrold made no attempt to stop him. The speaker did not instruct his audience, he appeared to forget that his listeners knew less than he did about such things as stem cups, incense-burners, ewers, water-pourers, Buddhist and Taoist symbolic vases and statuettes. He treated them to such entrancing words as Fukien—whites, peach-bloom shades, celedon and bleu-fouetée, signs of longevity and emblems of happy augury; they heard unpronounceable Chinese names and incredible Chinese legends. And all the time Brade looked, rapt in worship, at the leering fish on the mantelpiece, while the clock ticked on and the wind found its way into the room in spite of shut casements and heavy, close-drawn curtains.

"How much you know about the subject!" said Prentice, when Brade paused to accept a cup of tea from

Jerrold. "It is remarkable that a man as busy as you must be should find time for such an absorbing hobby."

"Hobby?" Brade looked at him vaguely. "Oh, I suppose you mean my little excursions into the investigation of crime. That's not a hobby, Mr. Prentice. That's the sinister blot on an otherwise harmless, not to say useful, career. Tell him about it, Jerry. He seems to want to know."

Dr. Jerrold replied to his host's lifted eyebrow.

"Brade regards his collection of porcelain and glass as his justification in life, not as a hobby. As for his work as a detective—"

"What a word, Jerry!" sighed Brade.

"As for that, he does it to earn a living, and he doesn't like it at all. He hates sending a man to prison, and the one or two cases he has had when he has helped to expose a murderer have very nearly killed him. So you can't call that business a hobby either. If he has a hobby at all, it's thinking up ways to make people believe he's even sillier than he is." Jerrold spoke affectionately.

"Well, Mr. Brade, will you take the fish? And if you write me a cheque for it, so much the better. Like you, I need money. We Socialists need it more than the lady of fashion herself. We never have enough. I was told that specimen was worth four hundred pounds, but that's rather fantastic I'm afraid."

"Four hundred pounds!" Brade set down his tea-cup and drew out his tobacco-pouch and cigarette-papers, which he always carried. Probably the occupation of rolling cigarettes gave him some satisfaction, but the cigarettes themselves certainly did not. No one had ever succeeded in smoking one. "Four hundred pounds!" he cried in an outraged voice.

"Oh, I'd take much less of course!"

"My dear man"—Brade moderated his tone to an indulgent sweetness—"you don't know what you are saying. Do you know there's just one other specimen of the San Ts'ai as perfect as this in Europe, and that's under lock and key in a museum? I'll write you a cheque for four thousand pounds. It's all I've got at the moment."

Jerrold laughed. "I wonder what that old Chinaman you were talking about would have said if he'd known his precious fish would swell the war chest of the iconoclasts to the tune of four thousand pounds!"

Prentice retorted amiably: "We're not image-breakers, my friend—not in the sense you're using the word. We destroy nothing beautiful unless it is rooted and grounded on the unspeakable ugliness of poverty and cruelty. Those must go!"

And when he had said it the other two men looked at him for a moment, believing that as he said, so would it be. That was the magic of Selford Prentice's gift.

Jerrold rose. "If I may, I think I'll pay my respects to Lady Charlotte and go back to the inn. Mimi will be home from her hunt, I expect. Brade, you'll stop on your way to London. Dinner I can't promise, but there'll be supper of sorts. The Blue Boar, Medbury, opposite the Town Hall. I'll leave you to settle the size of that cheque with Prentice." He chuckled to himself at the picture of these two men, greedy in their opposing enthusiasms, and unbusinesslike as they were greedy, striking a bargain over the porcelain fish.

The door opened. Stephen Litton stood there, his pale and agreeable face turned on the guests.

"Oh, how are you, Litton?" Jerrold got out of his chair to shake hands with him, and Prentice introduced Brade.

"I only came to bring you your letters to sign, Mr. Prentice. The postman will take them when he comes. It's nearly half past five now."

"No hurry, Stephen. Your sister Rachel has promised to stop here to see me on her way home. She'll post them at Hartover. It'll be quicker. Put them down on the table, that's a good chap. And take Dr. Jerrold to Charlotte. She'll fix up a date with you, and you'll bring your wife to dine, Jerrold?"

Stephen Litton put the letters down and glanced at the fish.

"Is it genuine?" he asked.

Brade made up his monocle and inspected the young man through it, not because he could see him better that way, but because the gesture sometimes had an intimidating effect. Brade's monocle was in fact a magnifying glass of unusual strength, so that the buttons on Litton's coat, the holes in the buttons, and the cotton used in sewing them on were plainer seen through it than the man himself.

"Genuine!" was all Brade said.

Litton, not intimidated, replied: "I had a feeling that it was a rare piece."

"Did you?" Brade dropped the monocle. "Why?"

"Because Stephen always says the right thing," Prentice cut in, with a hint of impatience.

"A rare piece"—Brade looked again at his treasure— "and there it was, tucked away in a Victorian what-not with a cracked Sèvres and inferior Dresden for company, dusted daily by the housemaid, I am told. An Irish housemaid! And not a crack, not a blemish, anywhere. A miracle."

Dr. Jerrold and Stephen Litton went out together. They crossed a hall and Litton led the way along a passage, through the entrance lobby into the former studio, now a living-room.

Jerrold paused.

"What a long way Mr. Prentice is from everyone else in this house!" he said to Litton. "Is it wise? He is so helpless."

"He likes it. His bell rings in three places—the library where I work, Braythorpe's pantry, and Nurse's bedroom."

"Could anyone hear him call out?"

"I don't think so, unless someone happened to be passing through the hall. The library is separated from his room by the wall of the old house, three feet thick, and the door is at the far end. Braythorpe and I were uneasy about some anonymous letters Mr. Prentice has been getting and lately all the garden doors have been fitted with special catches. They can't be opened from the outside, once they are closed. And we take care that one or another of us is always on duty to answer his bell."

Jerrold said no more.

When they opened the door of the studio a lash at the end of the wind that whipped the house blew in at the garden door which opened southward from the big bay in the west wall. Lady Charlotte looked up from her tea-pot, and a woman dressed in the white uniform of a nurse turned her face toward the two men. Dr. Jerrold looked up in surprise at her appearance. She had a powerful body, red hair arranged close to her head, lovely, sleepy eyes with red lights in the brown iris, and a fine pale skin. This was the woman referred to so rudely by Tassy Litton in her thoughts.

"How are you, Dr. Jerrold?" Lady Charlotte put out her hand. "Or ought I to say Mr. Jerrold? I never can remember though I know surgeons and vets are one thing and general practitioners another, and then there are dentists and osteopaths besides, so it's really no wonder people forget, but I don't think you're an osteopath. Is it something to do with asylums? This is Nurse Jonsen; Nurse—Dr. Jerrold. China?" She offered Jerrold a cup of tea. "You've had tea?" She set down the full tea-cup, and her glance strayed to the window. "I wonder if those stakes were pounded in deep enough. I fastened the standards to them myself, but if the stakes give—That's the worst of living so high up, Mr. Jerrold. The wind! Oh, Stephen, you can have the doctor's tea. Nurse, the muffins, or is it scones? Did I introduce Nurse Jonsen, Mr. Jerrold? We've never had such a pretty nurse before, though we've had younger ones. But of course Selford can't walk, so I suppose the doctors thought it would be all right, and I must say she can arrange flowers"—she glanced at the huge bowls of chrysanthemums that glorified the room—"even if Tom will insist on helping her. The doctors didn't think about Tom. He's so healthy."

Nurse Jonsen did not seem to be embarrassed, but passed the muffin-dish to Stephen Litton, reluctantly, like a person too comfortable to move. It was Litton, the tactful, who said smoothly: "Mr. Prentice suggested that Dr. Jerrold should bring his wife to dine one day next week, Lady Charlotte. They're staying at the Blue Boar for some hunting. What about Wednesday?"

"Yes, of course. Have you got a wife? What a pity!" She looked at Nurse Jonsen. "Why do doctors never marry nurses? In my young days they used to marry governesses, anyway in novels, but of course they used to be shown in at a side door, if there was one, and that's gone out with hip baths—though I'm sure I don't know what the connection is."

"Perhaps it has something to do with the increasing importance of hygiene," suggested Jerrold gravely. Nurse Jonsen laughed and Stephen looked relieved. The duty of rectifying Lady Charlotte's blunders fell to his lot frequently. Strangers sometimes made an effort to listen to what she said, and were not always amused.

"Does your wife garden?" Lady Charlotte continued. "I can give her some cuttings. But of course you live in Harley Street, don't you? Do the houses have gardens? I never go there myself, but if the Barretts had had a garden they wouldn't have been so unhealthy, or was it Wigmore Street?"

Suddenly Lady Charlotte said: "I couldn't think what it was about your wife, but I remember now. You were all in the papers and she didn't murder her husband after all. I don't mean you, of course—"

"You've forgotten, Lady Charlotte," Stephen interrupted her. "Mrs. Jerrold was never suspected of any complicity in her husband's death. You were thinking of someone else."

"On the contrary. I remember the case perfectly," Lady Charlotte reproved him, "because I was trying to repeat the colour of a sweet pea, a sport—and named it Pink Livery because there was something about a horse of that name in the papers, but it came out blue and I had to rewrite all the labels, so you see I know all about it, and I called the sweet pea Faithless instead, and I will give Mrs. Jerrold five seeds."

"It is very good of you, Lady Charlotte, and I shall be delighted to bring Mimi on Wednesday if that is really convenient. I only looked in to see you for a moment."

"Well, if you come on Wednesday I don't know what you'll sit on, because I've promised to lend most of the furniture to an exhibition for the new hospital. Most inconvenient."

Jerrold, though Brade complained of his lack of interest in porcelain, liked old furniture and said so.

"This is surely a very unusual piece?" He laid his hand on the back of a massive mahogany chair, set between the upholstery around the fireplace and the writing-table in the bay window. The carving of the loops and scrolls of the back and the arms, finished with eagles' heads, was uncommonly fine.

"That's what everyone says. It was made for the third Earl, and he was enormous. No one wanted it when Weleven was sold, because it is so big."

"Has Brade seen this chair?"

"The little man who fell on his knees to that absurd china fish? Really, Mr. Jerrold, is he a friend of yours? He said this room made him think of Henry VIII marrying the Empress Eugenie and having babies that consoled the Regicide Judges with cocktails. I don't know what he meant."

Litton said: "Surely Mr. Brade is famous for other things besides knowledge of porcelain? Wasn't he the detective they employed in the Marpen Hall affair?"

"Yes—but don't mention that to him!" Jerrold advised. "I really must go now, Lady Charlotte. Mimi will be waiting. Good night, Nurse. Don't bother to ring, Litton."

Stephen Litton jumped up and took Jerrold to the door. The wind veered in as he opened it. "It'll clear. The wind has gone round to the north."

"I hope that won't mean frost to stop the hunting. Mimi amd I are going into Oxfordshire tomorrow. She likes the Bicester country."

"We'll look forward to seeing you both on Wednesday—eight o'clock. What a night!"

CHAPTER 4

5.45 p.m.

Braythorpe was taking away the tea-tray from his master's sitting-room, and Chen trotted at his heels. He set down the tray, with its soiled cups and saucers, on the pantry shelf and went into the servants' hall, where the Medbury Grange staff were finishing a meal. Chen went with him.

Mrs. Myster, the cook, was a person of character, who had worked her way up to her present authority and made the most of it. She had a sallow face, a heavy body, and vigorous opinions. She disliked Braythorpe and he disliked her, but they presented a united front to the remaining staff. Molly Hegan, head housemaid, Irish, and inclined to trade on her blue eyes and quick wit, Bernice Langrove, the new under-housemaid from Medbury, bony, dark-haired, dark eyed, and untidy, Lily Sawyer, kitchen-maid, who came from the black country and whose twin passions were a greed for sweet food and a curiosity about the doings of the rich, and Phelps, an ex-soldier. Once every so often he went to Medbury and came home unobtrusively drunk.

They had been discussing the visit of Brade and Dr. Jerrold when Braythorpe came in and frowned on them.

"I don't suppose you know how to so much as turn down a bed," Molly Hegan changed the subject, addressing new under-housemaid.

"I don't even know whose beds have got to be turned down, nor why either," Bernie retorted.

"Not that tone if you please, my girl," Mrs. Myster interposed severely. "Now you listen. There's Mr. Selford Prentice, the master. You've nothing to do in his room at all, barring the weekly turn-out. His sitting-room is right at the end of the house, and his bedroom opposite. Then the Lady Charlotte Prentice and mind you remember to say yes, m'lady, or no, m'lady, if she speaks to you."

"She's Aristocracy, is she?" Bernice's eyes gleamed.

"She is. And don't you say it like that, either, or off you go tomorrow. I said it was a mistake taking a girl from Medbury, and mark my words, I'm right. Communists and heathens."

"Is she Mr. Prentice's wife?"

"No, she's not. She's his dead brother's widow. Have you got that straight?"

"I ain't a half wit."

"And Mr. Maurice Prentice—he's Mr. Prentice's son."

"Where's Mrs. Prentice, or is she a 'lady' too?"

"She lives abroad. She's a foreigner. None of us have ever seen her, and Mr. Prentice hasn't seen her for thirty years, they say. I tell you so you'll ask no questions." She looked severely at Molly Hegan. "And Mr. Tom Prentice is Lady Charlotte's son and Mr. Prentice's nephew. He's master of hounds."

Bernice sniffed. "I know 'im. Riding round in a pink coat while better men work for a roof to cover 'em and a loaf of bread."

"You keep them remarks to yourself, or off you go, as said before."

"And who's Mr. Litton?"

"He's the secretary and no relation, but Mr. Prentice was guardian to the family. Mr. Litton, Miss Tassy, and Norbury. Now you know. And it's time to clear. Get the tray and put the tea-things on it and see if you can do so without breaking everything, and keep that tongue of yours quiet."

Bernice obeyed, contemptuously.

"I've got her ladyship's frock to press before dinner," Molly Hegan said without moving. "Not that she'll notice. Not she. What's the use of maiding a lady like that? I wish Mr. Maurice or Mr. Tom would get married. I do that. There might be some life in the house then."

"Likely. And you'd be the first to complain of the work, my girl. Here, give me that piece of bread. That dog stares his eyes out if I don't give it to him." She buttered bread and fed Chen. "Lily, get the dog's supper. There's the bell. It'll be Mr. Maurice for his eggs."

Braythorpe, who had been discussing the racing news with Phelps, got up quickly and glanced at the clock. "Time to see to Mr. Maurice and Mr. Tom," he remarked, "but don't you forget, Molly, if one of them wants his bath turned after six, it's your job. And you can take their riding kit straight to the drying-room and not put their boots on their hats either, and hang Mr. Tom's cap on the dryer careful this time. And, Phelps, if you'd make a start on the tea things, or I don't know how everything'll get done before midnight." He went out, passing Selford Prentice's room on his left, and turned down the passage toward the front door and the studio beyond.

Maurice Prentice and Rachel Norbury were shaking off wet mackintoshes in the lobby.

"Good evening, Braythorpe," said Rachel. She had a swift way of speaking that discouraged slower tongues than hers, but Braythorpe was quick too, and admired her. She slipped off her silk hat, removed her gloves, and stood in her riding habit, neat and charming, faintly Jewish, a woman of vigorous, clear-running thoughts and a face that showed it, without showing at all what the thoughts were as they came and went. She had a look of attentiveness and intolerance, and those sensitive to personality were sometimes afraid of her. She was a traveller through life, not a wayfarer, as anyone could see, and all books were Bradshaws, and every hill and steeple a landmark on the way to her destination.

"Shall I dry them for you, Mrs. Norbury?"

"No, thanks, just leave them here. Mr. Prentice wants to see me before I go. Will you let him know I'm here?"

"Mr. Prentice is engaged just now, but I will inform him."

"Thanks." She walked into the studio.

Maurice gave his hat and gloves to Braythorpe and said: "I'll have tea before I change, Braythorpe. Mr. Prentice all right?"

"Yes, sir. There's a gentleman with him. It's about that china fish, sir, and I think he's bought it. Mr. Prentice told me to find something to pack it in, and to put it ready upstairs, as the gentleman wants to pack it himself."

"Good. That'll swell the election fund, Braythorpe."

"The gentleman's name is Mr. Brade, and Dr. Jerrold was here too," added Braythorpe.

Maurice stopped. "You don't mean the detective?"

"I think it must be the same, sir. I heard he was partial to china at the time." As Maurice made no reply, he asked: "A good day, sir?"

"Yes. I wanted it. I've got three meetings tonight."

"That'll be your morning coat and the grey tie, sir?"

"That's right, Braythorpe. You always know. Three boiled eggs? Can you wangle that out of the kitchen?"

Braythorpe smiled; and Maurice, stooping from the hips and walking deliberately to hide this awkwardness, followed Rachel.

Stephen Litton got up as they came in. "Hello, Rachel," he said to his sister; "good day?"

Rachel said: "Quite good." She unfastened her hunting skirt and stepped out of it in perfectly fitting breeches. "Awfully wet," she explained, hanging it over the carved back of the chair Dr. Jerrold had admired. "I'll wait to see Selford, Stephen. He wants to talk to me."

"He said you'd take his letters. They're rather urgent. If you post them in Hartover it'll save time. And just ask when you're there if there's a parcel for us. His electioneering pamphlets ought to be out today. I'm going back to work for an hour. I've got those notes ready for you, Maurice."

"Thanks. I feel a lot fitter for my day off. Glad I went. Not that we stand a chance in South Bramshire this time. Aunt Charlie, you've only given me two lumps!"

"Nonsense. I put three in. Everybody will say I'm absent-minded, and I'm not at all. I remembered all about that Marpen Hall affair though it happened ages ago, didn't I, Nurse?"

'You've hurt your hand, Mr. Prentice!" Nurse Jonsen exclaimed. Maurice explained. She got up, went out of the and came back with a roll of bandages.

Litton went back to the small room called the library. It was part of the old house, and a thick wall separated it from Selford Prentice's study. He began to type at once. In the drying-room Braythorpe hung up Maurice's wet clothes. In the passage sat Chen, staring at the door as if he could open it in time by force of will. Braythorpe opened the door and let the cairn into the garden. The night was black and the wind stronger than ever. Braythorpe went back to his pantry.

In Prentice's sitting-room Simon Brade, holding the porcelain fish securely under one arm, was taking leave of his host.

"I'll go and pack him up and I'll send that cheque by return of post," he said briskly, looking at Prentice apprehensively, as if he feared, now it had come to the point, Prentice might repent. Then he fumbled with his eye-glass and added suddenly: "See here, Prentice, I've got other things, you know, almost as interesting as this. I—I'll send you a sixteenth-century incense-burner. It'll cheer you up."

Prentice laughed and took his hand. "It's really awfully good of you, but I don't like that fish and I'll be glad of the money."

"Don't like him?" The fish leered as Brade held him out, reverently. "Like him? My God!"

He glanced around the room and saw only books, shaded lamps, crimson hangings, and dark red chrysanthemums. "But you haven't got anything else," he protested, in infinite pity.

Prentice shook his head. He was tired. "I like having nothing else," he explained. "I like walls and books and a

fire to look at. I couldn't think if I had to see that thing
grinning at me every time I looked up. Take him away,
that's a good fellow, but before you go, do you mind
handing me a couple of sheets of notepaper and an
envelope from that desk? If there is any there. The fact is
I never use the stuff."

Brade found the paper and an envelope and brought it
to Prentice. He had recovered his spirits, and his painful
spasm of generosity was over. He went out, closing the
door carefully, and carried his new possession upstairs to
the end of the corridor where a packing-case, straw, and
papers were set out on a dust-sheet. He knelt down and
picked up a piece of paper. Then he sat down on the floor,
turning the fish round and round in his hands,
scrutinizing every moulded scale all over again for the
flaw he thought must be there though he knew it was not.

The front door bell rang, and Braythorpe came to
answer it. Tom Prentice stamped in. "Damn that door. I
never have my latch-key. Why the devil does it have to be
locked? Here, take these. I'm in the hell of a mess. And
bring the whisky, will you? I suppose there's nothing but
tea." His pink coat was splashed and spotted with the
black loam of the Vale, and his stock sat string-like
around his neck. He was much untidier than Maurice,
but then, he had to keep with his hounds wherever they
went. He entered the studio and looked first at Nurse
Jonsen's smooth red hair gleaming under its lawn cap.

6 p.m.

Chen sniffed the wind. Then he lowered his muzzle
and trotted down the drive to the lodge, but found
nothing of any interest there. He made his usual round,
stopping to examine any significant smell. He picked up
plenty of interesting news. He learned, for instance, that
the butcher's dog had come along with the last delivery of
meat and that pheasants in the covert a mile away were
roosting low in the new plantation of larches. A rabbit

had crossed the lawn and there were moles in the orchard.

The window of the studio was open, but he did not go in that way. Instead he trotted straight past the front door. The postman was coming up the drive. Chen knew the bicycle lamp and told the time by it. The light picked out his small shape against the dark shrubs that sheltered against the house. He lingered, engaged in his own investigations, while the postman dismounted and rang the bell. Then he trotted round the corner to the garden door of his master's room. He sniffed at the threshold, examined the flower-beds on either side, his nose wriggling with displeasure. Cats! Having settled this, he sat down in the warm corner by the garden window and cleaned his paws.

Someone was coming across the room. Chen knew that this was not his time for being let in. It was too soon. The garden door opened. He sniffed. He trotted across the threshold. Then he stopped, taut with suspicion. He crouched, and curled back his lips, staring, his throat stiffening in a long growl of fear.

6.28 p.m.

Brade had finished packing his treasure, but the string provided by Braythorpe did not satisfy him, and the wooden pin to be inserted in the straw loop of the hamper was too short for security. He shook his head, made deprecating sounds, and finally picked up the hamper with both hands and carried it carefully along the passage to the top of the stairs. Here he stopped short.

A dog was barking shrilly below. There was a smell of smoke faint but distinct. He leaned over the banister and saw Nurse Jonsen's red hair under its white cap as she ran across the hall to the door of Selford Prentice's room. She struggled for a moment with the handle.

As Brade set the hamper down on a table at the head of the stairs, Tom Prentice, dressed in a bath-robe, a towel over his arm, was looking down from the opposite side of the landing. Brade scuttled down the stairs, with Tom behind him, just as Nurse threw open the door and cried: "Help! Fire!"

Chen, standing half inside the garden door, was barking, the shrill sound interrupted by long sobbing intakes of breath. On the hearth, before the fire, between it and Selford Prentice's chair, a file of newspapers was alight, and nearly burned out. The flames had run around the cretonne valance of the chair and veered across the hearth toward the other chair opposite. Selford Prentice was lying on the rug, his head over the fender, his hair and face scorched, his dressing-gown smouldering.

Nurse and Brade ran to him, and Tom beat out the flames with his feet and hands. They lifted the body of the crippled man away from the fire and laid it on the carpet. Suddenly it was over. The flames were out, and crowding into the room came Braythorpe first, then Maurice, Rachel Norbury, Lady Charlotte, Stephen Litton. The body of Selford Prentice lay quietly, his white face, under his white hair, unchanged by death, his eyes open and unseeing. Chen barked.

"He's dead," Nurse said, drawing back.

Brade knelt there, but he was no longer looking at the dead man. His eyes, bright and quick, were studying the room. "Oh, for God's sake, put that dog out," Nurse Jonsen cried, making a gesture, while Maurice obeyed. She picked up Selford Prentice's handkerchief from the floor, smoothed it out, and laid it over his face. Maurice, with Chen in his arms, walked to the window. Braythorpe held back the curtains, turned the knob, and opened the garden door. Maurice put the dog outside and closed the doors.

"Who let the dog in?" cried Braythorpe. "How did it happen?" His face began to twitch. "Has anyone been in this room? Mr. Brade, sir, when did you leave him?"

Lady Charlotte was looking from the dead man to Rachel, who stood erect and still in her riding clothes, her palms right shut on her fingers. Maurice moved slowly to the hearth. He looked at the blackened remains of the pile of newspapers. Then at the table on the other side of the chair where closely written pages of manuscript lay. "He must have leaned forward when the fire started, afraid his manuscript would be destroyed, and fallen," he said hoarsely. "Tom, will you call the doctor?"

"And a priest," Nurse Jonsen added.

"And the police?" said Brade.

Everyone looked at him.

"In a case of accident it is necessary," said the little man.

"I suppose it is. I can't think—" Maurice faltered.

"Mr. Brade is right." Nurse Jonsen looked startled. "When did you leave him, Mr. Brade?"

"Before six. I gave him a sheet of notepaper. He said he wanted to write a letter."

"Where are his letters?" demanded Stephen Litton suddenly. "They have not been posted. I put them down on top of his manuscript for him to sign. They are gone."

"They were there when I left him," Brade said. He had his monocle in his eye and was studying the small stand beside Prentice's chair. "Isn't this his bell? Did he ring it? Don't touch it please."

Nurse Jonsen's gaze was still on him. "What were you doing after you left him?" she asked.

He gave her his attention.

"Packing a piece of porcelain upstairs in the hall. Looking at it, rather."

"Mr. Brade came to see that fish Chen hated so," sobbed Lady Charlotte. "He's a friend of that nice Mr. Jerrold's. I don't think he'd do Selford any harm."

"Of course, it was an accident," Maurice said quickly, painfully. "Why are we standing here? Aunt Charlie— Rachel, please go. I'll wait till the doctor comes."

Brade walked carefully to the fire, stepping between the fender and Prentice's body. The grate was of the basket type and stood in the square chimney, leaving the hearth clear, except where the ashes sifted through. He

leaned down, took the tongs, and extracted some scraps of
paper which had dropped out of the fire. He showed these
to Litton, who exclaimed: "They are parts of the letters I
typed for him. Why have they been burned? Who did it?
And this—" He held a fragment of blue notepaper. "I
know nothing about this. It must be part of the letter he
wrote after Mr. Brade left him."

"May I see?" Brade took the scraps.

Tom had re-entered. He stood there, in his red
dressing-gown, looking angry and dismayed. "I don't
think we need keep Brade here, do we?" he said, roughly.
"Come, Mother, Rachel—no use standing here." He went
to Maurice and id a hand on his shoulder. "Go and have a
drink, Maurice, I'll wait."

"Of course," said Brade, "I will go if you say so, but the
inspector is sure to want me. He'll want us all. But I can
wait outside in my car."

"No—no." Maurice shook his head. "Tom is upset. We
all are." Suddenly he collapsed, sat down by the desk, and
let his head fall on his arms, sobbing.

Rachel went to him. "Don't, Maurice," she said. "This
is no time for behaving like a child. There'll be work to do.
Stephen—" she turned back to her brother—"take charge
of Selford's manuscript. Don't let anyone touch it. That,
at least, is safe."

Braythorpe, shivering, left the room. He came back
carrying a tray and set it down on the writing-table.
"That's that," said Tom, "we'd better all have one. Nurse
Jonsen, you too."

"I'll take Lady Charlotte away," said Rachel. "It's too
much for her." Indeed, Lady Charlotte's sudden silence
and pallor were alarming.

Outside the door she recovered a little. "But I don't
think he can be dead, Rachel—Dr. Garnet will do
something, I'm sure he will." They heard her protesting
as she went away. Brade stood swinging his monocle,
uneasily, while they aired. Nurse Jonsen had recovered
her self-possession. Maurice was quiet now, his face still

hidden on his arms. Stephen Litton wandered from door to window and back again.

Tom said gruffly: "What do you make of it, Mr. Brade? You're a detective, of sorts?"

Brade jumped. He was nearly as pale as Lady Charlotte had been. The others welcomed Tom's voice. The silence had become unendurable.

Maurice looked up. "Detective? But it is obviously a horrible accident."

"Look here, Maurice," Stephen Litton spoke. "I hate to say this now, but the doctor will be here soon and the Chief Constable after him. I think we ought to face facts. It looks queer. How did Chen happen to be in the room, and why were these letters burned? I'll swear your father didn't do that himself."

Maurice looked at the fire, fallen low. "Those files of newspapers," he began.

"Yes—but pull yourself together. They were lying there near the fire. The letters were on the table. Look." He went up to the hearth and picked up some charred scrap under the grate. "These letters must have been tossed on the fire carefully with the object of burning them. Only the bits that fell out of the grate are left. The papers may have caught fire from a spark, or a bit of burning paper from the fire, blown out by a draught of wind. But the burning of those letters was no accident. And why did Mr. Prentice not ring his bell? Why?"

"He couldn't," Brade remarked. "At least, I don't think he could."

Stephen looked at the little man quickly, then at the bell an old-fashioned contrivance of metal standing on the table near the chair Prentice had used.

"What do you mean?"

"I think he couldn't reach it."

"Why? It was under his hand."

"I don't think so. I wouldn't touch it if I were you."

Stephen drew back, looking at the table, arranged exactly as it always was, with the bell close to the arm of the chair. Brade handed him his eye-glass. "Just look through this, Mr. Litton, and you'll see what I mean. When I turned after helping Nurse move Mr. Prentice, I was kneeling and my eye was on a level with the table. If you look you'll see for yourself. The bell has been dragged across the table. There's a clear track where it has displaced the dust. And there is no dust on the bell, and there are no fingermarks on it either. There ought to be. I saw Mr. Prentice handle it himself, when he rang for Braythorpe to take away the tea. Someone has wiped it clean after replacing it."

"Then—" Stephen turned on them—"then someone was in this room after you left it, someone who burned those letters, and let in Chen, and removed the bell so that Mr. Prentice could not ring for help."

"But—he might have shouted. Someone would have heard him, surely?" Brade suggested.

"They couldn't!" Stephen exclaimed. "My room is nearest, and it is separated from it by the thick wall of the old house. Everyone else was either in the studio or in the servants' wing upstairs. He was dependent on his bell."

Braythorpe had come in and heard this remark.

"He was, sir, and I've often been uneasy about it. That was partly why I asked Mr. Maurice's permission to have patent catches on the doors, after those letters began coming."

"What letters?" asked Brade.

Stephen Litton said: "He'd often received anonymous letters containing vague threats. He did not believe in force of any kind, not even strikes, and lately he intervened in a dispute involving the Medbury chair-factories and persuaded the men's leaders to come to terms. It made him very unpopular locally. These letters were written by someone who hated him, and we suspected a man called Langrove. He would not allow us to take any action. He used to read them and tear them up."

"Patent catches?"

"Yes, anyone could get out of the house, but no one could get in, without a key."

"Except through the studio window which was alway open," put in Stephen, "and that room was usually occupied; and when it wasn't, Lady Charlotte was working in the garden outside. Anyone coming in that way, even if he missed being seen by the gardeners or Lady Charlotte would have to come down the long corridor and pas through the hall."

"Yet someone was here after I left the room this evening," Brade said. "Someone came in, argued with Mr. Prentice, threw his letters into the fire, snatched the bell away when he attempted to ring, and let in the dog." His glance went to the scorched cretonnes and the body of the dead man. He knelt down and examined the black silk dressing-gown. He did not move the handkerchief from the face, but he looked at it so long that Maurice cried out: "Must we go into this now?"

Stephen put a hand on Maurice's shoulder. "We've got to tell all this to the police," he reminded him. "As things stand we can't make a clear story of it. What's that?"

The wind was still blowing noisily outside the windows, but they could hear voices outside, shouting and menacing voices, and Chen's bark. Then the sound of a motor. Braythorpe went out and ran down the passage to the front door.

The deputation from Medbury gathered in front of the Grange.

A little dog stood in their way barking. He was under the light of the front door and they saw his coat bristling. And a car dashed up to the step, and out of it jumped Captain Stair, Chief Constable of the county, and an Inspector. "What's all this?" Stair faced the men scattered by the onrush of the car. "What are you men doing? Langrove, I see you. What's all this about?"

"A deputation to interview Mr. Selford Prentice," retorted Langrove promptly, "and within our rights, we are. We want to see Mr. Prentice and see him we will."

Some of the men were retreating already. Not so Langrove. He faced the Chief Constable, too exalted in his dream to be afraid of any man.

"Well, you can't see him."

The door was opened and a manservant stood there wild-eyed and haggard.

"Why not?" Langrove defied him.

"Because—he's dead."

The Chief Constable and the Inspector went in. The door was shut. Already the group around Langrove had dwindled to a few, too stupid or too curious to leave him.

"Dead!" Langrove stared at the silent house. "A judgment. Struck down by the God of the workers." He began to sing *The Red Flag*, his shrill voice mounting on the wind that swept it away.

While Captain Stair and Inspector Pennleaf were standing inside the front door and Braythorpe was trying to tell them what had happened, Dr. Garnet arrived.

When the three men came into the room, Maurice and Tom faced them, expectant; Stephen Litton was talking to Nurse Jonsen in a low voice; but Brade was kneeling by the body of Selford Prentice, still staring at the hand chief that covered the dead face.

CHAPTER 5

"WHEN did the dog begin to bark?" asked Inspector Penn-leaf, laboriously, note-book in hand.

No one replied. Lady Charlotte twittered the pages of her catalogue and sniffed helplessly.

"I was in the flower-pantry with the door open for a moment or two just after the postman came," Nurse Jonsen ended the silence. "If he had been barking then, I should have heard him. I think he began to bark when I was halfway down the passage on the way to Mr. Prentice's room."

"You were going to Mr. Prentice? Why?" asked the Chief Constable, Captain Stair.

"Mrs. Norbury wished to see him. I was actually going to see if Mr. Brade was still with him. I thought he had had enough visitors for one day. He was looking tired. I meant to send Mr. Brade out if I found him there."

"I see. Then it seems quite clear. If anyone did visit Prentice after Mr. Brade left him he went out by the garden door and let Chen in not more than five minutes before you reached the room. The dog would have given the alarm at once."

"It's been a horrible evening," Lady Charlotte intervened between sniffs. "Simply horrible. Rachel and Nurse quarrelling and Tom going to the Union meeting and Maurice going to three Labour ones and I thought someone ought to go with Tom, but Maurice wanted the Vauxhall— and Rachel telling Maurice that Nurse was unsuitable because she'd had her face lifted—that was when Nurse was putting fresh water in the chrysanthemum vase because those copper ones were really too good to throw away—it seems as if everything went wrong just to prepare us!"

"Was there a quarrel? What about?" asked Stair bluntly

Rachel had gone home. Maurice, Stephen Litton, Tom Nurse, and Lady Charlotte were huddled near the fire in the studio. Brade and Jerrold sat farther away by the east windows. Stair had taken up his post at the big writing table in the west bay and Pennleaf stood beside him.

Maurice spoke. "Mrs. Norbury and my father were close friends. She has a very acute mind and he relied on her. Nurse thought she tired him and said so. Unfortunately Rachel resented this and went so far as to say that Nurse was trying to keep her away from my father."

"But you approved of Nurse?"

Nurse Jonsen did not look up as Maurice answered "Certainly. My father liked her. She is Swedish and a trained masseuse. The average nurse is not strong enough to do the lifting."

"Why was Rachel so determined to see Mr. Prentice tonight?" asked Stephen Litton.

Brade, busily rolling cigarettes, did not seem to be listening, but his fingers paused in the work as Maurice answered. "She said she had an urgent message from my father asking her to come in after the hunt and see him on a matter of importance."

"And after all," Lady Charlotte whimpered, "it's perfectly true that Nurse does talk to Selford at the oddest hours of the night and I'm very sorry I told anyone because it made Tom jealous and upset Rachel, and after all Nurse does arrange flowers nicely and doesn't spill ink on the sheets or talk about her titled patients, but I told Nurse if everyone started quarrelling about her it might be better if she left. I don't mind people not knowing the difference between an Anemone japonica and a St. Brigid anemone so long as they're happy, hunting or writing books or making speeches or buying clothes. I dare say there are other interesting things besides flowers. But I do mind everyone getting upset and saying unpleasant things—"

"What I want to know is who was in this room say from six twenty to six thirty," Stair asked.

"I wasn't," Stephen Litton said, "so I can't answer."

"Rachel, Aunt Charlie, Nurse, and I, I think," Maurice volunteered after a moment's thought. "I don't think anyone went out after that. Nurse took out a bowl of chrysanthemums, to change the water, but that was directly after the postman came. I remember because that was when Rachel spoke to me about Nurse and said she did not like her. Nurse came back with the flowers and I went over to the writing-table to answer a letter that had come by the post. It was while I was writing that the three ladies were arguing and finally I couldn't stand it any longer so I told Rachel that I agreed with Nurse and that I thought she urged my father to do more than he ought to do."

"It's quite true," Lady Charlotte agreed, "we were all here. Everyone was so disagreeable I remember it perfectly."

"You can check that, Nurse?"

"Yes. Mr. Tom Prentice came in about six, had a drink, and went upstairs. Mr. Litton went back to his work before that, I think. Otherwise no one left the room so far as I remember except myself once to do the flowers and once to get a bandage for Mr. Maurice Prentice's hand, but that was earlier, just after he came in."

"And she and Rachel quarrelled even about that," Lady Charlotte complained. "Rachel asked her why she didn't sew it and Nurse said she preferred to fold it in and that she'd learned to do it that way in the war and Rachel said: 'But the war was over seventeen years ago,' and Nurse looked furious because no one knew she was as old as that. And as for anyone being out of the room, I went out of that window myself to see if the clematis I'd trained was holding in the wind, and it was." She pointed to the window in the west bay opening on the flagged path of the garden.

"That must have been before the postman came, Aunt Charlie. You were certainly here when Rachel and Nurse were talking, because you were always interrupting them. Besides, I was writing and would have noticed it if you had passed me."

"Can anyone establish the exact moment when the dog began to bark?"

Pennleaf thumbed the leaves of his note-book and found what he was looking for.

"Yes, sir. Must have been between six twenty-five and six thirty. Braythorpe, the butler, goes to Mr. Prentice sharp at six thirty and lets the dog in then. He says he was just starting for his master's room and heard the dog begin to bark when he was turning down the servants' passage toward the hall."

"There are no foot-marks outside the window, but that doesn't help us," Captain Stair explained to Brade with the air of one expert addressing another. "Anyone could have walked round by the flagged path as far as the orchard, and the orchard is full of marks where those men from Medbury came over. Or he could have walked round to the drive and out that way and the composition is too hard to keep impressions. We'll have a finger-print expert here in half an hour. That may tell us something."

"I don't think so," Brade answered mildly. "There's the bell, you know."

Stair looked at Pennleaf, and Pennleaf looked at Stair, like schoolboys bewildered by a question.

Jerrold explained. "I think Brade means that whoever was in the room remembered to wipe the bell he had handled and would certainly have remembered to treat the door-handle and anything else he had touched."

"Of course," Stair agreed.

"But why be so sure anyone was in the room?" asked Litton nervously. "After all, Mr. Prentice may have burned his own letters. The dog may have got in through the house."

Brade stared at Litton for a second. Then he resumed his cigarette-rolling. Quite a pile of uninviting cylinders of tobacco lay on the table beside him.

"We can't find anyone who admits letting him in and Nurse Jonsen says the hall door was tight shut," Stair remarked obstinately.

Nurse Jonsen opened her lips to speak, glanced at Lady Charlotte and then at Dr. Jerrold. Then she said resolutely: "I'm sorry to distress anyone, but after the first few moments when I thought of nothing but doing what was necessary, I realized that if Mr. Prentice had fallen accidentally, his attitude was unnatural."

Braythorpe knocked at the door and entered. "The doctors are asking for Nurse," he answered, as if he were short of breath, "and the postman is here to see the Chief Constable."

"Show him in," Stair directed.

The man came forward and stood there uncomfortable and expectant. Questioned, he said: "No, sir, I didn't see anything unusual. Mr. Braythorpe opened the door and took the letters like he always does. The little dog was running round the side of the house when I got off my bicycle at the door."

"Which way was he going?" asked Stair.

"Toward the lawn on the south side. Like he always does. I see him most nights."

"That would be toward his master's room?" asked Stair of Maurice.

"Yes."

"Did he bark at you?" asked Brade sympathetically. "Dogs are a nuisance to postmen."

"No, he don't bark at me." The postman smiled. "He knows me. He don't bother. He only barks at strangers."

"You came at six fifteen as usual?"

"Well, sir, no. I was early. The fact is it's election time and the post office has got a van on the service and it saves me a bit of work. It wasn't much after six ten. I know because I had to wait three minutes at the pillar box. My time for emptying that is six twenty and usually I have to be sharp to make it. But I got there six seventeen by my watch, and that was on the tick with the post-office clock when I got back to Medbury."

Pennleaf made a note and Stair nodded.

"You saw no one but Braythorpe?"

"Well, sir, just as I was starting to wheel my cycle over the flags, Braythorpe opened the door again to call after me about a parcel her ladyship was expecting—"

"Those primulas. They didn't come. And the frost—" murmured Lady Charlotte.

"Go on," Stair directed.

"And I was going to say—" the postman, confused, stammered.

"You saw someone else?"

"It was only Nurse going into the little room opposite the front door with a vase of flowers."

"No one else?"

"No, sir."

"No one outside the house?"

"No, sir."

"Then that's all, I think."

When the postman had gone, Stair turned to Tom. "You were upstairs from six o'clock, about, until you left your room and heard Nurse call?"

"Yes."

"What were you doing?"

"Well, I took off my clothes and put on a dressing-gown."

"And then?"

"My bath was running and I waited."

"Did it take nearly half an hour to run your bath?"

"Oh, no."

"Why did you wait so long?"

"I was writing a letter." Tom's face flushed slowly.

"Writing a letter? Was it so important?"

"It was, rather."

"I suppose you have the letter to show us."

"No, I haven't."

"Why not?"

"I burned it."

"Why?"

Tom stopped, faced the Chief Constable angrily, and then glanced at his mother.

"Don't you worry, Mother," he said. "I burned it because it was no good."

"Did anyone come into the room while you were writing?"

"No. Who should?"

Tom was beginning to be truculent.

"Then we've only your word for it that you were in your room at all?"

"That's all. Take it or leave it."

"That's not the tone to take," Stair said. "Someone went to your uncle's room and you had the best chance to do it. If you did why don't you say so?"

"I didn't."

"Dear me!" sighed Brade almost inaudibly.

"I think," Dr. Jerrold remarked, looking around him, "I think, Captain Stair, that the ladies have had enough for the moment. Would it be as well to go into the library and talk things over? Then you can send for your witnesses one by one. More satisfactory to you, perhaps?"

Stair, looking doubtful, assented. "Strike while the iron is hot, is my motto," he said; "still—"

"And Tom never was a liar," Lady Charlotte was saying. "None of the Weleven men are, and he's exactly like my great-grandfather who threw a hammer at the carpenter because he kissed his favourite housemaid."

Maurice said brokenly: "You are all going too far. Nothing has been proved. A horrible accident—"

Litton broke in: "For God's sake, Captain Stair, can't you realize what a shock we've all had?"

Tom patted his mother's arm. Stair and Pennleaf went in with Maurice.

Brade dropped his tobacco-pouch and came forward. He asked Tom urgently: "Mr. Prentice, let me look at your nails!"

Tom stared at his hands, dazed for a moment by the absurdity of the request. Then he swore, roundly, loudly, and at length. Brade listened with awed attention to the abuse flung at him, and when Tom bolted noisily from the room he remarked to Jerrold: "You see, Jerry, I'm always warning you against boyish men. I was positively boyish. I was upset. It doesn't do. Because someone has cleaned his nails on Tom Prentice's file, and Pennleaf has got it and it's going to make trouble for Tom, I think."

CHAPTER 6

TASSY'S day was never done until she had seen her mount stabled and fed. While she helped the man prepare the linseed gruel and examined the fine legs of the pretty mare, she thought over the day. "A grand day, Jenn," she said, and Jennifer J. responded with the pointing backward of a dainty ear and a toss of the head. These two agreed. Given hounds in full cry, the Vale of the Med before her, and nothing but clean November fences, a brook, or a stout post and rails to stop her, Jennifer J. would have broken her young heart in preference to being left behind, and so, she knew, felt Tassy.

When the mare was comfortable, busy at her manger, Tassy walked across the stable-yard and in at the side door of the house.

Here she was met by Mullie and all the dogs.

Mullie was old now, and beautiful. Nothing seemed to be left of her but the love that removes mountains. She had nursed Rachel, and later Tassy, when they were babies, disciplined and made them happy later on, and continued to mix the offices of nurse, adviser, disciplinarian, mother, father, and friend ever since. She kept their house, mended their clothes, made them well again if they were ill, consoled them if they were unhappy, shielded them from troubles if she could and wept over it if she couldn't, rejoiced with them, scolded them, and adored them. Where Mullie was there was home.

"Tea's ready, Miss Tassy, but you'd best have a bath first. And where's that new mackintosh and why have ye not got it on and where's Miss Rachel, herself?" Mullie had been reared in County Cork.

"A grand day, Mullie. Come along and I'll tell you about it while I have my bath. Miss Rachel's at the Grange and the car's gone for her. She had her mackintosh on and her skirt kept her legs dry, so she'll be all right. Don't fuss. I brought Big Ben home."

Tassy's bedroom was gay with the glory of a huge coal fire. The curtains were drawn over big windows, and her hunting trophies, photographs of horses and dogs, sporting prints, prize cups, and other reminders of her adventurous young life welcomed her. All the dogs came in and disposed themselves near the fire, Pocahontas, the golden spaniel languishing with adoring eyes, Nails, the fox-terrier blinking at her curiously, Chaing-Yung, Rachel's Peke, usurping the centre of the hearth-rug, and Jake, the old setter, flopping down beside him and going promptly to sleep.

Tassy peeled off her damp clothes, and Mullie took them, listening with intent interest to the story of the day's sport. "That was a fine cast of Mr. Tom's," Mullie agreed sagely.

"Ah, he's a man for the game, Miss Tassy. I always said so and I always will. 'It's not enough to guess,' my old father'd say, and him the best huntsman of his day in the old country, as any man'll tell ye, Miss Tassy, 'it's not enough to guess. You've got to think with the fox's mind and smell with the hound's nose. That's what ye've got to do to hunt hounds, Mary Mulholland, and never forget it!'"

Tassy, who had heard this maxim before, continued her account, recalled by Mullie's admonition to the business of undressing and getting into her bath. "Heavenly," she interrupted herself as she sank into the steaming water. "And then, Mullie, Mendleson spoke and Anarchy took it up and in no time we were off again. But Tom says we were on to a fresh fox. You never saw anything like the pace, and Jennifer J. never faltered. We went straight for the stream. I didn't dare steady her much—you know how it is with Jennifer J.—doesn't do to cool her—" this to Mullie, who had never mounted anything swifter than a donkey, and that sixty years ago—"so I just headed her for a willow and took my chance, and did she spread herself—" Mullie leaned forward and clasped her hands in her excitement. "Well, Mullie, the way she measured those last few strides and gathered herself up for the take-off, and the feel of her resting on her forehand on the other side and bringing her hocks well under, safe as the Rock of Gibraltar and twice as easy—you wouldn't beat it, not in a hundred years."

"Oh, Miss Tassy! But then, you've the hands. As my old father said, 'It's the hands that does it, Mary Mulholland, and not the heels, and if you tell me otherwise I'll tell you you'll never see a fox killed in the Meath country, not while banks is banks and horse-flesh different to mules.' And you better lie down, Miss Tassy, and not shake that sponge on Pocahontas or you'll have her in the bath too."

Tassy, drying herself, finished her story. Thinking of the ride home, her face changed.

"Mullie, what's the matter with them all at the Grange? I can remember the last time we stayed there, while Rachel was getting her divorce, and it was awfully jolly and cheerful then. Maurice was so nice and used to make me laugh a lot. Now—I hate to go there. They're so deadly serious. Is it because they're Socialists, or what? I'm so sorry for Tom. I wish Rachel had married happily, Mullie. Then she wouldn't want to reform everybody."

Mullie shook her wise head. "Miss Rachel was always contrary," she admitted benignly, "but don't you go criticizing your sister, Miss Tassy. Your mother was a clever lady and Jewish, so they say. She was a kind and loving mistress, but she was sad. Seemed the troubles of the world were her troubles and she couldn't bear them. That's what brought her and Mr. Selford Prentice together. And it's wrong, Miss Tassy. Father O'Flarty explained it to me long ago. 'You do what you can for your neighbour, Mary,' says he to me, 'and don't you fret about the stars in their courses. You leave them to their Maker.' And that's what I've done. Your mother, she couldn't see a sick child and not want to cure every sick child whether over the way or in the deepest jungle in Africa. And Miss Rachel—she thinks more of those she can't see or understand than those she can. And that husband of hers, he made it worse. Miss Rachel will not beg for anything, not even happiness, so when life said no to her, she said no to life, and now she cares only for thinking and planning for a grand future where there'll be no poor and no rich, and none will suffer—a future that'll not fail her, because she does not think for it to come in a lifetime."

Mullie had this way of drifting into a crooning chant, and Tassy was used to it. She had told them fairytales in just that voice. So now Tassy, drying herself vigorously, listened without attending to the sense of the words. "What a funny world it is!" she thought. Rachel and Maurice and Selford Prentice all so bothered about things that would come right just as quickly if they never gave them a thought. The trouble was that they and their sort threatened the precious things she and her sort would fight to keep. Tassy's picture of the triumph of Socialism in England was made up of rows upon rows of glaring white pill-box houses, with brisk young women carrying attaché cases walking in and out, accompanied by long-haired and spectacled young men, just about to attend or just having attended high-brow concerts or lectures in barrack-like assembly halls, or in dismantled drawing-rooms of such houses as Medbury Park, where the Flaxman mantelpieces would be blocked up with steel radiators and the Adams decorations replaced with modern nudes not in the least resembling the thin brown body under the rough towel in her hand. That was the bright side of the picture. The ugly side did not bear dwelling on at all. Dracy, the groom, for instance. What would they do with him? Lock him up? Shoot him? They'd never get him to take orders from such people as Langrove, father to the new under-housemaid at the Grange, who waved his arms and chattered death and damnation to everyone who had ever served champagne at a dinner party or worn a tail coat. And what would become of Jennifer J., the aristocrat Jenn, with her loathing of a heavy hand? And what of the face of England, its park-lands and lawns, its flowering gardens, its shaded lanes, and the funny little houses stooping over crooked streets, its square-built churches resting in quiet churchyards, its pasture-lands and beechy woods? The things English people thought of when they were far away and returned to if they could?

Perhaps Tassy was more tired than she knew, for she felt her eyes smarting, and rubbed them savagely with the towel. She and Rachel never talked politics. Rachel was always absent-mindedly indulgent to Tassy and kept open house for her friends, found the money for her horses, and encouraged her to buy the tweeds and jumpers and trim little evening frocks she liked. Tassy, in return, made no comment on the odd people Rachel entertained from time to time, and quietly withdrew when the conversation soared or delved out of her range. Her admiration for Rachel knew no bounds. Rachel was beautiful, brilliant, and altogether marvellous, and Tassy herself was just a girl with a good figure who understood horses. Politics had nothing whatever to do with it. Rachel might have practised Yoga and spent most of the day squatting on a straw mat, and still Tassy, though regretting these symptoms, would have held to her view of her intelligence and superiority, and thought herself too stupid and ordinary to understand. The point was that the world was largely composed of stupid and ordinary people, and Tassy's sympathy was with them.

Cheerfully disregarding the fact that the clock had chimed seven and dinner was set for eight o'clock, Tassy made a warm nest for herself on the Chesterfield, beside the fire, and settled down to enjoy her tea, while Mullie hovered over her. She had eaten her first egg and was beginning on the second when the parlour-maid came to the door, her professional calm missing. "The car is back and Hines would like to speak to Mrs. Mulholland," she said, breathing hard.

"Where's Mrs. Norbury? Hasn't she come?"

"No, Miss Tassy. If you'll just speak to Hines, Mrs. Mulholland."

Mullie went. Tassy considered following her, but thought better of it. They were probably keeping Rachel for dinner. Hadley, the parlour-maid, was a goose anyway, outside of the radius of pantry and dining-room, the sort of servant who changed her voice in the servants' hall and put on composure with her cap. But when Mullie had been absent for five minutes, Tassy felt disturbed, for she had been in the middle of an animated discussion of plans for the hunt ball, and Mullie was far more interested in such things than in any gossip Hines might be spreading in the servants' hall. Something must be wrong.

Tassy sat up. She heard Mullie coming along the passage, slowly, more slowly still as she neared the drawing-room door. Why was she hesitating, her hand on the door-knob?

"Mullie, come in at once and tell me what's wrong." Tassy jumped up and ran to the door and flung it open. Her nurse's face, noble and staunch, gleamed pallid in the light.

"It's Mr. Selford, Miss Tassy. There's been an accident. Hines says he's dead."

Was that all? For a moment Tassy had thought it might be worse. Mullie would not look like that unless she was afraid for Rachel and herself. Bad enough, indeed, but Selford Prentice had been so near to dying many times before that the news could not shock her as it might otherwise have done.

"I'll see Hines myself. Where is Miss Rachel?"

"Oh, Miss Tassy, there's police at the Grange. They're questioning everyone. Hines has to go back himself. He got there just after it happened."

"Police? Well, of course, Mullie. If it was an accident they had to notify the police. There's nothing alarming about that. But Rachel! She'll be frantic. I ought to go back with Hines and fetch her."

"No, Miss Tassy, my dear, don't do that. Miss Rachel told Hines you're not to go. There's nothing to be done for the poor gentleman."

Tassy ran down the hall and pushed aside the baize door that led to the servants' quarters. Mullie followed her. Hines was standing in the broad stone passage, the three maids grouped around him; a smell of burnt pudding came from the open kitchen door.

"Kate, go back to your stove; the dinner's spoiling," said Mullie severely.

"Come into the hall, Hines. Now tell me what happened," Tassy demanded.

Hines was a little man who had once been a stable-boy and could lend a hand to the two grooms and did frequently. He followed Tassy, hat in hand.

"I got there soon after the half-hour. Then I begun to think something was wrong. I went round to the kitchen and rang, but nobody came. So then I saw the studio window was open and I looked in and just then Mrs. Norbury come in with her ladyship and they looked terrible, miss. So I made so bold as to walk into the studio and speak to Mrs. Norbury. She said I was to drive home and tell Mrs. Mulholland that there'd been an accident and Mr. Prentice was dead, but Lady Charlotte, she was talking too, though I couldn't quite follow what she said, but it was something about a Mr. Brade, I believe, and—" Hines looked at Mullie, who was frowning—"and that's all, miss, and I'm to go back to wait for Mrs. Norbury."

"There's something else, Hines."

He shifted his position uneasily, watching Mullie. "Hines had better go," said Mullie. "Miss Rachel may be waiting."

Tassy stamped her foot. "There's something else. What is it?" she demanded.

Hines, being an outdoor servant, was not afraid of Mullie. He answered: "It's only what Molly Hegan said. She came in with some brandy for the ladies, and she followed me out. She said there'd been some newspapers on the floor by the fire and they'd caught somehow and Mr. Prentice must have leaned forward and tried to save his writing-papers on the table, and fallen. And she said: 'He was alone, they say, but if he was, how did that dog get in?' That's all I know, miss. Just servants' gossip."

Mullie and Tassy went back to the drawing-room.

"You finish your tea, my pretty. And don't you fret. The poor gentleman had to die soon. Maybe 'twas better to come quick and sudden. He was a good man, and the Lord is merciful. Holy Mary rest his soul." Mullie crossed herself.

Tassy had no great experience of human tragedy and sorrow. She had been too young at her mother's death to feel any shock, and she had never seen her father. Rachel, ten years older, had borne all that, and she and Mullie between them had made up the loss to Tassy. Selford Prentice had been an invalid ever since she could remember, and she had loved him, but not as Rachel did. Now, as she occupied herself telephoning to friends, helping Mullie to make the room bright with firelight and flowers for Rachel, she thought of the tragedy from her sister's point of view. And every moment or two, Hines's words came back to her. "Who let the dog in?"

Tassy knew Chen. She knew the precision of his habits.

He was never known to leave his master's side, except for two walks a day and after tea when he went to get bread and butter from the servants and after his supper was let out into the garden and let in again at his master's garden door at six thirty. The accident must have happened before six thirty. Then, if Chen was in the room, who let him in?

"Absurd," Tassy told herself, looking down at the Peke, who was restless, knowing that her mistress should be at home and was not. "Absurd!" she said aloud, and Nails, the fox-terrier, sat up expectantly, Pocahontas waved her tail, her mournful eyes on Tassy, and Jake, the retriever, grunted and flopped over on his other side. Was it absurd? If Pocahontas, for instance, failed to scratch at her door at seven-thirty, would she not know that the housemaid had overslept and failed to open the upstairs windows, or if Jake suddenly dropped five years off his age and made the room into a cage by his wild entreaties to leave it, would she not know he had heard a shot in the Hartover coverts, or if Nails came in with his tail tucked in and flattened ears, would she not look for a dead chicken? Chen had not altered his routine. If he had been in the room when his master was found dead, who let him in?

The car was coming. Tassy ran to the front door and threw it wide open. Rachel stepped out. She was wearing her motor coat and had her riding skirt over her arm. Under the other arm she carried Chen, the cairn.

She went silently into the drawing-room, put Chen down among the other dogs, and stood in front of the fire, while Pocahontas, Nails, Jake, and Chaing-Yung walked round and round the bristling cairn. Tassy and Rachel and Mullie waited for their verdict. Chen growled. He said, in effect: "You keep your places, and I'll keep mine." This was agreed.

Five dogs instead of four lay down on the rug, but Nails kept an eye on the stranger.

"I had to bring him. Maurice couldn't stand seeing him." Rachel shook off her coat into Mullie's arms and gave her a kiss. "Don't fuss. I'm all right. But there's the devil to pay up there." She looked away from them and at the fire. "Captain Stair thinks it was an accident, but no one else does."

CHAPTER 7

RACHEL NORBURY despised crying women, and because she was neither cold nor heartless she expressed her emotions in a way far more trying to other people than tears and hysteria would have been. Tassy and Mullie were left with nothing to do, unless their obedience to the negative request not to fuss could be called a form of activity.

"I'll tell you more about it after dinner, Tassy. Now I'm going to have a bath and change," she said, as she went out of the room.

Half an hour later she returned, and they went into the dining-room. Tassy loved this room with its rounded walls and moulded ceiling. The paint was white and the wide curtains crimson. In the narrow spaces between dividing pillars hung engravings from the family portraits in the collection of the head of the house of Lyste. It was a formal, graceful room, with an air of expecting like qualities from the people who used it, and Tassy always remembered her manners when she was in it.

Tonight she regarded her sister with despairing admiration, while Hadley waited on them, awed, too, by her mistress's calm. Everyone knew that Rachel had been devoted to Selford Prentice and that her life would be altered by his death. Yet she ate and drank as if nothing had happened, talking to Tassy fitfully about arrangements and the immediate problems arising from the event.

"I think you ought to go to see Lady Charlotte in the morning. She is terribly upset and does not like Nurse Jonsen. She's much fonder of you than she is of me. We'll both go about ten o'clock. Stephen has a lot to do, and reporters were calling up when I left. They'll all be there tomorrow. Happening at election time, it won't attract quite so much attention perhaps, though of course, as Maurice is contesting the division, public interest may be excited."

"I suppose so," Tassy replied, miserably.

"Luckily, Selford himself was not a public figure." Rachel finished her glass of claret and allowed Hadley to remove her plate, ignoring the extra solicitude the servant managed to convey in the act of routine. "Very few people outside the party leaders realized his importance. But Maurice being so popular socially, the gossip-writers will be busy. I think he wants me to deal with the newspapers. There'll be a lot to do."

"I suppose so," Tassy said again.

Eventually, when Tassy had repeated this phrase for the tenth time, Rachel turned to her with something like a smile. "Poor Tassy. Do I seem very inhuman?"

Hadley came in with the coffee, so Tassy did not have to answer and Rachel allowed the maid to serve them in silence. As soon as the door was shut, Tassy said: "It's all very well, Rachel, and I know you've had a ghastly shock and I hate to worry you, but what did you mean?"

Rachel stirred her coffee, her eyes on her teaspoon.

"I'd rather not say. Wait a little, Tassy. I'll tell you all there is to go on, but my private opinion I'd better keep to myself. There's no reason to burden you with it—not yet anyway. Come into the drawing-room and ask me any questions you like."

The two young women went together to the drawing-room, and there Mullie was waiting for them. She was not afraid of Rachel, although she obeyed her.

"Now, Miss Rachel, ma'am, you light your cigarette and tell us all about it." Mullie held out a box full of Turks and found matches for both girls. Then she sat down herself in an upright chair beside them, while Tassy perched on the stool before the fire, and Rachel took her usual seat.

"I don't know very much, Mullie. I had a message from Selford before I started for the meet this morning. Here it is." She took a note out of her bag and gave it to Tassy, who read out loud.

My dear Rachel:

I want to see you urgently before posting a letter which must go tonight. If you come to the Grange after hunting we can have a talk and then you can post my letter in Hartover. Will you send a message to say you will not fail me?

Yours ever,
Selford Prentice

"You see, he wrote it himself and sent the car with it, and as he never writes letters, it must have been something he wanted to keep from Stephen. I have no idea what it was. Anyway, of course I went, but when I got there a man named Brade was with him, discussing a piece of porcelain Selford wanted to sell. Nurse Jonsen tried to persuade me not to see him. She said he had already had a long talk with Dr. Jerrold—do you remember him, Mullie? He stayed at the Grange once about five years ago when Tassy and I were living there."

"I remember him." Tassy did. She had shown him over the stables and found him intelligent. He had picked out her favourites to admire and asked the right questions. He had also remarked on Tom's horsemanship, when they went out to see a new hunter tried over the artificial jumps in the paddock.

Mullie remembered him too.

"A fine figure of a man, he was, though doctors aren't what they were, Miss Rachel. How can you expect it with motor cars to whisk 'em off to another case before they've passed the time of day with ye? Write something ye can't read on a bit of paper and a shake of the hand, and they're off, too busy earning fees to listen to your troubles. Just as if listening to troubles wasn't half the cure!"

"I believe that is just what Dr. Jerrold does, as a matter of fact, Mullie. Listen to people's troubles. But anyway, Selford liked him and he brought Mr. Brade, who is a friend of his." Rachel braced herself and told them all that had happened. "The only things that puzzled them were that Selford had not rung his bell, which was in its usual place on the table beside him, that all the letters Stephen had brought him to sign were burned, and no one could account for the presence of the dog in the room."

At that moment all the dogs were admitted by Hadley. "I thought you'd like me to feed them tonight, miss," she told Tassy, "so I gave them their usual supper, and the little one had a bone. He didn't seem hungry."

Pocahontas sat down by Tassy's chair and rested her head on her mistress's knee. Chaing-Yung bagged the centre of the hearth-rug as usual. Jake compressed his stout body into a heaving mound as close as he dared to the Peke, and Nails went in search of his ball, which had rolled under the sofa before dinner. Chen looked with disapproval at the occupants of the hearth-rug and then sat down and stared at Rachel.

"But how did Chen get in?" Tassy asked. "Braythorpe always let him in at the garden door when he went to wheel Uncle Selford to his room. Was he let out as usual after his supper?"

"The servants say so. But the postman came about six ten and Captain Stair has made up his mind that Chen slipped in then and somehow got into the room just before Nurse opened the door."

"Was the door ajar?"

"She says it wasn't. So does Tom. So does Braythorpe."

"Or the door to the garden?"

"Shut, and the latch caught as usual. It could be opened from the inside—not from outside."

"One of the house maids let him in and won't own to it," Mullie suggested. "You can't trust these servants nowadays, Miss Rachel."

"But—well, perhaps, Mullie. Anyway, he was there and he couldn't have been there long. You know how sharp his bark is, and Tom and Mr. Brade and Nurse all say they heard him just as soon as they got to the hall. Tom and Mr. Brade heard him from the top of the stairs, and Molly Hegan passed the staircase going from Lady Charlotte's room toward the back stairs and he wasn't barking then, though the fire must have started by that time—between twenty and twenty-five past six."

"Where was Stephen?"

"Typing in the library."

"I don't understand." Tassy screwed up her eyes a little, a trick she had when she wanted to think about what she saw. "Why did you say you didn't think it was an accident? What else could explain it?"

Rachel did not answer. Instead she said: "Push Jake farther over so Chen can be down on the rug."

Tassy moved Jake, who grunted, and Chaing-Yung, who growled. Chen stalked into the vacant place by the fire, exchanged remarks with Chaing-Yung, and lay down, his earthy eyes open on the Peke. Apparently, though unfriendly, the two dogs respected each other, for Chaing Yung lay down too, quite six inches farther along than usual, and Chen pushed him no farther.

"What you think is that someone who was with Uncle Selford went out the garden door and Chen slipped in?" Tassy persisted.

"Don't let us guess, Tassy. Remember Selford and Tom were not on very good terms."

The telephone bell rang.

"I'll go." Tassy jumped up, glad to do something. The telephone was in the hall, with an extension upstairs in the room where Rachel worked. Tassy went to the hall,

leaving the drawing-room door open. She heard Mullie
say something to Rachel, and Rachel reply sharply: "Be
quiet, Mullie."

"It's Braythorpe. He says that Dr. Jerrold and Mr.
Brade are on their way to see you, Rachel." Tassy re-
entered the drawing-room. "Why do you suppose they
want to see you?"

"I don't know."

"Must you see them tonight?"

"Why not? I shall have to some time, I suppose.
Maurice must have sent them to clear up some question.
The sooner the whole thing is straightened out, the better
for us all."

Mullie's square face, turned on her nurslings, was
alight with protective devotion.

"You're not fit for questions tonight, Miss Rachel, my
dear. Let me put you to bed and see the two gentlemen
myself. I'll soon explain."

"No, Mullie. I must see them. There'll have to be an
inquest, you know. This Mr. Brade happened to be there
when Selford died and I suppose Captain Stair has asked
him to help. But you might send Hadley to bed and let
them in yourself. The less servants' hall gossip, the
better."

Mullie went to carry out the suggestion about the
servants and returned just in time to forestall a ring at
the bell. Tassy quieted the dogs, who resented being
disturbed. Nails barked, Chaing-Yung growled, and Jake
grunted, while Pocahontas, under Tassy's hand, brooded,
sensitive to her trouble. Chen opened his eyes and
watched everyone without moving.

Outside in the hall Mullie was talking to Dr. Jerrold.
He answered her reassuringly, somewhat at length, and
she opened the door for him to enter. Simon Brade
followed.

Rachel pointed to the sofa opposite her chair, and
Tassy stood hesitating after she had shaken hands with
Jerrold. Rachel introduced Brade.

Tassy could see that Dr. Jerrold was deeply troubled. "We've come to you for help, Mrs. Norbury," he said abruptly. "Captain Stair has asked Brade to help in the investigation. Everyone is anxious to get things clear before the inquest. Maurice is impossible—he is too broken up to help much. I advised Brade to come to you because you knew Prentice so well. Can you tell us anything about these anonymous letters?"

"I don't think they were important," Rachel answered. "We're almost sure Langrove sent them, but he is only a tub-thumper."

"Did you know he headed a raid on the Grange this evening? He's been examined. He says it was a deputation of workers from the factory to put before Prentice some grievance or other."

"I didn't know that, but what of it?"

"Only that they seem to have arrived at the Grange by different ways and Langrove may have been there about the time Mr. Prentice died."

"He couldn't have got in—and anyway isn't it clear that Selford died by accident?"

"We want to make it perfectly certain that the Coroner's jury will think so—if we can."

"You think there is some doubt?"

"A good deal of doubt, I'm afraid."

Brade was looking at Chen, and Chen, who had seen Brade last in charge of the detested effigy of the fish, returned his scrutiny. Then Brade turned to Rachel and made a deprecating gesture. "You don't think I like it, do you?" he said. "Mrs. Norbury, I assure you that I didn't want to have anything to do with the case. I'm not allowed to deal with anything more distressing than forgery or blackmail. Jerry, here, forbids it. And this is very distressing. I liked Mr. Prentice. I liked him so much that I nearly tried to persuade him not to sell me that specimen of San Ts'ai. When I tell you that, you'll understand I've told you everything. The fact remains that I was the last person to see him alive, apparently, and we think that somebody was in the room when he died, and there's no particular reason why it shouldn't have been me, and I've a natural preference for proving it wasn't. I don't know if you follow me."

Tassy felt a perverse inclination to giggle. The little man was the opposite of her idea of a sleuth and far more suited to the role of a music-hall comedian, one of those born mirth-makers, whose gravity is funnier than another's grimaces. While she was thinking this he fumbled in all his pockets for something which was not there and she felt sorry for him. "Jerry dear, I've left my cigarette-papers somewhere. What shall I do?"

"Sit still. Have one of mine if you want to smoke."

"But I don't. I want to roll some cigarettes. My one talent, Mrs. Norbury. You don't happen to have any Manila paper and tobacco about, I suppose?"

Rachel had not.

"What is it you want to ask me?" Rachel turned to Jerrold.

"Questions may be asked about Prentice's reason for wishing to see you particularly tonight, as I understand he did. If you feel inclined to tell us, it might be as well."

"But I don't know." Rachel opened her bag and handed him the note she had received from Selford Prentice. "You see it tells me nothing."

Jerrold read the short note and handed it to Brade, who glanced at it and gave it back to Rachel.

"And you can't guess?"

"Only that it must have been a personal matter or he would have dictated the note or telephoned. I can only imagine he did not want even my brother Stephen, who was his secretary, to know how urgent it was. You see he refers to a letter he wanted me to post for him. Perhaps that was the secret. But I don't see the connection, in any case—with the accident, I mean."

Brade was wandering around the room looking at things. Rachel's way of furnishing a room was to make the necessities of comfort as attractive as she could and push everything else out of the way, but Mullie, with quiet firmness, had preserved a few ornaments from this treatment. There was a show-stand for miniatures and Brade seemed to be engrossed by these, his monocle in use as he examined a fine Collins.

"Surprising, the connection between things that you wouldn't sort together in a catalogue," he said suddenly. "Now, this lady and my water-pourer. Had Collins ever studied just that purple-brown at its fountain-head? If so, where? You could string a whole inquiry out of that, you know. So distracting when you're trying to keep to the point. That's why I never do. A point if it's anything at all is nothing. A vanishing in space of converging lines. Are you interested in metaphysics, Mrs. Norbury?"

"Not tonight," Rachel answered shortly.

"That's a pity!"

"Why?"

"Oh, because if you are about to travel by road, a compass isn't much use!"

"I don't know what you mean, Mr. Brade."

"Well, you see"—Brade glanced uncomfortably at Jerrold—"we are all thinking about one thing so hard that we miss everything else. If you're catching a train and likely to be late, you don't notice the scenery. Now, in this case it's the scenery that matters, so it's far better to forget all about the train. If we all discussed Berkeley or Kant or Hegel for a few moments, it would help a lot."

Rachel turned to Jerrold with a gesture that dismissed Brade from the inquiry. "What is it you want to know?" she asked stiffly.

Jerrold hesitated and then, seeming to receive some signal from Brade, said: "You can help us by telling us, as nearly as you can, what everyone was doing and where they were at the time of the accident. It is a question of making it clear that no one in the house saw Prentice after Brade left the room at five forty-five."

"Yes, I see. Maurice, Lady Charlotte, and Nurse Jonsen were in the studio all that time. Tom and my brother were not there after six."

"No one left the room at all except Tom and your brother?"

Rachel stopped to think. "Lady Charlotte went outside for a moment to look at a clematis she had trained against the wall. Nurse Jonsen went out once—no, twice—the first time to get a bandage for Maurice's hand—he had injured it—the second time to rearrange some flowers.

"Can you time her absence?"

"The first time was soon after we came in—and she was only away two or three minutes. The second time was later and she was away from five to ten minutes. But the postman came just after she returned, and that was at six ten, so she was in the room for that last fifteen minutes."

"She could have walked down the passage, entered Mr. Prentice's room, burned his letters, and returned in that time."

"She could, but why should she?"

"Why indeed!"

"Besides," Rachel added, "it seems quite clear that the whole tragedy must have taken place during the last ten minutes before it was discovered. If Chen had barked sooner, someone would have heard him. Molly Hegan was passing along the landing about twenty past six, Braythorpe came through the hall to let in the postman at six ten. They must have heard him if he had been barking then. We all heard him as soon as the door was opened. And that is another point. When Nurse opened the door to go to speak to Selford, there was no sound. She says Chen began to bark just before she reached the hall, and Mr. Brade and Tom agree that they heard him begin to bark while they were still upstairs. If anyone was with Selford he must have gone out by the garden door just about the time Nurse left the studio about six twenty-five."

"So it seems. Though Chen may have spent a moment or two investigating before he raised the alarm, I suppose. However, to get back to the point—you yourself, Lady Charlotte, and Maurice were together in the room from the time the postman came at six ten until you heard of the accident. You're sure?"

"Yes. Certain."

Brade had produced a pencil and a minute diary from his pocket and was drawing in it. "Is this right?" he asked. "I do love to draw, don't you, Mrs. Norbury? Everyone does especially people who can't."

"I think that's right," Rachel agreed.

Brade handed the plan of the studio to Jerrold.

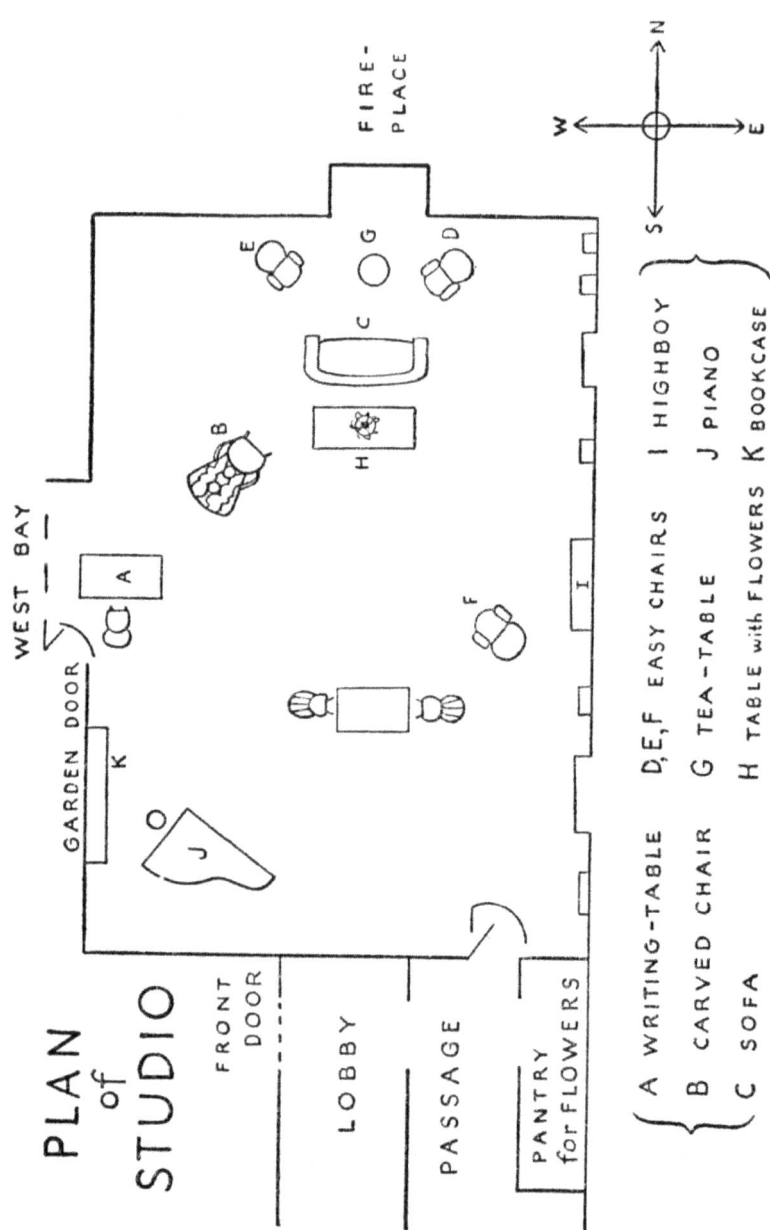

PLAN of STUDIO

FRONT DOOR

LOBBY

PASSAGE

PANTRY for FLOWERS

GARDEN DOOR

WEST BAY

FIRE-PLACE

N
W — E
S

A WRITING-TABLE
B CARVED CHAIR
C SOFA
D,E,F EASY CHAIRS
G TEA-TABLE
H TABLE with FLOWERS
I HIGHBOY
J PIANO
K BOOKCASE

"Well, that's the room. Where were you sitting?"
Jerrold asked.

"In the chair marked E."

"All the time?"

"I got up once to speak to Maurice, I think, and to feel of my skirt, drying on a chair by the radiator."

"Where was Maurice?"

"Writing a letter at the table A. I told you the postman came about six ten and he had a letter to answer."

"Nurse Jonsen?"

"On the sofa, C."

"And you could see each other all the time?"

"Nurse Jonsen had her back to the room. She could only see Maurice by looking over her shoulder, I should think. Lady Charlotte and I could see him, and he could see all of us. Besides, we were talking to each other."

"Even Maurice?"

"He interrupted us when he thought we were beginning to quarrel."

Jerrold looked at the plan. "Maurice was sitting near the open window. The room is full of furniture. Are you sure you could see him? It's important, you see, to place everyone as far as we can. There was no screen or other obstacle between you?"

"Why, no. There's that enormous chair, but it has an open carved back, and the writing-table has only a narrow top. There wasn't even a table with flowers on it between us. You can see for yourself."

"When did Tom Prentice go out?"

"Some time before the letters came."

"And your brother?"

"Stephen was there just at first."

"So you, Nurse, Lady Charlotte, and Maurice Prentice were together except when Nurse was arranging the flowers. That's something. Braythorpe says he could hear Mr. Litton typing all the time he was in the pantry, and the kitchen servants say Braythorpe was in the pantry between six twenty and six thirty. The cook and kitchen-maid account for each other and for the under-housemaid, who was washing up the servants' tea-things, and the head housemaid and I were upstairs, though we can't prove it," Brade remarked.

"What about Tom?" asked Tassy suddenly. All this time Tassy had been remembering what Rachel had said about Tom's quarrel with his uncle, but she had not seen its possible meaning until now.

"He says he was in his room till six thirty, when he came along the upstairs landing to go to his bath. Molly Hegan ran it for him and knocked on his door to let him know it was ready."

"Did he answer her?"

Brade turned an innocent face on Tassy. "I don't know," he said.

Up to now Tassy had felt bewildered, anxious, painfully sorry for Rachel, and distressed for herself, in turns. Now all at once she felt angry.

"What do you mean by that, Mr. Brade! You've acquitted everyone else in the house of being near that room at that time. Why not take the same trouble about Tom?"

Brade looked at Jerrold helplessly, and Jerrold explained: "Tom has taken rather a dislike to Simon, I'm afraid. Brade never asked him if he heard the maid knock. Tom stopped him before that. In fact, he lost his temper!"

Tom would, thought Tassy. And why not? If you have ridden straight all your life, taking your fences as they came, and then found yourself in a maze of barbed wire spun to trip you by some malignant enemy of sport, you would lose your temper. Tom had told the truth patiently enough, no doubt. It was when questions began to have the object of confusing and obscuring his memory that he would turn ugly.

"I don't see what you are driving at, at all." Tassy attacked Brade. "Why don't you speak out? Uncle Selford was in his own house with his own family and friends, and servants who were devoted to him. There was an accident and he died. Why make a mystery of it?"

"That's just what we're trying to avoid, Miss Litton," said Jerrold gravely.

"Then leave it alone. Any English jury will see it straight. It's only people who like to make problems and difficulties who'll find any mystery. The more questions you ask, the worse it will be. Everyone will start thinking of suspicious circumstances. Everyone will begin doubting everyone else. Do you mean to say you think someone in the house went in and burned Uncle Selford's letters and then, when he tried to save them, saw him fall and left him there, with the papers on fire? Is that what you mean? When everybody around him spent their lives saving him worry and trouble and pain and carrying out his least wish? Everyone loved him—"

She stopped abruptly. Did Tom love him? Tom, like herself, had kept free of the influence he exerted over almost everyone. Tom had resented his uncle's hold on the income which he felt should have been his without restrictions. Tom wanted to live his own life in his own way and meant to do it. But, until lately, he and his uncle had been fond of each other and as friendly as such two men of such opposite temperaments could be. It was only since the unfortunate mishap to Tom's mare Parasina, and the unexpected losses involved, that Selford Prentice had put any pressure on Tom to alter his way of life, and only since Nurse Jonsen came to the Grange that the uncle and nephew had actually quarrelled. Did Mr. Brade know all this? He did not look as if he knew anything. And Dr. Jerrold? Tassy knew that it was his business to understand people. Surely he would understand, then, that, whatever Tom did, he would not conceal it or try to avoid the consequences. If he had been there when Selford Prentice fell he would have called for help. What could be clearer than that? She looked at him to see if she was right in counting on him, and found him looking at her.

Tassy knew that putting her thoughts into words was not her strong point, but the thoughts were all right if she could get them out clear and straight. The thoughts themselves were both clear and straight. But Rachel's weren't. Rachel was sitting there in armour, thinking what? Mr. Brade was swinging his monocle on its dark ribbon, thinking what?

"Everyone loved him?" Jerrold turned from Tassy to Rachel with the question.

"Everyone near him loved him, I should say," she answered. "You know, of course, that he was separated from his wife."

"But that was an old story. I mean, they had agreed to live apart?"

Rachel moved suddenly as if faced with an intolerable choice and Tassy understood her trouble. To discuss Selford Prentice's private life with anyone at any time would have been distasteful, but tonight it was torture. Tassy spoke, defending her sister. "Uncle Selford had not seen his wife for thirty years."

"But they were not divorced?"

"No. He was a Roman Catholic, of course, and so was she."

"Then she was satisfied with the position?" Jerrold asked Rachel.

"No. She was never satisfied. She wanted an annulment and a legal divorce. Lately she has urged it again."

"Why?"

"I don't know. I understand she is still very lovely. The family is highly placed. She may have wished to remarry, for all I know. The marriage was hasty. In fact, they eloped. They lived together a few months. She was only seventeen. Selford told me she married him to get away from the irksome restraint of her life at home and an arranged alliance. Then when she found that he was not disposed to give way in all matters to her caprices, she came to hate him. Apparently she was a girl of violent passions, great beauty, and exaggerated ambitions. She cared for nothing but excitement and power. When they parted, Selford was very generous to her family, on the understanding that they should take over all responsibility for her control. I know he allowed them a large part of his income. Her father and mother are dead, but her two brothers look after her. That is all I know."

"I understand that they are the sole representatives of the former reigning house?"

"Yes. By a series of accidents and war casualties, they are. But of course the country was always a dependency of one great power or another. The island itself is important only because of its strategic position in war time. I believe there is an element favourable to Albania and Italy. I suppose it is humiliating to a Princess Velbesco to find herself the wife of an Englishman and a commoner. The brothers, apparently, do not mind so long as they get the cash."

"I see. Where is the Princess now?"

"In a nursing home in Austria. Lady Charlotte gave me the address and I sent her a telegram." Rachel stood silent.

"I'm so sorry to have to ask you all these questions, Mrs. Norbury, but you are so much the best person to answer them. Mr. Prentice and Tom had quarrelled?"

"Yes. About money. Selford's brother left everything in trust when he died and Selford had absolute control. Both brothers were Socialists, but Tom's mother's family was traditionally sporting and pleasure-loving. Selford would not allow Tom to spend everything on horses, and Tom resented his position. The friction had increased very much lately."

"Why?"

"Tom lost money on racing, and things came to a climax."

"Mr. Prentice had written his lawyer indicating proposed alterations to his will, and these would make Tom's position of dependency permanent. Did you know that?"

"No."

"The letter was among those that were burned. Your brother, Mr. Litton, had a copy, of course."

Tassy said: "Why should Tom burn a letter when he knew a copy would be kept!"

Rachel answered sharply: "Don't be silly, Tassy. No one is suggesting that Tom did."

"That's not true. It has been suggested. Tom quarrelled with Uncle Selford; Tom was in his room upstairs and might have come down any time in that half-hour. You're all thinking so." She stood up, ready to fight for Tom.

Rachel answered. "As a matter of fact, burning that letter in a temper is just what Tom might have done. He'd not have stopped to remember the copy. You'd better keep quiet, Tassy. You aren't helping Tom."

"I'm not trying to help him. Why should I? He has nothing to do with it!" Tassy protested, aware that Rachel was right.

"There's something in what Tassy says," Jerrold put in quickly. "The person subtle enough to do all the other things he seems to have done—wiped the bell, burned all the letters to mask his reason for burning one, and other things—would have remembered that copies were held of every letter except one. That was the one Mr. Prentice wrote in his own hand after Brade left him. That was burned so carefully that a mere fragment of blue paper is all that is left. There are scraps of others. They fell on the hearth out of the basket grate. But there is not one word of that handwritten letter to tell us what it was about or why it was written. Evidently you cannot help us there, Mrs. Norbury, not even with a guess."

"I hope I have not given the impression that I don't want to help you." Rachel stiffened.

"You are not very communicative, but that is only natural."

"Maurice Prentice and his father were on the best of terms, I believe?" asked Brade.

"Maurice?" The abruptness of this query took Rachel by surprise. "Why do you ask that?"

"Well, you know people aren't my province. I never understand them. I take Jerry's word for everything. But Maurice Prentice did see his father that morning, and Mr. Prentice did not tell him why he wanted to see you so urgently, or even that he had asked you to come. And Jerry thinks that's odd. Jerry is like that. He's thinking about the way people behave when I'm thinking about burned cretonnes and barking dogs and handkerchiefs."

Rachel turned to Jerrold. There was no apparent confusion in her speech or manner. The even flow of her sentences was noticeably deliberate and studied.

"There were a few things Selford consulted me about in preference to Maurice. Maurice, being half foreign, perhaps inherits a tendency to dramatize and exaggerate situations. He chafed under his father's dislike of publicity. Maurice is so built and equipped that he is at his best on a platform. He is not as patient nor as wise nor as disinterested as his father. No doubt he wants personal power. Their temperaments were different. I was in closer union with Selford's mind and views than Maurice or anyone else. Selford would not advocate any form of violence. He believed that change must come by the illumination of mankind. He believed in the League of Nations as a moral force and that if we steadily supported it the world would be on our side. Maurice thought it must be backed by physical force. That was one difference between them. Then, too, there were other and more personal matters in which Selford turned to me as a woman." She paused. "There were three ideas that occurred to me any one of which might account for Selford wishing to see me privately. His book. I was the only one who had read it. It might be something about that, or it might be something about my brother Stephen. We three were his wards, and he took Stephen as his secretary at a time when Stephen was under a cloud. We often discussed Stephen's future and he would prefer me to Maurice if that were the problem. Then, I did not understand Nurse Jonsen. There is no doubt that she tried to keep me away from Selford, and no doubt that she exceeded her duties as a nurse in the short time she has held the post. He was a remarkably attractive man in spite of being a cripple. He may have felt some difficulty in regard to her and thought that I, being a woman, could advise him."

"Charming woman, Nurse Jonsen!" murmured Brade.

"Quite! Tom thought so," Rachel agreed. It was not like Rachel to say that.

"Of course he thought so," Tassy said. "She sympathized with him. I don't believe he'd have had that quarrel with Uncle Selford if she hadn't."

"But she seems to be a good nurse," Jerrold said.

"Yes, she seemed to be. She is very strong and Selford had to have a powerful person as there was so much lifting to be done, though Braythorpe helped with that. She has good hands too. I noticed how quickly and cleverly she bandaged Maurice's hand, and she arranged flowers beautifully. I expect Selford liked having a nurse so deft and expert. Of course, she is Swedish and a trained masseuse."

"She isn't a Socialist!" Brade remarked conversationally. "I've seen her room. She has lots of pretty things. Socialists don't approve of pretty things, do they, Mrs. Norbury?"

Rachel showed now the restraint she had placed upon herself, by giving way to irritation. "Pretty things—Mr. Brade, don't you think you are rather insulting? We have Dr. Jerrold's word for it that you are a clever detective; otherwise I should think the reverse!"

It seemed that Brade went from blunder to blunder. "That's dear Jerry's one illusion, you know," he confided in her. "A clever detective is the last thing I am, Mrs. Norbury. The clever detectives like to have me about because they shine in my company. Everybody likes that. Look how intelligent Jerry seems just because I'm not. And yet," he sighed, "no one of you clever people can tell me why that handkerchief was lying in the middle of the room or who dropped it there, or anything else I really want to know."

Jerrold got up. As he did so the telephone bell rang sharply. Tassy, glad to have something to do, ran to answer it.

"Mr. Brade is wanted on the phone," she said.

"You go, Jerry," Brade begged.

They could hear Jerrold speaking. "Yes. Yes. I see. I'll bring him along."

When he came back he said: "Captain Stair wants us to go to the Grange at once."

"Is there anything new?" Rachel demanded.

"I'm afraid so. He says that the doctors agree. They do not think Mr. Prentice died by accident."

No one moved or spoke for a second. Then Rachel said: "It was Tom?"

Tassy faced her, every line of her small brown face and active body newly drawn. "Rachel, how can you!" she said.

Rachel, cruel in her suffering, did not answer. She did not seem to hear. It was Dr. Jerrold who spoke.

"I don't believe Tom Prentice had anything to do with it," he said, looking at Tassy's anguished face.

CHAPTER 8

MULLIE was there to let the two men out.

There was a question in the face she turned on them, her twisted hand on the door. Her faded blue eyes opened first on Jerrold's, then on Brade and rested there as she barred their way.

"'Tis a black house, the Grange, this night," she said in her singsong voice. "Mr. Brade, sir, ye'll understand, there's been blackness there this long time, and I've felt it, oozing up like the mud of the bogs though all ye'll see when ye look from a distance is the brightness of the sedge and moss on the top and the water shining back at the sky. The Prentices, they're good men, but bad at marrying. Mr. Gervaise, Mr. Selford's brother, he married a wild Weleven, with the tempers and the gambling and the longing for excitement of the whole race, even though her ladyship has dug it all into good garden soil and it comes up in flowers. But Mr. Tom is a good Weleven, for all his hot blood and quick fists. And Mr. Selford Prentice, he married a foreign woman with dark secrets. If ye're looking for evil, look there, sir. Ye cannot change what's built into the bones of ye, the blood that keeps ye living, the breath that moves the breast, no, sir. Ye can never do that. Mrs. Selford Prentice was beautiful, I've heard, but the line she came from was crooked, bad, bad! And there in the Grange was living strife, with a thin floor laid over it, where they walked safe for years, till now. That's all an old woman has to say, sir."

"Can you tell us anything—anything we should know, Mrs. Mulholland?" Jerrold asked.

"No—I know nothing. It's what I feel. No—no, I can tell ye nothing. Nothing at all."

"But she has told us, Jerry." Brade laid his hand on his friend's arm. "She's told us lots. If you had even so much as an Irish grandmother you'd understand."

"Good night, sirs. Ye'll not hurt my young ladies nor my Mr. Stephen? I never wished him to go into that house. I felt the trouble coming long ago."

"No, we'll take care of them."

She looked at Brade with trust.

Jerrold laughed as they stepped into the car. "You've made a great impression on Mullie, Simon. She's getting old and childish, but she has been a good friend to those two girls. What did she mean?"

"She meant what she said, of course."

"What she said was moonshine."

"Well, there is such a thing as moonshine and occasionally it lights up the scenery."

"You are being mysterious."

Brade was silent. Then he said:

"Jerry, I didn't mean to take this case, but now I've got to!"

"Why?"

"Because if Tom Prentice is accused of the crime and convicted I'd think always I might have saved him."

"You don't think he did it, then?"

"I don't know. If he did, I can't save him, but I shan't see him hanged or imprisoned for murder without finding out whether he is guilty or not, if I can. You don't think he is."

"No, Simon, I don't." Jerrold was emphatic. "And I'll tell you why. Prentice was a cripple. Tom might have killed a sound man, but not a helpless one. Why did you play the fool tonight? You've made an enemy of Rachel."

"But she told us a lot."

"Because I asked her."

"No. Because I annoyed her. Once or twice she forgot what she meant to say and said something else instead. Will you write it all down as soon as you can, Jerry? Everything?"

Jerrold sighed. "A jolly holiday I'm going to get!" he remarked to the darkness. "However, I admired Prentice and I'm bound to help clear up his death if I can. I

suppose Rachel and Maurice, Lady Charlotte and Nurse
are ruled out of the list of suspects? Prentice must have
died between six ten or a little later and six thirty."

"It seems so. But I'm not ruling anyone out. I've got to
explain everything before I shall find out the truth, and
the most puzzling thing of all is that handkerchief."

There was a short silence. Then Brade said: "It's
unlucky I met all these people before the accident."

"Why?"

"Because—don't you see?—I like them!" Brade was
plaintive.

"Wouldn't you have liked them if you'd met them
afterwards?"

"No. I'd have turned them all into puppets so I could
think about them. You don't think about people you like,
not as you have to think in a case like this. If I thought of
all these people as people, I couldn't work. I'd be too sorry
for them. I'm sorry for nearly everybody, but when a
tragedy like this happens I'm—well I'm too sorry for
them. I want to pat them on the back and say: 'There,
there!' Now, you know that wouldn't help anyone. In fact,
it would irritate them. I've tried it on people and I know.
It annoys almost anyone. I notice you said: 'Don't worry'
twice this evening. Doctors must say: 'Don't worry' in
their sleep and with their last breath I believe, and there
are even lusty persons who dare to go about the world
saying: 'Cheer up!' It seems a reckless form of bravery to
me, in a world like ours with guns so handy. So I try not
to say: 'There, there.' You understand me, Jerry?"

"Not more than usual, but go on."

"Well, now think of that household. There is Prentice,
the reformer. He lived for a cause. Maurice, his son. You
tell me that he is ambitious for personal power. Lady
Charlotte, who sublimates the Weleven temperament in
her flower-garden. Tom, a sportsman. I've turned them
all into things in my mind—collector's pieces—and shut
them up in the same cabinet. Do they fit? They do not. My
fingers itch to take them out—separate them. That

Victorian what-not upstairs at the Grange is an example.
There's a Russian ikon, symbol of love and sacrifice;
there's my fish, the creature that holds up the world and
convulses it, power; there's that cracked Dresden bowl,
with its forget-me-nots and rose leaves; and there's an old
drinking-horn that may have belonged to the fabulous
Weleven himself who hunted his hounds into the Irish
Sea and asked St. Peter if he'd viewed the fox. Now you
deal with people. Turn these things back into people and
all they stood for. Would you shut them up in the same
house? Wouldn't you feel afraid? Was Mullie wrong, do
you think?"

"No, I don't."

"And her fear has justified itself, Jerry."

"Do you mean you think Tom or Maurice, one or the
other, is guilty?"

Brade shook his head. "It needn't be either of them,
and still the truth may lie there somewhere, the result of
shutting up antagonistic forces within the barrier they
could not pass. St. Francis, Mussolini and John Peel
wouldn't exactly mix, would they?"

"Come, Brade, even if Prentice was a saint and Tom is
the British sportsman, Maurice has a record of devoted
service to the Socialist party."

"Have you seen his room?"

"I've seen it—yes."

"Have you looked at his books?"

"I don't remember."

"He has a complete set of Nietzsche, with marked
passages. And a thumbed copy of Machiavelli too. I
understand the Duce is partial to these works. And there
is that letter Prentice wrote. Why was it destroyed?
Suppose Selford Prentice found his son out. Suppose he
meant to take some action that threatened his career. I'm
asking you—I'm no psychologist and you are. What could
Maurice have done?"

"Brade, let's stick to facts. If Prentice was attacked, it
was between six twenty and six thirty and Maurice was

writing a letter in the studio at that time, and under observation."

"Can we be sure of that? It did not require more than three minutes to burn the letters and kill Prentice. We've got to see that room again. And the letter he wrote. And that bowl of chrysanthemums."

"Of all the people in the house it's Tom who had the clearest opportunity. And we have the word of three witnesses that he had quarrelled with his uncle."

"Yes, Jerry. So we have. And that would be all right but for Chen. If Tom did it he came and went by the hall door. He had no reason to open the garden door at all. But Chen came in by the garden."

"That's not proved. Brade, you are being fanciful. I don't think Tom did it, but there's no reason to think Maurice did. And what have the chrysanthemums to do with it, pray? Don't be silly."

They drew up before the Grange and got out, waiting in the wind till Braythorpe let them in. Brade walked straight into the studio. It was empty. Even the fire had gone out.

Brade went over to the hearth. "Sit down at that writing-table, Jerry, just as Maurice did. I want to see. Nurse was here." He sat in a corner of the sofa and looked over his shoulder. "Yes, I can see you. Lean lower as if you were bending over a letter. Yes, I can see your head and right arm." He moved to a chair by the fire. "Yes, I can see you plainly, through the carved back of that chair, and if I were talking to someone sitting on the sofa I should be facing you all the time." He moved to the opposite chair. "I can see you from here if I happen to look that way." He got up and went to the table behind the sofa. "Yes. Fresh water in this vase." He smelt of the bowl. He went to each vase in turn. "Fresh water, and each flower placed separately. It takes time to arrange flowers like that. Lady Charlotte said Nurse was good at the flowers!" He paused, puzzled. Then he went to the writing-table. "The letter Maurice wrote. Where is that?

Was it finished? When he left the house he was in no
condition to remember a letter left lying here when he
was called away—but there is no letter. Shall we ask
him?"

Braythorpe appeared in the doorway.

"Captain Stair is asking for you, Mr. Brade. He is in
the library with Mr. Litton and the Inspector."
Braythorpe was unsteady with suppressed excitement
and his eyes black in his pale face.

"Braythorpe, have you seen a letter?" began Jerrold,
impulsively.

Maurice Prentice pushed Braythorpe aside and
entered the room. He shut the door on the servant. "Is
this the letter?" he asked. "I intended to ask someone to
post it for me." He held out a sealed and addressed
envelope. Then, looking from Brade to Jerrold and back
again, he deliberately tore the letter open and held it out.
"I began it at that table while my father was meeting his
death. Read it if you like. Oh, read it! Well, if you won't,
I'll tell you what is in it and why I remembered it even
now. I am engaged to be married. I began the letter in
answer to one I had received from my fiancée. I had to
finish it, to tell her what had happened. I do not feel I can
see her again until this mystery is cleared up. There is a
shadow on the house. I cannot let it fall on her. Perhaps
you will be good enough to consider this confidential. My
father did not know."

His face, puffy and discoloured by tears, twisted
convulsively before he recovered himself.

"Please forgive me," he said with dignity. "You must
remember I am not all English. If I were I might be able
to hide my feelings better. I wish I could."

CHAPTER 9

WHEN the men had gone, Mullie came into the drawing-room with the evident intention of seeing her young ladies to their beds. They knew that rocklike demeanour against which they had tried defiance, remonstrances, and persuasion in vain. Mullie would just stay there till they went. You could tease her, be rude to her, cajole her, lose your temper with her, but she would have her way just the same. So they went meekly enough, as they had done before, and after they had been settled comfortably between the sheets in their separate rooms and Mullie had turned out the lights they waited for half an hour before they got up again.

Rachel, in her big, rather bare bedroom, wrapped herself in a quilted gown and went cautiously down the passage to her own sitting-room.

Tassy did not even turn on the light, but tied a mannish wrap around her and went to the open window. The moon looked like a lighted balloon blowing across the sky.

"Why do things look so different from what they are?" she asked herself, foolishly; the moon was not blown by the wind—but the clouds were. She tried to fasten on that difficult thought, for her sensations were unfamiliar and rather terrifying. She was going to think and she was terrified of thinking. The attack was beginning in her stomach like the worst kind of indigestion, but it wasn't indigestion at all. It was something much uglier. What she thought first, when she had given up the effort of trying not to think, was:

"I love him. I won't have him hurt."

She had never denied even to herself that she loved Tom Prentice, but she had never known before that he belonged to her. She knew it now. She had leapt in one flight from an attitude of humble adoration to firmer ground, the right to defend and guard him. It was a long leap, one to be taken only under an emergency, even by a thoroughbred. Just as, to escape an enemy, Jennifer J. might safely cross an obstacle which her mistress would not dream of asking her to face on an ordinary hunting day, Tassy found herself well over, though the country ahead looked difficult and full of danger.

Tom, with his broad brown face, which she could not see clearly because it was so dear. His reluctant grin. His hands so clumsy with a pen and so skilful when they touched leather. His bewildered fury when he knew he was right and couldn't find words to say so. His placid enjoyment of everything natural, when all was right in the stables and no one was interfering with his job. Tom, who was part of life and nature, following the rhythm of changing seasons and weathers, who could be still with delight, like a tree on a windless day, or move toward his job with the painful patience of blades of grain thrusting through the soil. Tassy knew his goodness as she knew the goodness of a sound apple, or a rich ploughed field, or a wind blowing through the pines.

Rachel despised him, though Rachel liked to follow him on a hunting day. "Because hunting does one more good than any other kind of exercise," she had explained once to the question of a Socialist friend, "and the mental refreshment I get is used in my work. I'm willing to sacrifice human beings, if it's necessary, to advance Socialism. Why not a fox?"

But the devoted labour that went into the keeping of a pack of hounds and hunting them over a difficult country three days a week, she minimized and ignored. The courage too. Wasn't the hunting field the nursery of every virtue that had made England great? England wasn't great, Rachel would say. Only fat and rich. Tassy passionately disagreed, but she was no match for Rachel in an argument, and knew it. Let them despise Tom and his sort. The farmers knew better and so did ninety per cent of the working people. The same men who put on their hats when the orchestra played God Save the King at the cinema touched their caps to Tom mounted and wearing scarlet.

"I wish I were clever!" thought Tassy, "but I've never been any use at all at anything except horses. What am I trying to think about?" She took the window-sill in her two small hands and gripped it hard.

"The truth is I'm afraid to think of what I'm trying to think about, so I'm thinking of everything else instead. It's exactly like funking a fence and going round by a gate." She paused, shocked at this discovery. "The trouble is I've never had to think of things. I don't want to think of frightening things. I'm not really a coward, but I'm behaving exactly like a man alone in a field who knows no one can see how he behaves except himself. It's awful to funk things."

She stared out into the windy night.

These two men thought that Selford Prentice was not alone when he died, and everyone else in the house seemed to be accounted for at the time except Tom. What did this mean? Would Tom be accused of murder? The word was out and she stared at it, unbelieving. The sort of a word you read in the newspapers or in detective stories, which Tassy liked. Not a word that you expected to have to use in your thoughts at all. It didn't mean anything. It wasn't true.

Now that she had said it she felt better. There was no such thing as murder in the world Tassy knew. It was just like the terrors of the fairy-tales she still read sometimes, something people made up for the sake of the story. As for the things that happened in the newspapers, they were different too. They happened to people Tassy had never seen. Crippen, for instance.

Here she was, drifting away from the point again. Why couldn't she think as straight as she rode? "There's something in education, after all," she decided, aware that there was a distinction between learning to work the mind and "lessons," which she had managed to "do" with

a minimum of this exercise. "Now I'm thinking about
school!" Tassy reproached herself in despair. "Damn!"

Her window faced south-east and overlooked the
orchard, sloping down to the river. Behind the house, on
the northeast side, were the stables, and she could always
hear the horses if anything disturbed them in the night.
Now she found herself listening for a sound which had
come and gone, and was repeated as she turned her head.
Horses hoofs on the paved yard. Then silence. Then a step
on the ground under her window. Something hit the sill
and she leaned out, suddenly happy. Tom was standing
there, whistling to her. He always came that way—left
his horse in an empty stall and walked round the house,
whistling to bring her out.

"Wait," she said softly into the shadows, "I'll come
down."

She pulled on a pair of flannel trousers and a jumper,
pushed her feet into shoes, and got a coat from a peg in
the hall below. Then she let herself out at a side door and
saw Tom. "Come to the stables." She led him along. She
took the key of the harness-room from its peg. It was
warm in there for the stove was still hot; the leather
smelt of oil, and the felt linings of the saddles set out to
dry were rank with horse-sweat.

"Luck, you being up," said Tom. "Look here, Tassy,
what did those two chaps say to Rachel? Do you know?"

They sat down side by side on the broad table, and the
moon suddenly shone in at the window behind them.

"They didn't say much. They asked a lot of questions.
But they think someone was with Uncle Selford—
someone who won't admit it."

"And they think it was me."

"Dr. Jerrold doesn't. He told me so."

"He wouldn't have said that if there wasn't something
against me."

"What is there against you, Tom?"

"A lot." Tom scraped some mud off his boot with the
handle of his crop. "I was upstairs and Molly had run my

bath. She knocked on the door and told me it was ready, but I didn't go in at once, and I didn't answer her. Fact was I was writing a letter."

Tassy knew how Tom wrote a letter, a pen grasped firmly in one hand, dipped too deep in the ink-pot, and head and arms and shoulders working hard as if the words had to be wrung out like clothes through a mangle. She said nothing.

"Then I burned it up," Tom continued, "and I was at the bathroom door when Chen began to bark, and I looked over the banister and saw Nurse, and smelt smoke. You see, there's no reason why I shouldn't have been down there and just come up. But I wasn't."

"Why should they think you were?"

"Don't ask me. But you know how these detective people go on. They have to suspect somebody. And there's this, Tassy—I had a fight with Uncle Selford this morning. Stephen knew it. I had a reason, too, if you want to think so, for bumping him off. He'd written a letter to his lawyer about altering his will. And there was Selma Jonsen."

"Was there?"

"Don't be sarcastic. She's a stunner. And she was awfully nice to me till Uncle Selford started getting her on his side. You know, the way he had. She sympathized with me. She understood what a damnable position I was in—a man of thirty, who likes racing and hunting, having to go to his uncle for every halfpenny. Well, when Uncle Selford got at her she started trying to reform me. As if it was a sin to own a good horse and want to see it win a race! Talked about my duty to the common man. Just as if the crowds cheerin' a winner wasn't mostly the common man and about the only fun he gets, poor devil. Fact was, I was fed up with him all round and I lost my temper. There's no denying it. I wish he hadn't died before we made it up."

"Oh, Tom! Who knew about the quarrel?"

"Everybody in the house, I should think. Why not?"

"And the letter to the lawyer? That was burned with the others?"

"I suppose so."

"So you inherit your half after all?"

"Yes—and a fat lot of good it'll do me if they hang me."

"Don't be silly."

"Well, Tassy, I don't know if it's so silly. They've been in my room and taken away a lot of things. The blotting book, for one, and my slippers, and a nail-file."

"What?"

"My nail-file! I don't know why."

"Are you sure?"

"It's gone. I had to borrow Maurice's."

"But, Tom, are they certain that someone was there?"

"I don't know. Tassy, there must have been. Anyway, someone must have gone into his room after that man Brade went out, if he's telling the truth. Chen was in there, with all the doors shut, and nobody admits letting him in. Then all his letters were burned. I don't suppose he did that himself. And besides, the way he was lying. I'm not too bright, but I could see for myself that he didn't fall out of his chair into that position, and if he'd turned over himself he could have broken his neck. There's something ugly in it, but I swear I had nothing to do with it. Do you believe me?"

"Don't be silly," Tassy repeated.

"But, Tassy, do you?"

For some quite obscure reason Tassy was embarrassed by his urgency, or perhaps it was the futility of words to express her faith in him that embarrassed her. She only sat there looking toward him, and that wasn't much use, as the clouds hung over the moon now and they were in darkness.

Then she became aware that he misunderstood her silence. Suddenly, helplessly, she began to cry. She was not used to crying and she did it badly, gulping down her tears childishly and noisily and sniffing between sobs.

Tom stiffened.

"Never mind. I can see it looks bad. And you saw me hit Maurice today too. You know all about my vile temper. I suppose I can't expect anyone to believe me. Somehow I thought you might."

She grasped his arm. "Tom, it isn't that. It's because—I don't know why—but I think it's because you had to ask. It's so awful—that you asked me. I'll never forget it. Do you suppose I don't know? Just as if I'd seen you writing that letter and been with you all the time. Oh, surer than that! Much surer. I know what you're like and that's the surest thing of all."

Whoever else might have found her incoherent, Tom apparently did not. He put an arm around her and gave her shoulder a reassuring squeeze.

"Well, don't cry about it, old girl."

Tassy wiped her eyes, and probably her nose as well, on his coat-sleeve.

"I won't. I never do. But you oughtn't to have asked me that. It makes me feel worse than anything. See here, Tom." She sat up straight beside him and tugged at his coat. "You go to Dr. Jerrold and tell him everything. He'll believe you. And he's clever. You aren't and I'm not, but nearly all the others are. He'll tell you what to do. Will you do it? It's no use to keep anything back. They'll find it out, and then it'll look awful. Promise."

"All right. I like Jerrold, but that man Brade is a dark horse. Looks like the funny man in a revue and never says two sensible words running, and then suddenly asks somebody something they'd rather not tell. I'll talk to Jerrold."

"And you won't lose your temper?"

"I can't promise that. But I don't feel so down as I did when I came. You'll come up and see my mother and look after her if—well, you know, if I can't for any reason? She likes you though you're no gardener."

She knew that he was smiling there in the dark beside her. How could she know that? When Tom smiled he seemed all the time to be trying not to until at last he gave up and then there was the smile all over his face. Even his ears moved in sympathy. But when he chuckled he hardly smiled at all. Thinking of this and of the question he had asked, her throat hurt until she thought she could not bear it. She mustn't cry again. He would think she was a silly fool. So she said rather sternly: "You've got to keep your temper. Of course I'll come to see Aunt Charlie, even if she does tell me again that she can't understand how my mother's daughter can live in a gardener's garden."

"I suppose I'd better go and get some sleep. God knows what'll happen to the hunt. Tassy, will you give Leydon a hand? If you'd whip in for him he'll manage."

"You'll be out again next week."

"Hope so." Tom got off the table. "Go to bed, old girl, and don't you worry."

She went with him while he led out his horse and mounted. He rode away, out of the stable-yard, and she heard the click of the gate as it swung behind him. She waited till she could not hear his horse any longer.

When she went upstairs she thought of Rachel and turned aside to listen for a moment at her bedroom door. No sound came through, but down the hall a crack of light showed. Rachel was in her sitting-room.

Tassy hesitated. She felt, suddenly, how little she knew her sister. Once Rachel had told her, briefly, that she had been in love with her husband and was not likely to love a man again. "If I ever marry," she added, "it will be someone who thinks as I do and is working for the new world." That strange, chilly new world Rachel believed in, where, in Tassy's view, no one would know how to live at all. But Rachel had loved Selford Prentice with hero-worship and a protective devotion, and she must be suffering now. Tassy went toward the streak of light under her sister's door.

There she paused, startled. Rachel was speaking.

"Are you threatening me?"

There was no answer. Whoever was there with Rachel was silent. Tassy turned the handle of the door. She must see who was in the room with Rachel. Someone who threatened her sister. Her heart beat fast in her panic. "Rachel, let me in," she called. The stillness terrified her. She beat on the door.

"Be quiet. Is it you, Tassy? Wait!" The key turned and Rachel stood there in the gap. Tassy could see part of the room, but not the corner by the fire.

"Let me in," Tassy said. "Who is here, Rachel? I saw your light and I heard what you said."

Rachel was angry. "What are you doing, dressed and up at this hour—spying on me. You are always stupid, but you don't usually interfere with my affairs. There's no one here. I'd dropped off to sleep and was dreaming. You woke me. Go back to your room and leave me alone."

"I can't. I don't believe you. I know you were speaking to someone."

Rachel stood there, so angry that Tassy could feel her rage like lire. She could scarcely see Rachel for it. She had never imagined that Rachel could be so angry. Her physical strength was no use against this hideous fury. She could not remember afterwards if Rachel actually forced her way, down the hall, into her room, but there she found herself, with the door shut and the key turned in the lock outside.

Pocahontas rose from the hearth and ran to the door, listening and growling. Nails had found his way to Tassy's room somehow and he barked sharply. Both dogs seemed uneasy and alarmed. Tassy drew them to her and crouched down by the fire, shivering. Should she ring? Should she beat on the door and rouse the house? Had Rachel spoken the truth or was she lying?

The dogs were restive under her arms. They knew that something was wrong, so wrong that the whole familiar house felt alien. If, in a moment, the bricks of the walls had driven out some deathly smell, if suddenly the turns and twists of the staircase had altered their shape, it could not have seemed stranger, more unfriendly, to the girl it had sheltered till tonight. Pocahontas whined. Someone had tumbled on the narrow step that fell so unexpectedly halfway down the hall. Silence. The wind blew the trees about outside and rattled the window-panes. Nails barked again and huddled close to Tassy. Both dogs felt stiff and alert to her touch.

The key turned in the lock and Rachel came in.

"I'm sorry I was cross," she said, switching on the light. "But I'd had a horrible dream. It's all right, Tassy. Go to bed. I'm going to take some aspirin and get a little sleep myself. Tomorrow will be a busy day. I'm sorry I frightened you. What did I say?"

Tassy did not answer.

"Why are you dressed, you silly child? Where have you been?"

"Tom came. I went out to talk to him."

"He shouldn't have done that. I wish you'd keep away from Tom till this is over. Now will you go to bed? I'm too tired to argue with you. You must take my word for it. There was no one here. It was only a dream."

The dogs settled down, close to Tassy. If there had been a stranger in the house there was no one there now or the dogs would have known it. If danger had threatened, it had passed. The dogs knew.

"You're shivering, Tass. Go to bed. I'm going." Rachel went out.

Tassy drew off her clothes and got into bed, still shivering. The dogs lay quietly. She called Pocahontas to her, and the spaniel jumped on to the bed and curled her warm, comforting body into the curve of Tassy's knees. The fire gave a dying flicker, lighting up the hunting trophies over the mantel and the silver cups on it. The curtains blew in the wind. She could see the sky beyond the big apple tree. Everything was just as usual, but Tassy felt adrift and alone for the first time in her life. Mullie and Rachel had always been there. She had never felt a serious need of human support and sympathy that they could not or would not meet. Even her love for Tom had been a devotion that completed and fulfilled itself. Now she thought of Mullie as a voyager into lonely and uncharted seas might think of a friend, dear and comforting, left at home, and of Rachel as someone who had taken a different ship for another and unknown port.

And Tom, who had seemed so remote and far above any need of her in spite of the casual affection he showed for her always, had become the person she must defend and protect from danger of a sort he was not equipped to meet.

Was Rachel's explanation true? If not, what did it mean? That she knew something and was in danger because she knew it? If so, how would Rachel act? And if she meant to speak out, tell all the truth, why should she try to deceive Tassy now, try to make her believe that she had been alone in her room tonight?

"Suppose Rachel knew something that would clear Tom. Of course she would speak. Of course she would tell."

Tassy's mind was travelling over uncharted seas, indeed. She had judged other people by herself until tonight. Now for Tom's sake she tested this habit. Would Rachel behave as she herself would?

"I'd sacrifice human beings for the sake of my work if I had to. Why not the fox?"

Tassy was cold in spite of the warm bed-clothes. "I couldn't do that," she thought suddenly. "The fox—yes. But not a man. Would Rachel do that?"

That was what they had done in Russia. They thought it was right, and Rachel defended them. She said that cruelty in a good cause was justified. She said that the capitalist system killed thousands with the utmost cruelty and they had a right to use any means to fight it. But a system, even if wrong, cruel by accident, was one thing, and a person deliberately causing another to suffer was another. Would Rachel do that?

Pocahontas moved closer, uneasy at Tassy's wakefulness Not until her mistress's breathing slowed down, to the deep even rhythm that meant sleep, did Pocahontas close her eyes.

CHAPTER 10

BEFORE Rachel had gone to her sitting-room that night she had switched the telephone through from the hall downstairs to her own desk, and she had not been sitting there for five minutes before the bell rang.

"Is that you, Rachel?"

"Yes."

"Can I come and see you now? It is urgent."

"Yes. I'll open the front door. Come up to my sitting-room and be quiet. I don't want Tassy to hear you."

Tassy, sitting at her window, heard nothing, and before Tom, riding the short way across the fields, reached Hartover, Maurice had parked his car inside the gate, admitted himself, and mounted the stairs, passing Tassy's door noiselessly on his way to Rachel's room.

Rachel had lighted the fire and arranged a tray on a table beside it. "Sit there," she said, pointing to an easy chair, and mixing a stiff whisky and soda. "You look all in."

"I am. I've got to tell you something I'd give a lot to keep to myself."

"Well?"

"I needn't ask you to keep the secret. You will, Rachel. Father—" his voice seemed to fail him—"how can I say it? Father deceived you. He nearly deceived me. Father has been engineering the *Sentinel*."

"Don't be absurd."

"No wonder you say that. Almost—" Maurice raised his hand and brought it down with a gesture of despair. "Almost I could be glad that he is dead."

"You'd better go on."

"That's not all. Rachel—he sold himself. There's just one possible explanation. His mind was failing. From now on I mean to look back on what he was two years ago. I mean to forget the rest. But first you've got to know the truth. That book of his is one long lie. All the time he was writing it he was pledged to stir up trouble secretly in England. All the time he was preaching peace he was acting in the pay of foreign powers. And if you don't believe me I will prove it."

"You'll never do that. You must be mad!"

"Very well. Look at these letters."

He took from his pocket a thin packet and handed it to her.

"I won't touch them." She rose and stood above him.

"You'd better."

"Maurice, you're either lying or a fool. I don't know which."

"Wait. Hadn't you noticed a change in my father lately? Hadn't he been more insistent that we should all follow him slavishly, not only in principle but in every thought and word? If you didn't see it, it is because you were already his slave. But I wasn't. That was the first thing I saw to make me wonder. Then little things happened. Braythorpe was given orders that all letters written on a special paper should be brought straight to him. I found this out by accident. Then the *Sentinel* started. Have you ever heard of the Brothers of the New Order?"

"Fairy-tales."

"My father was always a visionary. I tell you the New Order is a fact. Many Catholics support it, not knowing its real character. It is a plan to establish a chain of dictatorships under a central power. And my father belonged to it. Nurse Jonsen is in it."

"Nurse Jonsen?"

"That impresses you! You were puzzled by her relationship with my father. Now listen. There is enough here," he tapped the letters, "to make it clear. But he is dead, and he has left a great work behind him. His book is magnificent. Whether you believe what I've told you or not, you and I must agree on one thing: the truth must not be known. The effect on our cause would be incalculable. You see that?"

"I would die denying it."

"What good could that do! The proof is here. And there is only one thing that might force me to make it public. That is if an innocent person should be in danger of conviction of the crime of murdering him. He killed himself. I am certain of it. He knew that I had learned the truth and would expose him if he persisted. But he was too involved to withdraw. He raised himself by the table and flung himself backward toward the fire. I'm certain of it."

"Maurice, he couldn't have done that." It was a cry of anguish.

"He could and he did. His arms were strong. He could lift himself by them. I've seen him do it. He could have pulled himself up, rested his weight on his arms, and thrown himself backward over that fender, hoping it would pass as an accident. And he did. I know it. But if I say that, I shall have to give my reasons for believing it. You and I have to protect his memory, and his work."

"Then you mean that you'll put forward this theory to save Tom?"

"Yes—or anyone else—not from suspicion, but from being hanged for murder. I'll hold my hand till the last possible moment, but then I'll speak and my father's name will be printed on the memory of millions—the name of a traitor!"

Rachel, on her feet, looked down at Maurice, who leaned forward in his chair, his elbow on his knee, his hand opened toward her in a pose she knew.

"I must think," she whispered.

"Rachel—can you deny honestly that you knew that my father was hiding something lately? You were jealous of Nurse. You showed it. You knew he turned to her, but you did not know why. You cannot deny it."

It was true. True that when she received her summons that morning she had hoped that the temporary estrangement from the man she adored was to be ended. Bitter, bitter that Maurice should know it too!

"For God's sake, take care what you say to that man Brade," Maurice besought her, his voice low and urgent. "What did you tell him tonight?"

"Nothing he could not have found out."

"Nothing?"

"You must let me think."

"If a case is made out against anyone by Brade or another I shall be forced to speak!"

"Are you threatening me?"

It was then that Tassy knocked on the door.

CHAPTER 11

TASSY awaked in bright sunshine, with Rachel standing beside her fully dressed.

"If you want to come to the Grange with me you'll have to get up," Rachel said. She looked and spoke exactly as usual.

Tassy sat up, startled. Gradually she remembered.

Uncharted seas! People lied to you sometimes. Inferior people, and you knew they lied. They twisted their hands, or shifted their eyes, or looked at you with innocent frankness to see just how much you believed. But if people lied to you, knowing that you trusted them, as you'd trust an engine-driver or the needle of a compass, then indeed you had to start life from a new angle and walk in a new way. It wouldn't be a footpath made simple to follow by a signpost here and there, but a treacherous trail where you'd have to watch your step. That was not Tassy's idea of life at all, and in the sunshine, with Mullie bringing in a breakfast tray and Nails, following her, jumping on the bed, a virtuous cock to his head and an invitation in his eye, she rejected it. She put her arms around Rachel's neck and hugged her. "I'm so sorry, darling Rachel," she said. "I'm so dreadfully, dreadfully sorry."

Rachel never enjoyed being touched, but it seemed to Tassy that she liked it less than usual this morning.

"Do be quick, Tassy. There'll be so much to do, with meetings to cancel, and speakers to arrange for in Maurice's place, and reporters to see, and God knows what." Rachel went away.

The clouds closed over Tassy's window while she was dressing, and by the time they reached the Grange, rain was streaming down the wind-shield so fast that the wiper busied itself in vain. Tassy, who was driving, nearly ran down a man with a camera coming out of the gate. He turned and looked after them. Before they drove into the flagged enclosure before the house, a policeman stopped them and took their names. Tassy thought indignantly: "As if anybody could do Uncle Selford any harm now!"

Braythorpe let them in.

They turned aside into the studio. No one was there, but the room had its usual aspect, the bowls of flame-coloured chrysanthemums freshly arranged, reflected in the walnut of a highboy, the shining sides of the grand piano, and the crowded pieces of mahogany in their usual places. Lady Charlotte had brought a good deal of furniture with her, selecting it for association rather than harmony of style. Most of it was good, some of it rare and valuable, but none of it matched. Someone had left the morning papers opened on the sofa, and the weekly magazines, sporting for Tom, the *New State*sman for Maurice, gossip journals for anyone, and gardening literature for Lady Charlotte, were arranged on a table behind the sofa. Tassy liked the room and understood it, but it seemed unnatural that it should be exactly the same as usual today. The big west bay looked like the side of an aquarium in streaming rain, and the floor inside the door to the garden ajar on its south end was wet. Rachel went over to it and looked out thoughtfully.

"You know, Tassy, the first thing Lady Charlotte always does when she comes into the room is to open this door. It was open last evening till Maurice shut it. He was writing here at the table with his back to it. Why shouldn't someone have come in that way, if the room was empty for even five minutes? He could have watched his chance from outside and hid somewhere in the house until the hall and passage were clear, got into Selford's room, and let himself out again by the garden door there. At first we took it for granted that Selford was alone and no one thought of looking for an intruder. Lady Charlotte might have been here without seeing anyone coming in and perhaps hiding behind the curtain till she was occupied with one of her precious catalogues. He could have slipped over to the door to the passage, and once he got through that into the hall, there are plenty of places where he could have waited without being seen."

In spite of herself Tassy looked at her sister, remembering the tormenting doubts of last night. It seemed to her that Rachel was suggesting a fantastic possibility for some reason of her own. It seemed to her, too, that Rachel was suffering unendurably.

"But, Rachel, it was so wet last night. Anyone coming in from the garden must have left marks on the floor." She looked at the polished boards, shining with beeswax.

Lady Charlotte, a mackintosh over her black dress and a weather-stained hat acting as an umbrella, came along the path, round the bay, and in at the window. She removed a pair of storm boots and set them down, dropped the raincoat from her shoulders, and took off the hat. Then she turned her cool wet cheek to the two girls in turn and went over to the fire. "Someone has to look after the gardeners," she explained defensively, "and of course it isn't as it used to be in my young day when people wore crepe for anything closer than a cousin. You could tell the degree of relationship by the size of the bands on one's skirt almost as surely as an officer's rank by the gold braid on his sleeve. No one could garden in crepe. I see you're not in black, Rachel, nor Tassy. Of course Selford didn't approve of mourning, but I always think that's rather like telling people not to give you Christmas presents. You're hurt just the same if they don't. And I remember a cousin of ours who was so particular about her widow's weeds that she wore them up to the very morning she was married to her second husband. She wasn't a very good wife, my mother used to say, but she was a most devoted widow. However—" Lady Charlotte continued and had transferred to the subject of the damage done by the pheasants when Braythorpe came in to say that Mr. Maurice would be pleased if Mrs. Norbury would go upstairs.

Rachel paused to ask Lady Charlotte: "Were you here in this room all yesterday evening or did you leave it empty at all?"

"Dear me, Rachel. I hope you aren't going to start asking questions like that. If you want to, go to the Inspector or Dr. Jerrold. They know all the answers by now. I think you'd better see to Maurice. Perhaps you can do something with him. I never did understand Maurice, and the only thing I can do for him is to keep out of his way, because I'm always saying the wrong thing. Tassy can stay here and help me write some letters. It takes me ages if I do it alone because I put down everything I think and never get out what I really want to say, and Tom's worse. He uses such a lot of muscle over a one-page note that it's tiring to watch him. I've a list of people to write to, I think it's here in my knitting-bag. Lady Ashtown, Lady Forteviot—no, those are roses."

Rachel had gone and Tassy was helping to turn out the knitting-bag when Stephen Litton came in. His face was paler than ever, and his pleasant manner disturbed. Tassy did not know her brother very well. Although she was fond of him in a pitying way, she considered him a good deal of bother. He had inherited a substantial income from his father, and Rachel and Tassy divided their mother's money between them. Stephen had begun life in the Foreign Office, where he stood an excellent chance of success, for he was intelligent, popular, and knew the right thing to say and just when to say it. But he had an incurable habit of falling in love, and in affairs of passion his tact failed him completely. A year ago he had suddenly been supplanted in his post abroad by a more discreet rival, and it was understood that his career as a diplomat was suspended if not finished. Selford Prentice had engaged him as secretary, although he was not a Socialist. So far as Tassy knew, he had not been in love with anyone since the episode in Prague had caused his downfall. He had not borrowed money from her lately at least, and she judged by that.

"Hello, Tass," said Stephen. He was always affectionate toward his young sister, but treated her with the amusement and slight disdain of a subtle mind toward a simple one—the man who expects women to understand the arts of beauty and flirtation. "You've got an attractive figure and a well-set head and good eyes," he said to her once. "Lots of fascinating women have less. But, damn it, Tassy, you don't seem to know it, and that's fatal."

"Where's Rachel?" asked Stephen.

"With Maurice."

"The Inspector wants to see us all. You see, the inquest's set for Monday, and Corry, the solicitor, is coming down this afternoon and they want everything clear. I've sent down to the stables for Tom. Mr. Brade and Dr. Jerrold will be here too. It seems Jerrold has taken notes of the case, and the Inspector wants him to read them to us all and get the points confirmed. Of course, the Inspector has our statements, but I think it was Brade's idea to use Dr. Jerrold's account. I don't like the job, Lady Charlotte, but I ought to warn you that one or two new difficulties have cropped up."

He hesitated and as usual Lady Charlotte took advantage of the pause. "Such a crowd of people all making difficulties about the most trivial things, Tassy. I thought that doctor was so nice, too, but he's just like all the others, and I shouldn't dream of blaming Selford for anything now, but I always said he was careless about the fire with all those papers lying around and I know they're saying Tom quarrelled with him and of course he did, but that isn't the same thing as pushing helpless relations into the fire and you can't expect the Inspector to know about the Weleven men's tempers, though I told him about my grandfather throwing the port at Lord Beaconsfield, and it was much worse than it would be nowadays because of his waistcoats, and this was a good one embroidered for him by the Queen, it was said, and port stains—"

Tassy took firm hold of Lady Charlotte's hand. "You mustn't say anything like that about Tom," she said, "and, for mercy's sake, don't cry. Dr. Jerrold is all right. You can trust him. I'm so glad he's here."

"It's quite true. I do talk far too much. If you'll just hold my hand, Tassy, and squeeze it when I'm to stop and I'll keep this catalogue of Smithers here and start reading it out loud instead, for if I think anything, I say it sooner or later, and as far as I can see I'm only safe when I'm talking about flowers."

Stephen had gone to collect the others and came back with Nurse Jonsen. Tassy was startled to see how old she looked. Maurice and Rachel came next. Maurice's cheeks and eyelids were puffy and his face was blurred like a man's after a week of hard drinking. "He's been crying," Tassy thought. "How awful!" Maurice, with his brilliant future, his dignity, and his charm, had always been someone to admire from a distance, a person remote and unheeding. She thought of him as moving through distinguished gatherings, attracting attention as he went. He would never have to please and flatter like Stephen. Others would try to please and flatter him. In spite of his politics or perhaps partly because of them he was much courted by society hostesses and frequently photographed in company with well-known people. To see him weakened by human emotion was a shock.

Tom, in riding breeches, smelling of the weather, came with the Inspector and Dr. Jerrold. Braythorpe came too, so that the room seemed full of people, saying good-morning with various degrees of stiffness and looking for seats, when the door swung open and Simon Brade stood there embracing a wicker basket such as picnic-makers used before fitted outfits were invented. His face was flushed, his thin hair dishevelled, and his monocle swinging over his arm. "The San Ts'ai—it's gone!" he shouted.

Dr. Jerrold said mildly: "My dear Brade—please! We've had quite enough shocks. What has happened?"

Brade lifted the lid of the basket and showed the packing inside. Then he set it down and walked forward into the group. "You all know—or perhaps you don't know—that Mr. Prentice sold me his porcelain water-pourer last night. I promised to pay him four thousand pounds for it."

No one appeared to understand. He looked from face to face, then he said, dancing with annoyance: "Water-pourer. Polychrome. San Ts'ai, post-Ming dynasty. Date, 1690. Valuable. Unique. Unparalleled. One other in existence to my knowledge. Worth four thousand pounds or more. Gone."

The Inspector rallied and turned to Jerrold.

"It's quite true," said Jerrold, staring at Brade. "You'll remember the jug upstairs in the cabinet in the far end of the hall, Lady Charlotte. Brade understands these things and Mr. Prentice asked me to bring him to see it. It proved to be unexpectedly valuable and Mr. Prentice agreed to sell it to Brade, who collects Ming porcelain. If it is gone, the matter is of considerable importance. Where did you leave it, Brade?"

But the little man was too disturbed to make a clear story. Apparently he had not quite finished packing the fish when he heard Nurse Jonsen call for help. He had picked up the basket and set it down on a table at the head of the stairs on his way down. Braythorpe had seen the hamper there later and, knowing what it contained, took it to the pantry, without opening it. This morning Brade had asked Braythorpe for it, opened the basket, and found that the porcelain fish was not there.

"That ridiculous fish! Of course I remember it. I never knew where it came from," Lady Charlotte explained. "Anyway, nobody wanted to look at it and Chen always barked at it, so I put it in the cabinet with the other things we couldn't throw away, exactly, but didn't want."

Brade groaned. "Didn't want!" he repeated. "Well," he rallied, "do you want it now you know it's worth four thousand pounds, and is anybody going to do anything about it?"

Tassy looked at Tom, and moved nearer to him. He had been waiting patiently enough for someone to explain what was wanted of him, but now he said: "Four thousand pounds —that's what I asked Uncle Selford for yesterday. That's what I wrote that letter about. Four thousand pounds for a China jug! My God!"

"Does anyone here remember seeing that basket?"

Braythorpe told what he knew, which was very little. He had noticed the hamper and had taken it just as it was to the pantry and locked it up in the silver-safe. No one could have touched it after that, but whether it was empty when he took charge of it or not he could not say. The catch was fastened and the peg run through.

Rachel said swiftly: "Does this mean that the fish has been stolen? Then someone was in the house last night— someone we don't know about. I've thought so all along."

Pennleaf, the Inspector, shook his head. "We can't find out how anyone could have got in, Mrs. Norbury."

"Have you considered the door in this room?" Rachel pointed to the bay, with its door opening on the south.

"Yes, ma'am, we have. The room was occupied by two or more people from four thirty until after Mr. Prentice died. Braythorpe closed the curtains when he laid tea. Earlier than that anyone would have been seen. The gardener and her ladyship were in the rose-garden and it was daylight. Besides, the floor is polished and there were no marks except just by the window. We looked most carefully to see if the little dog ran in that way."

"What about the latch-keys? Everyone seems to have owned one. Can they all be accounted for?" Jerrold asked.

"I had mine on my chain," Maurice said. "I always carried it. I let myself in with it last night."

"Yes," Braythorpe agreed, "but Mr. Tom is always forgetting his and he had to ring when he came in."

"I left it in my room." Tom turned to Braythorpe. "Did you see it there?"

"Yes, sir, I left it lying on the tray on your dressing-table as I thought you'd want it when you went to your meeting."

"Have you seen it since, Tom?" Jerrold asked.

Brade had recovered. He was rolling cigarettes with a pumping motion of his right elbow, scattering tobacco beside his chair. Tassy's spirits had lightened. If they could only find a way for some stranger to have entered the Grange last night, then, surely, no one would suspect Tom of anything. He had not stolen a porcelain fish certainly. No one would ever believe he knew enough.

"Have you seen the key since?" Jerrold asked Tom again. "I think so. I don't remember. I forgot it again this morning, but Braythorpe let me in."

"Why not use this window? It always seems to be open."

Tom looked bewildered. "I suppose we might, but the housemaids wouldn't like it. Our boots are generally pretty muddy, and there's no scraper or anything. Mother uses it, but she wears overshoes if it's wet, and takes them off." There indeed were Lady Charlotte's storm boots inside the window.

"Suppose you see if the key is there, Braythorpe," Jerrold suggested.

"I'll go too." The Inspector and Braythorpe went out together.

The key was nowhere to be found.

CHAPTER 12

CAPTAIN STAIR was a gentleman embarrassed by the unusual. He showed it by his manner. Normally he was hearty, occasionally he was noisy, at present he was bluff. But he was efficient. He had not had so important a responsibility since the war, and enjoyed his position.

Inspector Pennleaf, risen from the ranks through sheer merit, could be remembered by his black tidy hair, black untidy moustache, capacious waist-line, and trustworthy blue eyes. He was never silly, and sometimes he was shrewd.

Brade, Jerrold, and these two men were in consultation in the studio an hour after the disturbance about the porcelain fish, when a large van drove up to the door, and Braythorpe entered to say apologetically: "They've come for the furniture, sir."

There was general bewilderment until he explained: "Lady Charlotte promised to lend some articles for the exhibition at Medbury for the county hospital, I believe." Jerrold remembered then.

"She told me about it. What pieces were to go, Braythorpe?"

"The writing-table in the window, the work-table, the big chair, I think, sir, and those chairs too." He pointed to the pair of Queen Anne chairs on the east side of the room.

"They ought not to have come for them, under the circumstances," Stair remarked.

"They said nobody had countermanded the order for the van," Braythorpe explained, "and I asked Mr. Maurice and he said to let them go on with it. He said the committee was depending on the things."

"Well, under those circumstances—"

Brade looked unhappy, but he said nothing. It was Pennleaf who remarked: "I think they ought to be left where they are, sir."

"Why, Inspector?"

"We've still to reconstruct the position of every person in the house at the time of the accident."

"Ah, that's all right. We know Mr. Maurice Prentice was seated at the writing-table, whether the table's there or not, and they won't want the upholstery. Let them take the things, then, Braythorpe, since Mr. Maurice wishes it. We mustn't let the hospital fund suffer."

Brade still looked unhappy, but he followed the others in silence to the library as the van men came into the room.

"Now, Mr. Brade," said Stair as they settled themselves, "we'd like your position clear. Are you working with us or in the interests of the family?"

Brade looked doubtfully at Jerrold, who replied for him: "Brade works for no one's interests, Captain Stair. He finds out the truth if he can. It is true that I advised Maurice to ask him to help you, and Maurice agreed. But that does not tie his hands."

"Then we can speak plainly before him?"

"Of course."

"Then I'd better say what I think. Tom Prentice killed his uncle. Do you agree?"

No one answered.

"Do you agree, Jerrold?"

"No. I don't believe he did it."

"You, Pennleaf?"

"No, sir."

"You, Mr. Brade?"

"I don't know who did it." Brade was petulant. "You first, Jerrold."

"I don't think Tom did it, because I know Tom. If Mr. Prentice had been a sound man I might have had my doubts. But he was a cripple, and Tom's incapable of attacking a helpless man."

"Pennleaf?"

"Because of the dog. I think that Langrove got into the house some way and did it and let the dog in when he went out."

"Mr. Brade?"

"Well, I haven't got very far, but there are a few little things—"

"Can't you specify?"

Brade twisted and turned on his chair, helplessly. "The trouble is, if I tell you, you'll think I'm silly. I'm sure I don't know why people want to listen to me. They always either laugh at me, which I don't mind, or get annoyed, which I do. But one thing you'll admit: Jerry understands people, and he says Tom didn't do it."

"I don't know why. We have any amount of evidence that Tom has an ungovernable temper. It's the talk of the hunt. He thrashed his own cousin before everyone the other day—the very day his uncle died."

"But you never heard of his losing control over himself with an animal or a child, did you?" Jerrold asked. "If Mr. Prentice was shaken against that fender and killed, the criminal was no sportsman; that I'll swear."

Captain Stair, himself a sportsman, made doubtful noises in his throat. Then he said: "Well, your other reasons, Mr. Brade? Maybe we'll follow those better, not being psychologists like the doctor here."

"Must I, Jerry?" Brade seemed distressed.

"Don't be shy!" Stair urged. "Speak out like a man."

"Oh, dear!" Brade retreated as Stair charged him. "I've forgotten."

"Now, look here, Mr. Brade, if we're to help each other, let's do it, and no false modesty. They say we officials object to amateur aid. I don't. I'm prepared to accept any help from anyone. After all," he observed generously, "I'm an amateur myself. Pennleaf isn't, but he's not jealous either, are you, Pennleaf? If we are baffled we'll call in Scotland Yard, and no nonsense about it either. But not till we've sifted the facts for ourselves

and seen what we can make of them. Come on, now—
what are these little things? Do you agree with the
Inspector about the dog?"

"I don't know," Brade replied unhappily.

"Come, you must know what you think?"

"Which?" asked Brade.

"Which what?"

"Which think!" Brade almost shouted.

The two men confronted each other, Stair red under
his greyish hair, standing four-square to his audience,
Brade swinging his glass by its ribbon in a frenzy of
irritation. Jerrold intervened.

"Brade apparently hasn't made up his mind what he
thinks about Chen. Can't you tell us why you are so sure
Tom had nothing to do with it, Brade? You must see
Captain Stair is right. We have to collaborate."

"Very well, I'll tell you. I don't think Tom did it
because I know somebody else did." He smiled, evidently
pleased with himself.

"Who?" shouted Stair.

"I don't know who. It was either someone much
cleverer than Tom or someone much stupider, someone
who planned it all carefully and waited his chance or
someone who did it on the spur of the moment and was
lucky enough not to be caught at it. And if you want to
know why, you've seen that nail-file, you've heard about
that latch-key, you know all about Chen, you've seen Mr.
Prentice's room and the track of the fire, and you all saw
that handkerchief. It was lying out of reach of Mr.
Prentice's chair. And you know that the bell had been
moved, replaced, and wiped clean."

Pennleaf said: "Yes, sir. The flames worked away from
the chimney, then they turned across the body and
caught the chair on the opposite side, as if a draught from
the window had blown them back. So I say that window
was opened and Chen came in then. That's why I don't
see Mr. Tom guilty. He had to get back through the hall
door. He hadn't any time to lose and he didn't let the dog

in for him to give him away. The dog was sure to bark. It don't fit the facts. I say the murderer got out by the window, however he got in, and that was just before the accident was discovered, because, from all accounts, that's when he started to bark. But I don't understand about the handkerchief."

Brade beamed on him. "Nor do I, Inspector. And that's why it's so important. There are three things I don't understand and can't explain in any reasonable way. One is the handkerchief, one is the disappearance of my San Ts'ai—the fish, you know—and one is something Mrs. Norbury said, and I can't even tell you what that was, for I don't know."

"Come, Mr. Brade, you must know, even if you can't explain it."

"But I don't. Jerry's got it all written down in his book, but he won't show me."

"I told you. I've a typed copy. You can read that."

"I only know that while she was talking I could see this room and everything and everyone in it and then suddenly the picture was blurred and I didn't know why, and I don't know yet."

"Too vague for me by half!" Captain Stair grunted. "Will you read us your account of that interview, doctor?"

Dr. Jerrold hesitated. "I'd like Mrs. Norbury's permission to do that. I hold no position in this inquiry, nor did Brade then. She spoke freely to us, but she might wish to reconsider her account before it goes on record. I have no doubt she'll tell you all she told us, Captain."

"Let's have her in. Ring the bell, Inspector."

When Rachel came in response to a message from Braythorpe, the men rose and Jerrold placed a chair for her.

"Now, Mrs. Norbury, we've asked Dr. Jerrold to read us his account of the interview you had with him last night." Captain Stair's manner was evidently intended to be soothing and Rachel put up with it, without protest.

"He feels a difficulty in doing so and would like your permission first. I suppose you have no objection?"

"Yes," answered Rachel, "I have. It is one thing to speak plainly to a friend, another to make a statement which you are willing to sign on oath. In so serious a matter I should wish, naturally, to be perfectly accurate in every detail. If Dr. Jerrold will give me his notes I will read them and alter anything I am doubtful about."

"But it's just those things that we want to know," Brade suggested, uneasily. "It's impressions we are interested in."

"I should have thought it would have been facts," Rachel replied. "For instance, I remember expressing my personal feelings about at least one person present last night. I cannot allow such remarks to enter into a formal statement."

"I quite understand," Stair agreed, with robust sympathy. "Dr. Jerrold, will you hand your notes to Mrs. Norbury for correction?"

Jerrold, who had taken his note-book out of the small attaché case beside him, shook his head. "I'm sorry. I can't pass this on to anyone. I've already refused to let Brade read what I've written here. It is full of my private comments and conjectures. I make a habit of keeping very full notes of conversations, and my observations of people, in my work. I will let Mrs. Norbury have a typed copy— including all she told us last night."

"Well, that's all right, then," Stair agreed.

The door was flung open by Lady Charlotte, who stood there twisting her hands in distress. "Will you please come, Dr. Jerrold? Oh, come at once! Mrs. Myster's killing Bernice Langrove and Lily's fainted." Women's screams could be heard from the kitchen wing, and Dr. Jerrold ran down the hall toward the sound. Pennleaf and Stair followed, and Brade, after a second, followed them. But outside the door he hesitated, twirling his glass thoughtfully. The screams grew louder, masculine voices joined in. Nurse Jonsen passed him, her white skirts swinging round the corner and out of sight. Tom came downstairs with Tassy Litton. Rachel walked out of the library, saw Brade standing there, and smiled at him. The screaming had diminished and now stopped.

Tom came back. "It's only a fit of hysterics. Mrs. Myster went for Bernice like a wildcat. For God's sake, come out to the stables with me, Tass."

"Perhaps I'd better go," Rachel remarked. "Aunt Charlie can't deal with those servants. They've all lost their wits, I think."

Tom and Tassy went out.

Brade returned to the library. He looked around the room quickly and saw Dr. Jerrold's note-book lying on a chair. He picked it up and it fell open at a gap where several pages had been torn out. As he stood there looking at it, Jerrold came into the room.

"I thought you might do that," he said angrily. "You did once before, but that time you didn't know that what I'd written wasn't meant for you to see. This time you did. Don't do it again, Simon." He took the book into his own hands.

"But, Jerry, I wasn't reading what is there—honestly I wasn't."

"What were you doing?"

"I was looking to see if what was there five minutes ago was still there, and it isn't."

Jerrold opened the book quickly and saw the gap in its leaves.

"Who did this?" he asked.

"Mrs. Norbury didn't want us to re-read your account of that interview. She said so."

"She tore out these leaves!"

"She was the only person in the room."

"Then—Brade, if she did let out something she wants to hide and it's written down there, we'll know what it is. I typed a copy last night for you. She doesn't know that."

"I shall be interested in that copy, Jerry. We'd better go back to the inn and have a look at it before someone burgles the copy too."

"Right. But first I wish you'd come and have a word with the girl in the servants' hall. She's got something to tell us."

The scene in the servants' hall was farcically dramatic. Lily, the blonde kitchen-maid, was lying on the floor, and when Nurse Jonsen revived her with contemptuous efficiency, she began to sob. Near the fire Mrs. Myster had returned to her attack on Bernice, the young housemaid, who was resisting so vigorously that, just as the others came in, they both lost their balance and fell, sprawling, over a chair. "'Elp!" shrieked Bernice, "'Elp—she'll murder me, she will, the bloody bitch! 'Elp, for the love of God!"

The Inspector and Jerrold parted the fighting women. Mrs. Myster stood panting and smoothing her apron and then her hair.

"She's got something she won't give up," she said as well as she could for lack of breath, "and I'll have it out of her yet, if she kills me for it first. I always said she'd bring trouble to this house, and now likely I'll be believed. Like bull like calf!"

With this obscure saying, she glared at the company impartially and malevolently and then sat down, while Bernice, wild-eyed and gypsy-like, her straight dark hair hanging into her eyes, shrank, cornered, into her big chair, and Lily sobbed on Nurse Jonsen's arm.

"If you don't stop crying I'll throw a whole jug of water over you, my dear," said Nurse Jonsen calmly, pushing the girl to a sitting posture and removing the support of her arm. Lily gasped once and was silent.

"You open her hand!" Mrs. Myster pointed to Bernice, cowering before her. "She's got it there and she won't own up. Been pokin' and pryin', she has, and I'm doing no more than my duty, which is what I've always done and always will, whether it's appreciated or not. You open her hand. Then you'll believe me—though why I should be doubted, and me giving faithful service for half a lifetime, I don't know."

Bernice sought the watching faces for one that might be friendly. "I'll tell the doctor," she said, giving up the fight. "I'll tell 'im if you'll let me go 'ome. I can't stand this 'ouse no longer, I can't. My mother made me come and I wish I 'adn't! You're all parasites 'ere, and them as pretend different is the worst of the lot. You just wait till the next strike. You'll be breaking stones in the road for a livin', you will, and scourin' garbage-pails for a bit of stale bread. That's what the parasites do in Russia, and the working man's on top. Wait till my father gets you." There was more of the same thing, and all the time her thin fist was clutched on her secret.

Braythorpe stepped up to her. "Bernice, did you bring those letters? Did your father write them?"

Her eyes glittered as she returned his stare.

"Don't you wish you knew!" she retorted.

Braythorpe, without more words, leaned over and forced open her fingers. For a moment she struggled like a cat, then she wrenched her hand away and flung across the room something that dropped on the floor at Dr. Jerrold's feet. He picked it up, looked at it, and handed it to Brade. Brade in turn gave it to the Inspector.

It was a latch-key.

"Where did you get this?" he asked.

"In the garden. I went out to get some dusters that's been left out overnight. They was on the line yesterday to dry and then the rain came on, and Hegan said to leave 'em and then we forgot. That key was lying on the grass, beside the path."

"Are you telling the truth?"

"Well, tell them where it came from yourself if you don't believe me."

"Is this Mr. Tom Prentice's latch-key?" the Inspector asked Braythorpe.

"I think so, I'll try it." Braythorpe went out.

"Of course, Tom was always careless, but that's not the same thing," Lady Charlotte went on, and the others raised their voices over hers.

"Why didn't you bring it straight to us?"

"Because I knew what she'd say." Bernice pointed to Mrs. Myster. "She wouldn't believe me. She'd say my father got in last night and did in Mr. Prentice. She thinks so. She said so. I meant to 'ide it."

"Do you know the risk you were running?"

"Jail? What'd you send me to jail for? The whole of Medbury'll rise up and let me out. I'm a free citizen and I ain't done nothin'."

"You've nothing more to tell us about this key?"

"No, I ain't!" She jerked her head back with a gesture of defiance.

"Well, my girl, you come along with me and show me just where you picked it up." The Inspector took her arm and led her out of the room. No one followed them. Rachel spoke quickly to Mrs. Myster, and Lady Charlotte suddenly remembered that she had given no orders to the kitchen since the day before, and chose this unsuitable time for making a complaint about the soup. The men trailed back toward Stephen's office for a further consultation.

In the stables Tassy and Tom were engaged in discussing the points of a young horse which Tom was trying. Their language was technical and as obscure to the uninformed as that of eminent mathematicians, painters of the modernist school, or a pair of financiers discussing the bank rate. But they were comforted.

"I've made a damned fool of myself," Tom suddenly let out as they walked toward the house.

"Yes," Tassy agreed vigorously, "you have. But you can stop making a fool of yourself now."

"I have stopped—if you mean Nurse Jonsen. I don't know how it happened, but this morning everything seemed different. Why, she didn't even look pretty. She looked as old as Mother. I don't know what happened."

"Did she put you up to quarrelling with Uncle Selford?

"I don't know. No, it's not fair to blame her. It was me. I'll tell you something, Tass, I thought I was in love with her."

Tassy, not usually ironical, said: "No!"

"Did you guess it?" Tom seemed surprised.

"I shouldn't call it exactly guessing."

"Oh, come. I didn't say a word."

"Oh, Tom, didn't you?"

"What's come over you, Tass? You're sarcastic."

Tassy shook her head. Then she said: "You say it wasn't her fault, but it was. Didn't she sympathize with you—say how unjust the money arrangement was, and how marvellous you were to put up with it, when most men would go to law to get their rights? Didn't she come down to the stables with you and listen to you talking about the horses and the hounds and telling her about the hunt?"

"She was awfully interested—she was really, Tass."

"Was she? Look here, Tom, you aren't blind or as stupid as you try to be. Think. Tell me what you're remembering this second!"

Tassy stopped and made Tom stop too.

"It's nothing."

"Yes, it is. Tell me."

"Just the way she looked at her shoes when she came out of the stables. She wears awfully pretty shoes."

"She would."

They walked on in silence. Tom glanced at Tassy's grim little face. Things seemed reversed between them today. Only yesterday she had been a kid he liked and felt at home with, and he himself an experienced man of the world, who spared time every now and again to give her a treat, a ride on a new horse, or a jaunt to a sale of foxhound pups—even, once or twice, a run up to town to do a show. Today, he was feeling a fool, and she, somehow, was the person he turned to for reassurance.

"It'd be a lot worse if you weren't about the place, Tass," he said, surprised at his discovery.

"I'm not about the place," she replied shortly.

"Look here, Tass, what d'you mean?" They stopped short again, under bare cherry trees, and stared at each other.

Tassy herself did not know exactly what she meant. She, too, was bewildered and slightly aghast at the change in herself and Tom. She had worshipped him for a long time, and, seeing his faults, had regarded them much as she did splashes of mud on the scarlet of his hunting coat. Now she saw him otherwise. He was, after all, no hero. How could she know that, if that red-headed cat should turn his way again, he would not crawl back and let her pat him with her velvet paw?

It was one of those moments when familiar things seem to shiver into fragments, just as if they hitherto had seen each other only in a mirror, and the mirror had fallen at their feet. Neither Tassy nor Tom was prepared for the shock of facing the other, just as they were. It happened that Tassy's hair, which was fine and blew into soft curls when unrestrained, was bright in the scrappy sunlight, and the pupils of her eyes were big and black, and her cheeks flushed. The brown girl was faintly and tenderly coloured like the autumn day. There were two large freckles on her decided young nose. Tom, who saw very little, all told, saw plainly for once and was always to see her so, just as she was then, as long as he lived. This staunch young friend, whom he had liked to tease and spoil and teach, so securely his, as far as she went, or as far as he needed her, had suddenly been shown him as a delectable young woman slipping out of his reach. Tom, who would have said that he had fallen in love frequently, now did so for the first and last time in his life, but neither he nor Tassy knew it then. They only stared at each other, with the sunlight silvery around them, and the branches of the cherry trees writing faint shadows on the sheets of their faces, a pattern they could not read. Tom's question was forgotten, and Tassy's answer never said. Bewildered and disturbed as two puppies in a strange place, they looked away from each other and walked on toward the house.

CHAPTER 13

AFTER lunch Rachel, Maurice, and Stephen went upstairs to Maurice's study to work. Jerrold and Brade had gone back to Medbury, and Tom retreated to the kennels.

"Come into the studio with me, Tassy." Lady Charlotte took the girl's arm. "It will do me good to be alone with you. It's just as I've said all along: once you begin making mysteries you can't stop. Suspicion is exactly like convolvulus. It crawls along underground and comes up where you never expect to see it. Things seem odd to me now that never did at the time, like finding my gardening gloves on the writing-table when I'm sure I put them in the basket, and Braythorpe cleaning the silver just as usual, and Stephen smoking a cigarette. I really must check this order to the seedsmen or I shall be noticing something queer about you, and so far you're the only person I haven't suspected of anything." The bewildered lady sank into a chair by the fire, sighing as she hunted through her papers for the one she wanted. "How extraordinary the room looks with all the furniture gone!" she murmured. "Now, I do hope they haven't taken that seedsman's order. No, here it is." She became as nearly silent as she ever was.

Tassy took up a weekly gossip paper and looked at the pictures until she came on one of Maurice in a party of well-known people, photographed with smiles and champagne glasses all complete on the occasion of the opening of a new restaurant.

"From left to right, Lord Philip Haverley, Miss Pollie Calwell, Mr. Maurice Prentice, Miss Meg Lofield," she read.

"Is that the girl they call the Tin Princess?" she asked.

"It's a very good idea," Lady Charlotte answered; "I could name my dahlia that. She's silver-grey, you know, if she comes true next year. I never saw the girl, but she's pretty, isn't she? Of course, Maurice's friends are all fearfully useful. If they haven't got yachts, they've got influence, and if they're poor, they're brilliant, but I never heard of any as rich and pretty as that." They looked together at the striking and surprisingly grave young face. "Her father married the Duke of Davenhill's daughter, so he must have been rich then, because I remember when I was a girl hearing that he was a barber's son. His name was Mario and I always wondered what his wife called him in private, but he danced well, so some of the girls didn't mind, only my grandmother took me out and she was terribly unworldly and old-fashioned and preferred gentlemen who didn't have to remember to be gentlemen and she adored Tom's father because, of course, he was so different from the Weleven men, who like horses better than women, and she'd always wanted to travel and my grandfather said she could go anywhere a horse would take her, so, if you please, she sold the only string of pearls she had that wasn't an heirloom and took her own hack to the Continent and rode through France and Spain and got all the way to Granada before he found her and brought her home."

Maurice in the picture was off his guard. His face was turned toward the lovely girl beside him. How little anyone knew Maurice, Tassy thought. Rachel did, perhaps, but even Stephen, with his talent for people, took Maurice as everyone else seemed to, as a person with ambitions and a purpose and very few private feelings or interests. Perhaps that was the truth about him—but perhaps it was not. What was the truth?

Lady Charlotte was still talking, but Tassy did not know it. She looked across the room to the place where the writing-table had stood. Last night Maurice had been writing there in the bay, while the others had talked, sitting in a group near the fire. Could he have slipped out at the garden door, let himself in at the front door with his latch-key, gone to his father's room for some unknown purpose, and returned the same way without being seen? She moved over to the fire and sat down in one of the chairs. She could see the chair which Maurice must have occupied. No, some one of the three women would have seen if he had moved. Even Nurse Jonsen on the sofa facing the fire could have seen if she had been sitting in the corner as she usually did, propped up with cushions; or even if she hadn't, a mere turn of the shoulder would have brought his figure into view.

Besides, why? So far as Maurice's life and behaviour could be judged, he was the person most completely in sympathy with his father and most devoted to him. What Lady Charlotte had said was true. Everyone was suspicious of everyone else. The mystery had already warped her own mind. Last night she had been ready to suspect Rachel of some sinister secret. Rachel, her own sister. Today it was Maurice. Why had she picked him out? Only because he was one of the clever people, driven by enthusiasm for a cause she did not understand. She could suspect Maurice because she could not see into his mind. She could not suspect Tom, because, in spite of his temper and his simplicity with women, she knew how he would act under any circumstances she could imagine. Just, in fact, as she would act herself. "You can't go about thinking people are criminals because they aren't your own sort," Tassy pulled herself up.

Half an hour later Rachel came in and said it was time to go home. "Maurice has given me some work to do for him. I've promised to phone Colby, the agent, and to offer to speak in Maurice's place tonight and tomorrow. I've got some notes Selford made out yesterday. I want to work out my speech. Come along, Tassy."

The afternoon was dreamy with subdued brightness.

"Let me drive, Tass," said Rachel. "I want a rest from thinking." Tassy obediently acquiesced and Rachel started the engine.

Lady Charlotte's gardening took no account of the convenience of motors approaching the front door. The low wall of her rose-garden was built on the edge of the flagged circle on which the Vauxhall stood, and a large bed of flowering shrubs in the centre narrowed the turn, so that getting away from the Grange required skill and patience, unless the car had been backed from the gate at the edge of the flags to the doorstep.

Tassy felt in her bag for her cigarette-case, took it out, and found it empty. Like others accustomed to driving a car, she was irritated by Rachel's less efficient maneuvering of the gears. Rachel's bag was tucked into the seat between the two girls and Tassy reached for it, to rifle her sister's cigarette-case, but Rachel, seeing her gesture, took a hand off the steering wheel and grasped Tassy's arm. The moment was critical, the wheels skidded, the car plunged forward straight into the low wall, and Tassy gave a cry of pain as her arm twisted under Rachel's hand. The low wall, built of bricks and mortar rubble, crumbled. The brakes ground. The car jumped and stopped.

Lady Charlotte ran out from the house, and Braythorpe followed. Rachel picked up her bag, but the clasp had sprung open and Tassy saw that it was stuffed full of papers, covered with a fine script which looked like Greek to her. She recognized Dr. Jerrold's writing.

"I'm sorry, Tass," Rachel said, looking at her sister. "Is anything the matter? Are you hurt?"

"It's my shoulder." Tassy avoided Rachel's glance.

She climbed out, and she and Braythorpe examined the car. A mudguard was bent and the hood dented, but otherwise it seemed to have escaped disablement. "I'd be careful, though," Braythorpe advised; "you may have loosened the brakes, ma'am. It'll get you home all right, but I'd let Hines go over it before you take it out again."

Lady Charlotte was lamenting the damage done to the wall, and trying to replace the roots of a saxifrage plant which had been torn out when it crumbled. The two girls returned to their places, and Rachel backed away and, skimming the edge of the shrubs precariously, drove out of the gate and down the drive.

"Why did you want to open my bag?" demanded Rachel, watching the road.

"I wanted a cigarette. I didn't know—"

"I suppose you didn't. You are stupid, Tassy. I wish you'd leave my things alone. Is your arm hurting you?"

Tassy felt her shoulder cautiously. "I've put it out again," she said, despairingly. "Damn! I'll have to ride in a strap, I suppose." Tassy had dislocated her shoulder in a hunting accident a year ago and since then had to be careful not to do it again.

"We'll send for Dr. Garnet."

"Blast! He'll say I'm not to hunt for a fortnight, and I can't lie up, Rachel. Why did you do that? What does it mean?" Tassy, sick with pain and bewilderment, cried out.

They were driving down a winding hill between beech woods. Rachel deliberately drew the car aside into a track made for timber carts and stopped it.

"We may as well have this out here and now." She took her cigarette-case, helped herself, and passed it to Tassy. Her lips were stiff as she spoke. The less we discuss it at home, the better. There was one thing I told Dr. Jerrold last night that I didn't want him to remember. He may not have remembered it—he may not have written it down. But I don't want it on record. Now you know."

"You've no right to keep things back. I don't like it."

"I'm acting for Selford. There's no one else to do that."

"What about Maurice?"

"Maurice!" Rachel smoked for a moment in silence. Then she said: "You can't understand, Tassy. I can't expect you to. But since I gave up any idea of being happy, I've found just one thing in the world worth living and working for—worth dying for, too. Selford Prentice gave me that. I'm the only person who fully understands what he was working for. Maurice doesn't. He is a leader, he is eloquent, he'll climb to power, perhaps, but he is ambitious, and that's fatal. If the choice came between serving his father's ideal and gratifying his own ambitions, I'm afraid he'd hesitate, I'm afraid he'd choose to take the way that led to fame. Selford knew it. Maurice isn't great. He depended on his father's intellect. He's shrewd, he can make use of people, he knows good work when he sees it, but he wants his thinking done for him. I've got to do it now."

"I always thought Maurice cared more about getting on with his own career than anything else. Look at his smart friends. Uncle Selford had so few friends, except the people who worked for him. Is Meg Lofield a great friend of his, Rachel?"

"No. Why?" Tassy recognized that voice, since she had heard it last night, when Rachel had sent her away from the door. It had a rasp like that of some musical instrument pressed out of its range.

"I wondered. She's so rich and lovely and they say she is very serious, wants to use her money for the good of the world. I saw her picture with Maurice's in Talk of the Town."

"There's nothing in it." Rachel seemed to hesitate. Then she said: "This is between ourselves, Tassy, but I may marry Maurice. If I do, it will be because we can both work better that way. I haven't decided. But he won't marry anyone else."

"Don't do that, Rachel. Oh, don't marry Maurice!"

"You don't understand. You will never understand. But you'll do what I say. Leave me alone. And stop thinking about all this. You'll only make a muddle of it. Thinking isn't your strong point, you know."

Tassy realized suddenly how sure Rachel was of her.

"She's so much cleverer than I am, and I've always adored her so, she doesn't dream I won't do exactly as she wants," thought Tassy. "She doesn't know me after all. She understands Maurice all right because he's her sort.

She's never tried to understand me. I'm too simple and stupid. It would be like reading a copy-book. But there are quite a lot of things in my old copy-book she might remember if she'd ever thought about them: 'Love your neighbour,' 'Tell the truth,' 'Play the game.' She would laugh at them. But I don't. They seem right to me. If I don't tell the truth, if I'm unkind or mean, I feel uncomfortable. Damned uncomfortable. But she'd explain it to herself. She'd say you have to lie sometimes in the cause of truth, and if you love one neighbour too much a hundred may suffer, and that the 'Play the game' idea is behind a lot of wickedness. I've heard her say so. Rachel is beautiful and brilliant and I adore her. She's all I've got except Mullie. But she's not my sort and I'm not hers."

All this passed through Tassy's thoughts as she looked at her sister.

"Rachel, that bit you want Dr. Jerrold to forget—has it anything to do with the way Selford died?"

"Oh, no. Nothing at all."

Again that feeling of slipping off into space, just when you thought you stood firm. Tassy was not sure that Rachel was lying, but neither was she sure she was not.

"Was it something I said—or something you said?"

"I'm not going to tell you, so why ask questions?"

It must have been something Rachel herself had said. Tassy knew nothing and could give nothing away. But Rachel, with her caution and her power of concentration, had surely not told those two men more than she thought best. Then last night and today were different; something had happened between to alter Rachel's policy. All Tassy's doubts and suspicions returned. Someone had been there last night talking to Rachel. Who? Maurice? Another thought startled her. Stephen?

Rachel loved Stephen and hoped for great things from him. She loved him, as she loved Tassy herself, protectingly and admired him with a certain human weakness which was very nearly the only such lapse in her habit of detached judgment. She might scheme and lie to save Stephen. What possible motive could Stephen have for harming Selford?

There was money. Suppose Stephen had been in that room last night to try to persuade Selford to lend him money. Suppose he had been afraid to say so. Stephen might behave like that. Tassy's thoughts stumbled on in this unaccustomed field, awkwardly, but carefully too, for she knew she must not make mistakes. Her mind acted like a trustworthy mount finding his way home through the woodlands in the dark, his nose and his forefeet nearly touching.

Rachel was no longer watching Tassy. Tassy looked at her sister and tried for a second to guess how her thoughts ran, but she could not. Rachel would be racing ahead, covering miles to Tassy's inches, but would she be going straight, and did she want to? Tassy knew she must depend on herself, follow her own instinct, take her own line. She had no pilot and this was a strange country and all the fences were blind.

"Look here, Tassy, I want you to promise me something." Rachel turned on her with all her authority. "Don't talk to Dr. Jerrold or Mr. Brade. They've nothing to go on. Tom is the only person a breath of suspicion falls on and even if the jury isn't satisfied that it was an accident they aren't going to believe Tom had anything to do with it, especially now that the latch-key has been found in the garden. The worst they can do is to bring in a verdict of murder against some person or persons unknown. But we may be able to convince them it was an accident. Tom is tough enough to bear a little ill-natured gossip. He'll forget all about it in six weeks and other people will forget it sooner. Promise me you'll keep out of it."

"You mean you want me to promise I won't tell Mr. Brade about your taking those notes?"

"Well, yes. Or anything else."

"But I think he'll guess you did."

"Of course he will. But he can't prove it. And it's no crime. I'm not afraid of him."

Tassy said nothing. Beech leaves, browned and shrivelled, drifted past the wind-shield and settled lightly over those fallen earlier and already mingling with the soil. The wet trees glistened, their trunks black and green as snake-skins, and far away a woodpecker tapped noisily, and a tractor started up in a field beyond the road.

"Promise, Tass?"

"I'm not very likely to talk," Tassy said slowly, "but I don't understand. I can't understand. Why are you trying to cover something up, and what is it? Whatever it is, I know more trouble will come of it. You're clever, Rachel, and you think you're cleverer than anyone else, but somehow I believe Mr. Brade is a match for you. Besides—besides" —Tassy drew a deep breath—"it isn't worth it. Can't you see that?"

"You aren't very clear about it yourself."

"I know I'm no good at saying things, but that doesn't mean I can't see them. I'm so proud of you."

"What has that got to do with it, you silly kid?"

It had everything to do with it, but it was impossible to say why.

"I don't want you to hide things—and I hate and loathe your taking those pages out of Dr. Jerrold's book."

"He had no right to put down that conversation. I took the only way of preventing the harm he might do."

"I hate it," Tassy repeated helplessly. "And besides, if Tom's under suspicion and there's any way of clearing him, he must be cleared. I don't care who suffers."

"Even me?"

Tassy said nothing. Her shoulder was painful and she felt tired out. How could she answer? How could she act?

Then, looking at Rachel, she forgot herself, for Rachel's face was that of a woman in torment.

"Tassy, I loved Selford," she said. "I never knew how I loved him. And I don't know what to do. Oh, I don't know what to do!" She sheltered her grief and pain behind her two gloved hands and Tassy stared at the leather gauntlets not daring to speak.

"Can't you tell me?" begged Tassy at last. "Rachel, darling, I'd help you if I could. Can't you tell me all about it? Rachel, do! Oh, do tell me."

But the moment of release which might have brought the two women closer passed, leaving them separated by Rachel's secret. Her habit of control reasserted itself. She would not trust Tassy. How could she? Though she loved her she despised her, and that was a mistake. She took her hands from her face and said: "You can help me best by doing exactly what I tell you to do. Hold your tongue." The effort she was making chilled her voice, and her voice chilled Tassy's heart.

Rachel backed the car out into the road. She said no more, but her lovely inscrutable face was quiet and set in lines that made her seem older than she was.

"I'd like Dr. Jerrold to come and set my arm," said Tassy as they drove down Hartover High Street. "He won't fuss so much as Dr. Garnet."

"I'd rather you had your own doctor," Rachel answered. "Don't be silly, Tassy. You can't play about with that shoulder of yours. You'd better go to bed."

An hour later, propped up on pillows and made much of by Mullie, Tassy faced the situation.

Unless she defied Rachel and Mullie and the doctor and all the maids, she was practically a prisoner for the next three days. By that time the inquest would be over. Even if the jury brought in an open verdict, how many people would go away believing the worst of Tom? She could hear them talking—Tom's temper—his debts—Selford's will. And all the while there was someone, in the Grange or out of it, who would deserve what Tom would have to bear. Rachel knew it, but she did not care.

CHAPTER 14

RACHEL came in after dinner and brought Stephen with her.

She said: "Look here, Tassy. You've got to be sensible. Dr. Garnet says you must have caught a chill hunting yesterday. It was that long hack home in the wind after getting wet, I suppose. Your temperature's up. And the shock of all this trouble hasn't improved matters. You'll just have to stay where you are. The doctor will send you something to quiet you down and you'd better go to sleep. I'm going to be busy. We've got to carry on as well as we can, with the election next week. Of course Maurice can't appear till after the funeral. But everyone will be sorry for him and that'll help and I'll do my best. I've cancelled all my own engagements to speak for him and they'll send a woman to take my place. I've got my hands full, so promise you won't worry me by trying to get up."

"I may as well promise, since I can't get into my clothes." Tassy was ungracious.

"I'll stay and talk to Tass a bit," Stephen volunteered.

"Well, don't stay long. And she's not to see anyone else tonight. Settle her down at ten, Mullie, after she's had her medicine."

"I'll have to get back before that, anyway. There's a lot to do," Stephen answered. Rachel, preoccupied and lonely, went out to her meeting, and Mullie went down to supper.

Stephen sat down on the end of Tassy's bed.

"Can you lend me one thousand pounds?" he asked without preliminary. "I want it now."

"No, I can't," snapped Tassy. "I haven't got that much in the bank and shan't have till the end of January. Who's the new girl, Stee?"

"Don't be funny. It isn't a girl. At least, not exactly."

"Oh, I suppose she's well-preserved. You are a fool, you know. Won't you ever get over it?"

"It isn't that at all this time. I'm in the devil of a mess, and that's a fact. I've got to have the money. I've got to have it now."

Tassy sat up and her shoulder hurt.

"Why don't you ask Rachel?"

"Because she'd be furious."

"She isn't usually. She's rather a fool about you herself."

"She's been awfully good to me. But this is something I can't tell her. Be a sport, Tass. You're close as anything. The bank'll let you have an advance on your January dividends. You know they will. I tell you I've got to have it."

"When?"

"Before tomorrow."

"Why?"

"Oh, let me have it. I can't tell you why."

"Then I won't help you. And that's that. I don't want to."

"Will you give me the money if I tell you why I want it?"

"Perhaps."

Stephen took a turn around the room. Then he returned to Tassy's side.

"You'd better hurry up. Mullie'll be back," Tassy reminded him.

"Did you ever see Elena Prentice?"

"Selford's wife?"

"His widow. Yes."

"No, never."

"Well, they say she's the most gorgeous woman on earth."

"She must be fifty."

"I don't know how old she is. But she's grand, everybody says so. Carved and coloured by a master. Makes every other woman look cheap. And that's not all. There isn't a lift of her finger that isn't full of magnetism. Maurice has got a bit of that. She's—well, she's a marvel."

"Go on. You can skip, you know. Does she want a thousand pounds off you?"

"Don't be an ass. Of course not. What she wants—or wanted—is her freedom. Do you realize that Selford kept that glorious woman tied to him all these years—that he refused to let her divorce him or even to divorce her? They lived together a few weeks, and she went home to her father months before Maurice was born. It was far worse for her than it would have been for a European. It meant that she had to live, year in, year out, under the strictest sort of chaperonage. Even now her brothers won't allow her to go anywhere alone. Elena was expected to devote her life to good works. Good works! A woman like that! Watched and. guarded like a girl of sixteen. When she came to England last summer, a maid like a stone mountain came along and a female cousin besides. Of course she is a dazzling creature, besides being very tall, and so graceful that people watch her walk across the room even when they can't see her face, but—think of it, Tassy. Never to stir an inch without some watch-dog tagging along behind you—a woman of her temperament!"

"Get back to the thousand pounds," advised Tassy, wearily.

"You're an unsympathetic little brute. Well, anyway, Elena came to England hoping to see Selford and Maurice too and try to persuade Selford to free her. You see, before she could marry again her first marriage would have to be annulled, you see that, I suppose?"

"Are you going to marry her on a thousand pounds?"

"She's got plenty of money," Stephen replied, as if it did not matter, but Tassy knew it did. A glorious woman of fifty was one thing; a glorious woman, even of fifty, with plenty of money might be another. She considered Stephen without trying to disguise her disgust. "Have you ever seen her?" she asked.

"No, but I've heard about her."

"You'd better go on."

"The long and short of it is she wrote to me and I promised to help her."

"How?"

"I said I'd talk to Maurice. But that was about as much use as reasoning with a tea-kettle to make it sing. He's hopelessly prejudiced of course and wouldn't even see her. I couldn't use my position to pester Selford, even if I'd thought he'd listen, and I'd about given up hope when Nurse Jonsen came."

"So you promised her a thousand pounds to vamp Selford?"

"Tassy, you're vulgar. I did nothing of the sort. That isn't it at all. The truth is Nurse was with Elena for three months, and I got Selford to take her. Of course, he didn't know. Elena thought a woman might do what a man couldn't."

"Well, did she succeed?"

"No, she didn't. She might have, of course. Selford liked her. But—oh, Lord, Tass, can't you see how I'm fixed? If she blurts out the whole story on Monday, how am I going to look? Once this man Brade got hold of a tale like that, it wouldn't take long to fix up a good story. He'd make it out that I was in love with Elena, that I'd tried to bribe Selford's nurse to persuade him to free her, and when she failed I staged an accident. Now you know."

Stephen was frightened, and Tassy watched his unguarded face. Too young to be sorry for him, she was absorbed in her own sensations. He was a human being like herself, he was her brother and he could behave like this. She could not loathe him without loathing herself. It was just accident that he was a coward and a weakling and that she was not; or perhaps she was—perhaps just the circumstances to test her courage had never arisen.

"But you've an alibi," she said. "Braythorpe told Mr. Brade he heard you typing in the office."

"He lied."

"Stephen, what do you mean!"

"He didn't hear me typing because I wasn't using the typewriter."

"What were you doing?"

"If you must know, I was sound asleep."

"But Braythorpe—why should he lie?"

"I don't know unless it was to give himself an alibi. He's got that sort of tricky mind. If I had been using the machine all that time and he had heard me doing it he must have been in the pantry. I don't usually work until I've taken Selford's letters to him. He thought I'd jump at the chance to prove I was in the office. But suppose he should come out with it—say he made a mistake or something, under pressure?"

"So you want the one thousand pounds to shut Nurse Jonsen's mouth?"

"She won't tell. She's too much mixed up in it herself. It's Braythorpe."

"Do you think you can bribe him?"

"Of course I can. For the present, anyway, and it's the present that matters."

"Well, I see why you won't go to Rachel, anyway," Tassy told him.

"You seem to think better than usual in bed, my dear. Where's your cheque-book?"

"I'm not going to give you that money, Stee."

"You're not—"

"I'm not. Twelve Englishmen wouldn't like you any better for trying to bribe a witness, and if Braythorpe took that money, he'd just cut and come again. I'm not going to support him for the rest of my life. You can see what Rachel says if you like."

"My God, Tassy—" he gripped the wooden post of her bed and stared at her—"you shall help me."

"I've just rung for Mullie. You may as well go. If it's any comfort to you, Braythorpe isn't likely to tell that kind of a story about himself. He's just as dependent on that alibi as you are."

"Come in, Mullie. Mr. Stephen's going."

So this was what it was all about. Rachel must believe that Stephen had something to do with it. But why? And what was there in that conversation last night with Brade and Jerrold to give it away? Something so trivial that they were unlikely to notice it unless they had the written record before them to study word by word? Tassy could not remember that Stephen had been mentioned at all. She lay there trying to reconstruct the interview from memory, while Mullie stirred the fire and prepared the room for the night.

CHAPTER 15

"THINGS," said Brade, "not people. Things don't pretend. They are what they are. If they move, there's a reason for it. Stick to things, and, for preference, little things. Now, I've been looking at the house, Jerry. It's interesting, you know. Just a few examples. The smallest thing in Tom's room was that nail-file."

"Why the nail-file, Simon?"

Dr. Jerrold and Brade were sitting by the fire in the parlour of the Blue Boar Inn. The market square was quiet for the hour was nearly midnight.

"It wasn't the nail-file. It was even smaller than that. Just one black thread, too fine to see except through my glass. And very like other black threads taken from the frayed shoulders of Selford Prentice's dressing-gown."

"Is this a fact?"

"Oh, yes. The Inspector regards it as conclusive. The thread found in the nail-file and others from the dressing-gown have gone up to Scotland Yard for expert examination."

"And if that identifies them as being from the same garment, will they arrest Tom?"

"That would be hasty, Jerry. There's no padlock on Tom's door and anyone might have used his nail-file. Besides, anyone who touched the body might have caught that thread on a finger-nail. But no one will admit to using Tom's file."

"What else?"

"Lady Charlotte's room. Ink spilt on the carpet."

"Brade, you're fanciful."

"Why? Lady Charlotte is fond of things and it's a new carpet. But she's fonder of fresh air. Hence the window always open even in a gale of wind. Hence the overturned inkstand. Hence the stain. Therefore wherever Lady Charlotte was, an open window."

"Far-fetched, but still—"

"Nurse Jonsen's room. Lots of little things, and expensive ones too. For instance, a rare rosary."

"And the meaning of that?"

"It might have several meanings. Is she a Catholic and was she trying to convert her patient?"

"You're joking."

"Oh, no. Now Maurice. Those marked passages in his books. How's this? 'Not the corruption of man but the softening and moralizing of him is the curse.' 'To have and to wish to have more, in a word Growth—that is life itself.' Or 'Beyond good and evil—certainly—but we insist upon the strict preservation of herd morality.' Or 'Morality may be regarded as an illusion of the species.' How's that for mental food for a young politician?"

"It doesn't sound as if Maurice was in such perfect agreement with his father after all!"

"That is another little thing. Bright Jerry!"

"And the handkerchief—a little thing too."

"The folds in it are smaller still and more important."

"Are you honest in saying you don't know what they mean?"

"I can't even imagine, yet. In fact I'm the only person who seems to be thoroughly bewildered by the case. The Inspector is certain that Langrove is guilty, and the Chief Constable thinks Tom is his man. So does Mrs. Norbury, or I'm very much mistaken."

"Why? She hasn't said so. If she thought that, she'd keep away from Tom."

"She doesn't want to show she thinks he did it. That's obvious. She is still hoping the jury will bring in a verdict of accidental death."

"How do you know?"

"I'm surprised at you, Jerry! With your insight into the human mind! She has gone out of her way to point out that someone might have got in through the studio window. Why do that if not to absolve Tom? But she thinks he did it just the same, or she did last night, or why should her sister have been so ready to defend Tom? Obviously she'd said something before we came on the scene, and Miss Tassy was looking for a chance to speak for her friend."

"You are guessing. And whom does Maurice suspect?"

"I think he suspects the right person, but I don't think he'll admit it; perhaps he won't admit it to himself."

"And you don't know who that is?"

"Not yet, Jerry, not yet. You ought to be able to tell me."

"I—why, in God's name, Simon?"

"Because we know what he did! Listen. We'll call him X if you like. Let us be conventional at all costs. Now then, X had a quarrel with Prentice. He was afraid of him. He wanted to prevent his writing a certain letter—giving away some information it was imperative he should keep to himself." Brade leaned forward, his eyes the eyes of a seer, intent on the drama he was building. "He saw his opportunity and took it. He opened that door—from the hall—came into the room, demanded an answer from Prentice, and found him actually enclosing the fatal letter in its envelope. He snatched it away, threw it into the fire. Prentice told him that his mind was made up, and reached for the bell. X snatched the bell out of his reach, and, knowing that Prentice would not give in, picked him out of his chair and shook him over the fender till he died, and left him lying there. Then he considered the situation, threw all the letters on the fire to make the detection of that one improbable, wiped the bell, and let Chen in, going out by either the hall door or the garden door."

"He must have gone out by the garden door, or why let the dog in?"

"Why indeed? And what did he use the handkerchief for? Prentice did not drop it where it was lying, and it was not used to wipe the bell, for there was no dust on it at all."

"Could Chen have got in by the other door?"

"Perhaps. But the garden door was opened for a moment at least. Another little thing, Jerry: it was the draught from the open door that blew a scrap of the burning papers out of the fire on to the files of newspapers and set them alight, for the south-east wind never blows down that chimney. X may not have known anything about the fire until afterwards. Now reconstruct the person who did all that and tell me who it is."

"A man who acts quickly inflamed by passion, but thinks afterwards and then thinks coolly and cleverly."

"Yes? Go on!" Brade was writing in a note-book.

"Someone who knew Prentice well enough to be sure he would keep his word."

"Yes. Go on!"

"Someone with less natural aversion to violence than the average. However strong the motive, it would be revolting to a good many hardened characters to attack a crippled man."

"Yes. Go on, Jerry, go on."

"Someone—" Jerrold hesitated and stared in front of him before he went on—"someone capable of a second crime and a third if the need arose."

"Yes."

The two men looked at each other. Outside, the clock of the Town Hall struck the hour slowly. When it had stopped, and while the last stroke still vibrated, Brade said: "Who?"

And Jerrold answered: "Look for a man who wants something enough to pay any price. The world is full of them now, or the world would not be what it is."

CHAPTER 16

MULLIE had little faith in thermometers, but she knew a fever when she saw one, and she slept on the couch in Tassy's room that night. Tassy's sleep was a mixture of blank oblivion, produced by Dr. Garnet's prescription, and nightmare. More than once she woke crying out and found Mullie at her side with water, her heavy old hand comforting and cool. At last, wet with perspiration, she slept quietly, and the winter dawn did not wake her, nor did the church bells, though they seemed to ring in the house itself, nor did Pocahontas scratching at her door. It was a thought that woke her at last, clear and audible as the bells, themselves.

"I must see Dr. Jerrold or Mr. Brade and tell them what I know. Today."

But while she ate her breakfast and Rachel talked to her, she realized how difficult it would be for her to do any such thing. Inside the house Rachel's orders were obeyed, and after hers Mullie's. Tassy herself was indulgently treated, but was denied any kind of authority.

"I'm going to London with Maurice," Rachel said. "I've given my instructions. You are to rest and sleep, and see no one. Be good." She kissed Tassy lightly and went away.

"Here I lie," thought Tassy. "Tom's in danger, and Rachel is hiding something that might save him. Besides, it's all wrong, even if she's doing it for Stephen; but is she? Would she, even for him? There's only one thing she'd sacrifice everybody for, and that's her work. Is that at the bottom of it? Could the truth, somehow, hurt that? She thinks this new book of Uncle Selford's is the greatest thing of the kind that's ever been done. Suppose the truth is something disgraceful about him. She'd lie to hide that and think she was doing right. She thinks it doesn't matter who suffers if the cause is at stake. She defends all the horrible things the Russians do. And I'm doing nothing to stop her."

"Mullie," Tassy sat up, white and determined, "I'm going to get up. I'm going to ride to the Grange. I can manage all right. Bring me my things."

Mullie looked at her tenderly. "Now, me darlin', don't you be getting excited like. Look at all the nice books Miss Rachel's left, and there's a new Sporting and Dramatic come and nobody's opened it and I'll fetch it this minute and if ye're good and quiet I'll have cook make a chocolate soufflé for your lunch. There'll be no going out for you till the doctor says so, and that ye know well."

"Then telephone to Dr. Jerrold and tell him to come and see me. Mullie, I mean it. If you don't I'll get up by myself and you won't be able to stop me, and if I put my shoulder out again and it cripples me for life, it'll be your fault."

But Mullie could not be bullied like that. Not for nothing had she had her way with her charges all these years. They might do what they liked when they were well, but in sickness they never resisted her.

"Now, Miss Tassy, none of that, my dear. Ye can't so much as get into your coat, let alone mount your horse without help. And Dracey's got his orders and he and the lad are out with the horses this minute and the car's gone. As for Dr. Jerrold, it's Miss Rachel's instructions you're to see no visitors and it's my duty to make sure ye don't, but rest quiet and get well and do as the doctor says."

"And she's right," thought Tassy. "I can't dress myself with this shoulder. If I try I'll probably faint or something, or put it out again and be laid up for weeks. What am I to do?"

She took up a book at random. It did not help her, for it was the story of a Superman who framed a plot to destroy the civilized world.

She tried again. "Mullie, help me this once. Get Dr. Jerrold to come. I must see him. I must. Can't you understand? I've got to talk to somebody. You'll be sorry if you don't help me, Mullie. And Rachel will get into trouble too. Mullie, I've got to see Dr. Jerrold, I've got to."

Tassy's cheeks were feverish. She caught Mullie's hand and pleaded. She could not explain. Mullie would take it for granted that Rachel knew best. Rachel's masterful brain had dictated too long and her authority could not be evaded. Tassy was the baby, and Mullie did not expect her to be reasonable. But she showed her concern, as she poured out the medicine Dr. Garnet had left and gave it to Tassy to drink.

"What ever's got into ye, Miss Tassy, dear? It's a fever, that's what it is, and I'll not be lettin' ye out of my sight till Miss Rachel comes home. Ye haven't behaved like this, not since ye was six and threw the castor oil at the doctor himself because he wouldn't let ye hunt on Boxing Day, and ye sickening for measles, and Miss Rachel and I had to tie ye down or you'd have been out of bed and got pneumony like as not. If ye go on like this I'll have a hospital nurse to ye, and then we'd see, and how'd ye like that? With her starch and her haughty airs and upsettin' the whole house. There's the doctor this minute and we'll see what he says."

Dr. Garnet said just what he was expected to say. He, too, looked at Tassy's bright cheeks and hot eyes and gave peremptory orders for quiet and rest and no worry.

"You're all treating me like a baby. I won't stand it!" Tassy tried to turn over and thought better of it.

"Go to sleep, my dear. You'll feel better when you wake up."

"I can't sleep. I haven't slept properly for ages."

"Dear me, that's bad," the doctor sympathized. "I'm sorry, Tassy, but you'll have to behave sensibly. There's nothing for you to do but rest and get your temperature down. Take your medicine. It'll make you sleep. I'll call again this evening." She heard Mullie talking to him outside her door.

She knew she was ill now. Perhaps she would have pneunonia and die and Tom would go to jail. The draught she tad taken sent her into a semi-doze, disturbed by her burnig thoughts. She saw Rachel's face menacing and lovely. She saw Tom tied up, struggling to free his arms, pinned behind him. She saw the others looking on and smiling. "It's no use. Drink your medicine," they said. She fought and pushed the glass away. She must not take that medicine; if she did she would forget what it was she wanted to say.

They were forcing her to drink. She screamed with Mullie bending over her.

"Hush, my dear, hush, Miss Tassy, my lamb."

Tassy shrank back on her pillows. "Go away," she said, "I don't want you. I won't drink that. Leave me alone."

"I'll be telephoning the doctor," muttered the old nurse, bewildered and alarmed. She went out. Tassy could hear her going downstairs heavily, one step at a time. It would take Mullie minutes to get to the phone and longer to make the connection. She did not like telephoning.

Tassy slipped out of bed. Painfully she managed to open a drawer and pull on her underclothes and a pair of riding breeches, but the boots were not there and she could not have got into them if they had been. There were wollen stockings and a pair of brogues. Then a jersey. She was crying with pain. She couldn't do it. Yes. All but the right sleeve. She meant to walk to the Grange. She would make Lady Charlotte keep her. What a time it took! Mullie have finished by now. At any second she would hear her coming up, dragging her stiff right leg. Poor Mullie! Yet Mullie's face had seemed threatening to Tassy. Something was there, something she did not recognize, something hostile, something to outwit and escape. Never mind a coat. She'd go now, as she was, while Mullie was in the front hall. She'd go out the side door.

It was quite easy to walk. Surprisingly easy to get down the stairs. With thankfulness she heard Mullie speaking into the phone. "What did ye say? Can ye not spake up, then? In Medbury? Can ye not get him? Ye'll try, did ye say? Ye'll do better'n that, my girl. Ye'd say he's to come to Hartover House at once or Mrs. Norbury'll want to know the reason why not. Yes, it is urgent. Sh'd ye think I'd be afther sayin' so if it wasn't and my Miss Tassy sendin' me out of the room?"

Tassy was in the passage. She was at the door. It was locked and bolted and the key was not there. She could hear the servants moving about in the kitchen beyond. Hadley's voice came, so loud and vulgar when she addressed cook, so refined in the dining-room. Nails came running long and, seeing Tassy, barked for another walk, though he had just come in.

"What's that?" Cook asked.

"I don't know. And my nerves are all on edge. What with Miss Rachel giving orders for the house to be kept locked and Hines saying somebody got into the Grange last night and queer things said about Mr. Prentice. Come along with me, cook."

Tassy picked Nails up under her sound arm. Chen was there too, not barking, but staring at her.

"The window," she thought. "The dining-room." That was locked too, but the key was inside. She turned it, still carrying Nails. She was outside, and already the mist was in league with the waning light to shelter her. Chen came too, still silent. Now for it! The front of the house would be best. She walked boldly past the drawing-room windows, round the corner, and into the path that led to the hill field. She was free, but shaking with the effort of her escape. She dropped Nails, who bolted with resolution toward the hedge where lived a colony of white rabbits. Chen kept at her heels, curious and approving.

Suddenly she stopped short. Was she mad? She looked back at the house. Never before had it seemed other than a safe and welcome shelter. How often had she opened that door, thankful for the protection and love that would meet her there! The chimneys smoked lazily, the windows gay back the failing light, the friendly and intelligent window of a house inhabited by people who had always lived this same sort of life. Those windows had never guarded against anything worse than the English weather. They had never imprisoned anyone, and the brick walls were thick for comfort. Tassy looked at it as if she were leaving it for ever, leaving Rachel and Mullie and the stables and Jennifer J. Could she come back if she left it now, like this, shattered her loyalty to Rachel, behaved like a hysterical child? That was how it seemed. And why was she doing it? For Tom?

Chen, trotting at her heels, looked up at her, his mud coloured eyes intent. Then he passed her, indifferently, and set out along the footpath. At the stile he paused and looked back once. He gave a short sharp bark, squeezed through the rails, and waited for her on the other side, waited unit she climbed the stile, pain in her shoulder and a dizzy singing in her head, and followed him.

Chen led Tassy over the fields to the Grange and straight to the window of his master's sitting-room. The window, were dark, but he settled himself to wait as usual, expecting Braythorpe to let him in.

While Tassy hesitated, a light sprang out inside the room. Someone came in, walked straight to the window, opened it and looked out. Chen slipped between his legs and was in side. He trotted over to the cold hearth, examined it with his muzzle to the rug, and whined. For a moment he lost confidence. He sought frantically for understanding and looked up at the human faces turned his way, to find it there if he could. His small but competent intelligence was beaten by the mystery of his own distress. Then with supreme effort he stepped back, crying as he went. Step by step he moved away, staring and crying. Then he straightened, raised his head, trotted to the hall door, and nosed it, crying still.

The door was opened for him. He trotted down the hall, found his way to the servants' sitting-room. Tea was laid, and all the servants were there. He sat down and stared at Mrs. Myster until she gave him a piece of white bread spread thickly with butter.

He would never go into his master's room again. For just that moment, sniffing at the hearth-rug, something in his brain had threatened to snap. That was not a moment he would forget. There are some things a dog must not try to understand, and the reason for his desperate distress was one of them. Chen was himself again. He finished the bread and butter and looked at Mrs. Myster for more.

CHAPTER 17

IT WAS Simon Brade who let in the dog and the girl, and it was he who opened the hall door for Chen. When the dog had gone, Tassy found herself shrinking back against the curtains, shivering. For that moment when Chen snarled at the empty hearth she seemed to see what he had seen and share his terror.

"If he could only tell us!" she whispered.

She looked at Brade for comfort, but Brade was frightened too. She learned then what it is to turn to others for support and find that the only support we can expect is from our own courage, as long as that lasts.

"What is the matter? What has happened now?" she asked, afraid of the answer.

"It isn't what's happened—it's what may happen!" He stared at her. "They telephoned from Hartover that you had gone. That frightened me. You ran away because you knew something, and knowing anything in this case is dangerous. The man who killed Selford Prentice will do anything."

"But, Mr. Brade, are you sure anyone did kill him? Might it have been an accident?"

"No. The doctors agree. He was shaken against that fender until his neck broke. His dressing-gown was torn on the shoulders where the fingers of the murderer gripped him and there are black silk threads on the nail-file found in Tom's room."

"Tom!" Tassy cried in protest.

"Yes, Tom. And Tom did not kill his uncle!"

"You believe that?"

"I know it."

"How?"

"Jerry says so. And Chen came in by the garden door just as he did now. Tom never let him in. Why should he? But my opinion won't save Tom from hanging for another

man's crime. Help me, Miss Litton. No one else will. Tell
me what you know." The little man, white-faced with
dismay, appealed to Tassy.

"But everyone is helping you."

"They think they are, but they're not. Stair thinks
Tom did it, and is working to prove it. Pennleaf thinks it
was Langrove. Your sister is hiding the truth, whether
she knows it or not. Braythorpe is a coward and therefore
a liar. Jerry knows something he won't tell."

"You think Rachel is hiding something? Then—do you
suspect Stephen?"

"Do you? Might he have done it?"

"No—oh, no."

"Is that because he is your brother?"

Tassy stared at the hearth where Selford Prentice's
body had lain. "I wouldn't try to protect anyone who had
done that," she answered, "but Stephen couldn't. Oh, he
couldn't!"

"Not if he were angry enough?"

"He doesn't get as angry as that. But—"

"But?"

"But if he were terribly frightened—Oh, why did you
make me say that!"

"He lied when he said he was typing for that half-
hour. There was no typed work to be found. But then
Braythorpe lied too. They were both frightened!"

"But Stephen!"

"Are you frightened too? Are you too frightened to tell
the truth? To save Tom?"

"Will the truth save him?"

"I think it will if we can find out what it is."

"I'll tell all I know, but I'd like Dr. Jerrold to be here. I
came to tell him. I want to tell him now. I'm afraid Rachel
will stop me."

"Then I'll find him." Brade paused. "Jerry's keeping
something back, but that may be the one thing to help us.
If he hadn't typed out those notes because he didn't want
me to see them as he wrote them down we shouldn't have

had the record of that interview with your sister, for she took those pages out of his book. Why?"

"Oh, I don't know. I don't understand. Unless it was something that might hurt Uncle Selford's work. It's that she cares for. She'd sacrifice anyone for that. Find Dr. Jerrold, Mr. Brade."

Brade seemed to be recovering, for he paused, pulled down his coat, gave a touch to his tie and hair, much as a woman uses a powder-puff after a fit of hysterics, and went out.

Tassy tried not to look at the fender and the cold hearth. Then because she was afraid to look at them, she did, and her heart felt icy and heavy in her breast. There was someone who could take that helpless man and kill him there at his own fireside, leave him, and live on, hiding the truth. "It can't be anyone I've ever seen," she whispered. "He must look like the people they shut up in prisons and asylums. It can't be anyone in this house. It can't be." She glanced at the blackened windows. No one could get in. The garden door was shut and latched. Yet someone must have got in from outside. The person who had written those threatening letters, perhaps. Langrove, with his red eyes and gesticulating hands? He had come to the window, found it unlatched, crept in, and, in his madness, done this horrible thing, and gone away again. It must be so.

She was still feverish and her imagination painted its pictures against the blank glass, so that when she saw a face looking in she did not think it was real.

The handle rattled. Someone was trying to get in. "It's not what has happened, it's what may happen," Brade had said. She crouched back, staring at the window.

"Let me in, Tassy."

It was Tom. Now she knew his face and his voice. She went over to the window and opened it. He stepped in. His broad, ruddy face showed his anxiety. Tom was perplexed by his trouble, like a man called upon to fight an unknown enemy in the dark.

"I was frightened about you, Tass." He gripped her hands and hurt her injured shoulder. "Mullie phoned that you'd gone. How did you get in? Why did you come? I was going out to look for you. Are you all right?"

"I had to come. Rachel wouldn't let me see anyone and I wanted to talk to Dr. Jerrold. Tom, do you know that—" The door opened quietly and Jerrold and Brade came in.

"Tom saw the lights," Tassy explained.

"Will you go and telephone to Hartover House, Tom, and tell them Tassy is here?" asked Jerrold. "Mrs. Norbury was here when Mullie rang up and she went straight home."

"She'll come back," Tassy said. "She'll try to stop me telling you. Let me tell you quickly."

Tom went out and she began.

She told them about Tom's visit to Hartover and what he said. Dr. Jerrold stopped her.

"Repeat that," he said sharply

"What?"

"What you have just told me."

"Tom said he was trying to write to Uncle Selford when Molly Hegan knocked on his door to say the bath was ready. And then he—"

"Tom said that? You had not told him that Molly Hegan knocked?"

"No, of course I hadn't. I didn't know it."

"You can swear to that?"

"Why, yes. Oh, Dr. Jerrold, I see! You mean it proves Tom was in his room. He wouldn't have known she knocked, otherwise."

"He may have guessed. But just the same it has the sound of truth. He'd have had to think it all out very carefully to have planned that—telling you, I mean. Don't you see it's one of the strong points against him that the maid says he did not answer her?" He opened the door and came back in a second with Tom. "Did Molly Hegan say anything when she knocked on your door, Tom?"

"I don't remember. Oh, yes, she said the bath was ready."

Dr. Jerrold said nothing for a moment. Then he asked: "Is that all?"

"Yes." Jerrold watched him. Tom turned back, that perplexed pucker around his eyes. "I believe she said somehing else. Yes, she did." He worried over it.

"You can't remember?" Jerrold spoke sharply.

"It's there somewhere." Tom looked startled. "Does it matter?"

Jerrold turned away. Then he said: "If you do remember, come to me, or Brade or Tassy here, and tell us. It may be important."

"But it wasn't," Tom said. "It was just a remark about—No. I've forgotten." The bell rang as the connection with Hanover was put through and he went to answer it.

"Does it matter?" asked Tassy.

"Yes. But Tom ought not to know that. He's far more likely to recall it if he isn't trying too hard. Don't you see if he could repeat what she said it would prove that he heard her? You can help there. If Tom can remember what she said it may save him. You will be with him a good deal. Ask him casually some time when he's thinking of something else."

"I'll make him remember."

Jerrold shook his head.

"My dear, you must understand. We've all got a storehouse in our brains, packed full of forgotten things. If you press Tom, this particular memory will be pushed farther down with every effort to recall it. But if he's left alone it may come to him when he's thinking about feeding a sick horse or talking about the weather. If you forget a name, does it come to you when you are trying to remember or after you've given it up and are talking of something else?"

"I see. Why?"

"Never mind why. That's how our minds behave. Now go on."

She told them about the words she had heard Rachel speak behind the closed door. "I'm sure she was talking to some one. But she said afterwards that no one was there. I didn't hear or see anyone, but the dogs did. They couldn't settle down until afterwards, when Rachel came in."

Jerrold glanced at Brade.

"There's no way of knowing. We can't prove she wasn't alone." Brade replied to his glance. "And she won't tell us.'

Tassy went on hurriedly, watching the door. She told them about the pages from the note-book in Rachel's bag and all Rachel had said to her about them, and she told then about Stephen's appeal for money, feeling ashamed and wretched but going doggedly on. When she had finished she sat there knowing that Rachel would never forgive her for what she had done. "Must you tell Captain Stair about Stephen?" she asked.

Brade was busy rolling a cigarette. He looked up.

"I'd rather not," he said with a return to his usual manner. "He's so happy about that nail-file! Let's have a secret. Everybody else seems to have. I do want one of my own!'

Jerrold moved impatiently. "It's your imagination, Brade about my having a secret. You know perfectly well that when I write my notes I put in all sorts of details interesting to me but perfectly irrelevant."

"You might let me decide that."

"Well, I won't. You've a superstitious respect for my judgment and might go astray on some guess of mine which I myself wouldn't base a professional opinion on."

"And meanwhile nothing Miss Litton has said helps Tom."

Jerrold thought that over. "No—the case against Tom is still the strongest. He had the motive and the opportunity. There is the quarrel with his uncle and his uncle's threat to alter his will. Even the latch-key tells against him. If he had thrown it out of his window to suggest that an outsider might have found his way into the house that night, it might have fallen just where it was found."

"Tom! He'd never have thought of doing that!" Tassy protested desperately.

"Others won't know that."

Brade turned abruptly.

"Who could have done it? Of all the people who were here that night, which one would you suspect, Miss Litton?" Tassy stared at him. Then she said slowly:

"When I begin to think about people, of course I see not one of them could have done it. Just the same, Uncle Selford and Rachel and Maurice weren't kind, the way Tom is. Tom would never run over a dog because he wanted to get to a meeting on time, but they would. So I believe if Uncle Selford was killed by anyone, it was either a brute you'd know for a brute when you looked at him or else by someone who had taught himself to think like them—someone who had a reason. I know I can't explain, but I can see it awfully clearly."

"You think a political motive may be behind it?"

Tassy frowned. "I know some of the Socialist party hated Uncle Selford. You see, he was so powerful, in spite of being almost unknown to the general public. He interfered in a strike in the factory, and the leaders were furious. You know, lots of Socialists are cruel if you can believe what they say. I've heard them talking. Some of them wouldn't do the things they praise other people for doing, but I suppose others would, especially if—if—" Her eyes widened. "I've seen foxes killed. The hounds kill quickly to kill, because that's their business. But cats kill mice differently. They like to see the mouse suffer. There are people like cats. Suppose one of them thought it was right to hurt one person for the sake of society. Suppose he was cruel inside like a cat. He'd like being cruel, and he'd think he had an excuse. Do you see what I mean?"

"It's very good psychology, Tassy."

"I don't know anything about psychology, but I do know that people who are afraid of anything manage to get out of it, sometimes in ways they can't have planned deliberately. Well, if a cat-man believed anything was right that served the cause and it would serve the cause to get rid of Uncle Selford, he wouldn't be stopped because of Uncle Selford's being a cripple, but Tom would."

"You are right. We've a word for just the process you're describing, it's so well known. And there's a theory that most political violence can be explained in the same way, pathologically. Wreckers are needed when the house is past repair, but the born wrecker won't wait for that! And we who hate violence and suffering are bound to fight them." Jerrold smiled at Tassy, and Brade looked at his friend gratefully. Tassy knew how he felt. Dr. Jerrold was strong and wise, someone to hold to when everything else seemed to be slipping around them.

The door opened and Rachel stood there, silent, looking first at Brade and Jerrold and then at Tassy. Tassy started toward her sister. "Rachel, you are ill!" she exclaimed. She had never seen Rachel so haggard and pallid. Rachel stared at her. Then she wavered on her feet, gripping the handle of the door. Jerrold caught her arm and Brade pushed a chair forward.

"There's a tray with whisky in the studio—get it," Jerrold said. Tassy started to go, but met Braythorpe in the hall and sent him on the errand.

When he came back, Nurse came too. "Can I do anything?" she asked.

Brade was pouring whisky into a glass. Suddenly he paused and looked at Rachel.

"When you heard that Tassy had left Hanover, you were in the studio, Mrs. Norbury. You and Maurice Prentice asked Braythorpe for a tray. You had the glass in your hand, but you set it down and did not drink from it. Did you take away Mrs. Norbury's glass then, Braythorpe?"

"No, sir. I haven't touched the tray."

Jerrold took the glass and gave it to Rachel.

"Don't drink it," Brade exclaimed, snatching the glass from Rachel's hand.

"Aren't you being unnecessarily dramatic, Simon?" asked Jerrold mildly. Nurse Jonsen was smiling. Braythorpe hesitated and then went away.

"Shall I drink it?" asked Nurse. "What are you afraid of, Mr. Brade?"

"Just my nerves!" he answered. "I'll drink it myself." He did. "Mrs. Norbury shall have the second glass."

"I wish to speak to my sister." Rachel turned to Tassy. "Can you explain yourself?" she asked.

"You don't want me, then," said Nurse Jonsen. "I'd better go." She seemed to expect the two men to follow her, but Jerrold opened the door for her and came back.

"Tassy is not well," he said, "but she came here to tell Brade some things she thought he ought to know. I wish you would be open with us, Rachel. Can't you speak out?"

She met the attack with a stare of resentment. "What has Tassy said?" she demanded.

"I've told them all I know," Tassy answered. "Everything. What I heard you say on Friday night. Who was there, Rachel? Tell Mr. Brade and Dr. Jerrold. It isn't safe to keep anything secret now. I beg you to tell."

"No one was there. Tassy caught cold on Friday, hunting. I expect she had a fever then. I'd fallen asleep in my chair and was dreaming. Is that all?"

"You took my notes. Why?"

"I told you you had no right to use what I said in that interview until I had read what you had written and passed my statements. I said so and I meant it. When I have made up my mind, I act. Don't you, Dr. Jerrold?"

"You do, Jerry, you know," remarked Brade. "It's exactly what you do!"

There was silence in the room. Brade broke it by saying: "This isn't too cheerful a place. Suppose Nurse puts Miss Litton to bed and we all go and have some more drinks somewhere else."

"Are you coming home with me, Tassy?" Rachel asked. Tassy shook her head. "I'm going to stay here," she answered. "I'll go now and ask Aunt Charlie if I may."

CHAPTER 18

"I'M SURE I'll be only too pleased to have someone to help me," poor Lady Charlotte said, after Tassy had gone upstairs with Nurse. "Though I must say Tassy looks too ill to help anyone and I don't seem to have any medicine in the house but camphorated oil. Molly Hegan has gone home and left a note to say she wouldn't come back and Mrs. Myster says she won't have Bernie Langrove in the house another night and I haven't made beds or dusted a room since the fire at Weleven when I was a child and we lived for three days with the gardener."

Upstairs Tom knocked on Tassy's door and at her response poked his head in. "I just thought you'd like to know how that pup of Miracle's fought for his supper. He got the best bit and kept it, too, against all comers. He'll make a stallion hound before he's done, Tass." He shut the door and went downstairs again before Tassy could reply, but the world had suddenly improved for Tassy. The fire was bright, Tom was there, all this trouble would be over some day. She went to sleep.

"You'll stay to dinner, won't you, Rachel?" asked Maurice. "There's that leaflet to draw up and a lot of work to be done."

Brade and Dr. Jerrold had joined the others in the studio and now Braythorpe wheeled in a cocktail cabinet and began to mix the drinks with Tom beside him, giving advice. Brade wandered up to watch the proceedings, and began to talk to Tom. The names of horses, jockeys, and trainers were heard, between Lady Charlotte's comments on her garden catalogue: "Lady Gay is vulgar, of course, but useful in her place. I always think Lady Forteviot is stingy, don't you, Rachel?" Luckily those who heard understood that she was not slandering the aristocracy, but only expressing her views on the habits of roses.

"Well, that's what I was told," Brade was saying, deprecatingly, "and myself I think I'll have a flutter on the tip. What do you think, Mr. Tom?"

Braythorpe's hand trembled.

"May be something in it," Tom conceded, thoughtfully. "Sounds likely. Funny about the Limberly stables. Does nothing to speak of for years and then coins a pot in a fortnight. I'll have a word with a man I know—"

"Ever go racing, Braythorpe?" asked Brade, his monocle still trained on the cocktails.

"In a small way, sir," Braythorpe admitted.

"Well, just fetch the evening paper, if there is one, and I'll show you. I don't do much myself as a rule, but I'm not above taking a tip like this." Braythorpe set down the cocktail shaker. "I'll shake it up for you," Brade offered. "Go and fetch the paper."

No one was watching. Brade played with the bottles on the tray. He poured out a bit of the mixture in the shaker, added to it from a selection of liqueurs, and began to manipulate the shaker. When he had finished, he poured the finished cocktails into glasses and handed them around. He approached Dr. Jerrold last. "Have a care, Jerry," he warned his friend in an undertone. "If you want to keep your secret, that is! Ah, there's the paper. Now, Braythorpe, you see—" He turned to news of the Lincolnshire entries and drew Tom into the discussion, while Rachel, Nurse Jonsen, Maurice, and Jerrold sipped their drinks.

"You've got too much absinthe, haven't you, Braythorpe?" asked Rachel.

"Oh no, ma'am, the same as usual."

"Let's all have another," Brade suggested. "It won't hurt us." He looked around at the lifted faces. "After all," he said seriously and deliberately, "the day has been a relief, in a way. That latch-key was in the garden, and San Ts'ai is gone, Chen began to bark after Nurse opened that door. Everything points to an outsider having been in the house on Friday evening. Pennleaf agrees. That's better than thinking there's someone in this house with a sinister secret, isn't it?"

No one replied, but the second round of cocktails vanished, and only Lady Charlotte and Rachel refused a third, though Jerrold, with his eye on Brade, had not drunk much from his glass when it was refilled.

"I'm quite tight enough already," Rachel remarked, with a sudden and very charming smile.

"We're having dinner early," Maurice told them. "Will you stay, Jerrold, and Brade too?"

"It's very kind of you." Jerrold glanced at Brade.

"Very kind," murmured that gentleman. "I have just a few little matters to attend to yet. I think I made it clear that Captain Stair has asked me to help him? He seems to want to avoid calling on Scotland Yard, and personally I think there are enough people worrying you all as it is." He looked about him with unfeigned satisfaction.

Rachel's cheeks wore a slight flush, unusual to her pale skin. Tom was deep in the racing news and had dropped his restless and watchful manner, Maurice was standing in front of the fire, beside Rachel, and seemed about to begin to talk, Nurse Jonsen had not changed her position on the sofa and was finishing her third cocktail appreciatively. Braythorpe announced dinner.

There was no doubt about it, some of the tension had lifted from the party, and everyone talked to his neighbour. Jerrold remarked that he had given Tassy something to relieve her pain. "She'll be all right, Mrs. Norbury," he assured Rachel. "Of course, she has a temperature, and she'll have to rest that arm. You needn't worry. I'll keep an eye on her. All this has been a shock—and she's very young."

"Next year," Lady Charlotte was saying loudly, "I shall extend the Rock Garden into that hollow in the field and make a pond at the bottom—just the place for primulas, you know, and a collection of gentians at the top. I shall have to have rocks brought from the north I suppose. It is practically impossible to get the right colour nearer home, and I believe I'll try a group of ericas—yes, of course I will; why not?" She looked at Simon Brade as if he had objected. "Just because I've planted them everywhere else without success is no reason at all why they shouldn't do there, with masses of rhododendrons. No, Braythorpe, I think I won't have any more hock." The rhododendrons had momentarily sobered Lady Charlotte, for there was chalk in the soil and even the cocktails could not make her forget it.

Rachel was talking smoothly and brilliantly about Abyssinia. Everything she had read and everything she had heard seemed to be marshalled, ready for her use. Jerrold, who had been there, listened with interest and did not seem to be half so well informed as she was. "A mandate undertaken by the League—" she was saying.

Maurice broke in. "Nonsense," he said, thumping the table. "The only way to accomplish anything in this world is to find a man and give him power. It is the age of quick movement, quick thinking, quick action—no League, no parliament, no coalition is efficient enough. While it waits and talks and wonders, a man steps in and acts. You've only to look at the world to see that. I tell you—" he brought his fist down on the table so that the glasses rattled.

Braythorpe had finished off the cocktails in the pantry. He poured more hock into the glasses and his hand trembled. He had fifty pounds put by and he decided to stake it all on Mr. Brade's tip for the Lincolnshire. "I tell you—" Maurice had forgotten what he meant to tell them, but his voice rose. "England needs a master, and she will have one before long. The only question is: Which? I should say: Who?"

Rachel took this up. "Not a master, a servant," she said, quietly. "A servant of the people."

Maurice laughed. "Servants in plenty. One master, and no mistake about it. He must be master without rivals, or else—" Nurse Jonsen was watching him, smiling. He looked at her and stopped.

"Every man has his rivals unless he is powerful enough to eliminate them by force. Do you go so far as to applaud that?" Jerrold asked.

Maurice quoted: "'If the ruler has to get rid of possible rivals he must do so by any means whatsoever, for this must be done before anything else can be effected!'"

Jerrold added: "*'Que Messieurs les assassins commencent.'* Voltaire supports Machiavelli."

"*'Vive les assassins!'*" Maurice agreed. A silence fell, which Nurse Jonsen ended by saying in a quiet voice: "But in England, surely, such things are not needed. You are prosperous, happy; you trust your leaders. Reason prevails." She looked across the table at Brade and laughed lightly. "I have little time to think of such things," she went on, "but I feel sure that it is in England that true progress will be made, without bloodshed or violence. Do you not agree?" She turned to Jerrold. "In Sweden we think this."

He returned her glance. "I'm so sorry—you asked me? Ah, yes. I think I do agree with you, Nurse, on the whole, though, like you, I have little time to think such matters out."

Maurice attracted attention to himself again. "I have given my life to thought," he said; "I know what I believe now, and I am ready for action. I know what I know—" he raised his glass with an air of having said something startling and profound.

"Just like my rhododendrons," murmured Lady Charlotte, plaintively. "You can bring the coffee, Braythorpe."

"I know I'm being a terrible nuisance," Brade apologized, "but I do want to see you for a few moments, Nurse."

Brade was holding the door open for the ladies to pass out, and Nurse came last.

"Why, of course, Mr. Brade. Come into the library now. There will be no one there."

He followed her. When they were seated he said: "You see, I've been told that you know Mrs. Prentice—that you nursed her, indeed. We can't disregard the fact that she seems to have hated her husband. Would you mind telling me all you know about the situation?"

"Of course not. And I must explain first that I would have been quite frank about the matter if Mr. Litton had not begged me to be silent. You see the Princess—I am accustomed to calling her by her foreign title—persuaded him, through a friend, to get me engaged as her husband's nurse. I knew nothing about her plan until the letter came from the nursing home saying that they had had an inquiry about me and had recommended me to Mr. Prentice. I was free. The Princess—Mrs. Prentice— was going into a nursing home and I was to take her and leave her there. I had grown very fond of her and felt that her position was a cruel shame. Her brothers are peculiar men, completely idle, very arrogant, and selfish. She had been tied to her husband for over thirty years and had never seen him in all that time. She wished to be free. If her brothers had helped her she could have obtained an annulment of the marriage, but they would not make the necessary statements—that she was under age and had not the consent of her parents. She is subject to a nervous illness which they use as an excuse for a really maddening and humiliating supervision over all her movements. If she were free she would marry again—an old friend, who would give her the necessary care and far more independence. But, I gather, her brothers were unwilling to give up the allowance Mr. Prentice paid them, on the understanding that they would keep their sister watched and guarded and never assist her to a divorce. I could not understand why he took this line.

"To be brief, the Princess finally persuaded me to accept the post here and, if I got a chance, speak a word for her. She said that I could convince her husband better than anyone else could, that she was fit to lead a normal life. I had no idea of doing anything wrong. There seemed no reason why I should not come here in my professional capacity, do my job as well as I could, and if a personal friendship grew up between me and my patient, as does happen sometimes, I could mediate between him and his wife. But Mr. Prentice was, I think, a little unbalanced, shall we say, on this one matter. He looked back with such morbid horror on the final violent quarrel with his wife that he had convinced himself that she was unfit to live a normal life and would do herself or someone else an injury unless she was watched and guarded. As her husband he was able to impose his own conditions, particularly as the family is poor and they are all dependent on what he allowed them."

"And if he died?"

"I have no doubt he had made his own arrangements. Of course, I do not know."

"Thank you, Nurse. You have been most kind and helpful."

She opened her eyes wide to look at him.

"You are not thinking that his wife may have had something to do with his death, I hope? How could she?"

"No"—Brade shook his head—"but apparently it suited her, as it happened. And we have yet to find who did it and why. If she had done it we should have known why. In this case the people who had opportunity appear to lack motives and it is only those who couldn't be guilty who had any reason for committing the crime, which you'll admit, Nurse, makes things difficult."

"You would like me to stay on here for the present? Or can I take another case? I can't afford to be long out of work."

"If you could stay, just for the moment—? You might be needed."

"Then, of course, I will."

Jerrold, in the parlour of the Blue Boar Inn, folded up a typed manuscript and put it away. He looked with affectionate amusement at Brade, who was seated at the table arranging and re-arranging a set of ivory cubes, like nursery bricks.

"Well, Simon, have you discovered yet what Mrs. Norbury wanted to hide?"

"No, Jerry, I haven't. Nor what you want to hide either. Nor anything else to speak of. At the moment I'm not even trying to. One thing at a time."

"And what's the thing now?"

"That handkerchief. Come here, Jerry. Take my glass. Now look at those bricks. What do you make of them?"

The fine printing on the ivory was clear through the glass Brade handed to his friend.

On one side of the cube was written: "The handkerchief was used by the criminal for some purpose."

On the other side was written

"(a)? Wiping the bell?"
"(b)? Gagging his victim?"
"(c)? Blowing his own nose?"

"Must you be facetious?" asked Jerrold.

"Facetious? My good Jerry! There are three alternatives —the only three I can think of. Now turn the brick on this side, (a) 'wiping the bell.' On the other cube I've written what follows this assumption. If used for this purpose, first, the bell was already free from dust. There was no dust on the handkerchief, although there were discoloured spots where Chen must have trodden on it. But the table was dusty. Any table is if it stands beside a wood fire for ten hours, supposing it was dusted not later than eight a. m. Then why was the bell already clean when the finger-prints were wiped from it with a clean handkerchief? You'll find that line worked out on the sides of these bricks marked (a). The most reasonable conclusion is that I dusted it myself before I left the room. The bell is shiny and I hate dust and it might have caught my eye. But I didn't. Did Mr. Prentice do it himself? What with? His handkerchief? That leads to precisely the same difficulty. Did Braythorpe do it? He says not, and if he had I should have seen him doing it, unless he returned to the room after I left it, and he says he didn't. You see, if (a) stands, then someone was there before the murderer. Well you can work on that for yourself —it leads to an endless chain. Now (b). If Mr. Prentice had been gagged with the handkerchief it must have been tied, but it wasn't. It might of course have been held over his mouth for a moment or two, but not while he was being shaken against the fender. And why should it have lain so far from the body, in that case? Now (c). It's quite possible and not at all funny. Even criminals blow their noses. To tell the truth, I prefer that theory. It would lead us away from Tom. He had a perfectly good handkerchief in his dressing-gown pocket, and besides he never does blow his nose. I've watched him to see. He has a remarkably tough nose, lined with leather or something. Once in a while he sniffs. But there was no mucus on the linen—nothing to blow, in fact. What follows is a nervous creature who uses a handkerchief when he doesn't need one or a lachrymose creature who weeps when excited. Langrove?"

Jerrold, unimpressed, remarked that it was time to go. Brade stood up. "Did my cocktails do any good, Jerry?" he asked.

Jerrold hesitated.

"If you want to know a man, get him to drink with you. You've often told me so, Jerry. Well?" He quoted from a note-book: "'A man who acts quickly inflamed by passion, but thinks afterwards and then thinks coolly and cleverly. Someone who knew Prentice . . . with less natural aversion to violence than the average . . . capable of a second crime and a third.' That is how you described the criminal, Jerry. Was there anyone in that party who fits the description?"

"You're thinking of Maurice. But he can't have killed his father if he was not there at the time, and I'm bound to say that those cocktails just made him silly."

"Little things, Jerry. You're sound on character, but weak on trifles! I think you said it was time to go."

CHAPTER 19

NO AMOUNT of pleading could induce Dr. Garnet to allow Tassy to attend the inquest. Her temperature still wavered well over the normal, and when she moved, her shoulder ached and her head felt light and unfamiliar.

Mullie had been brought from Hartover to keep her company in the quiet house, and Tassy, defeated by her illness, lay still and waited, trying not to watch the clock.

"There they are!" she cried, hearing a car draw up below the window. "Oh, Mullie, make someone come and tell me what's happened."

The clock struck four.

Mullie, absent for an incredible time, came back. She held an envelope in her hand.

"It's not over yet, my lamb, and won't be. They've sent for Chen. The jury want to see him, Hines says. But here's a letter for you, and that kind Doctor Jerrold sent it. So read it while I get ye a cup of tea and by then maybe they'll be coming back. There, is that easy?" She fitted the pillows to Tassy's back and, giving her the letter, went away. It read:

Dear Tassy:

While Stephen is answering questions about those threatening letters I'll try to give you an idea of what has happened. The jury want a look at Chen, so Hines will take this.

Nothing new has come out so far. Nurse made it clear that everyone regarded the tragedy as the result of accident until Braythorpe said: 'Who let the dog in?' Brade told his story—testified to Stephen bringing in the letters for Prentice's signature, Braythorpe taking Chen out when he removed the tea-tray, and he himself handing Prentice the writing-materials asked for, and going out and shutting the door. It was made clear that the files of papers burnt were on the left side of the chair near the fire, while the letters were lying on top of the manuscript on the table at Prentice's right, and as the manuscript was safe, there was no connection between the burnt newspapers and the burnt letters. The scraps of letters found had actually fallen from the basket grate, and I think the jury is convinced that the letters must have been placed on the fire deliberately.

Next came the evidence of the tears on the frayed shoulders of the dressing-gown, and the black silk threads found on Tom's nail-file. Brade pointed out that anyone might have used the file.

Tom had to answer questions about the missing latch-key and his quarrel with his uncle. He told his story about trying to write a letter to his uncle, and then destroying it. And he could not remember what the maid said when she knocked on his door.

Stephen has been reading copies of the burnt letters. The one to the lawyer makes it plain that Prentice was serious in his threat to alter his will to Tom's disadvantage. The Coroner asked Stephen to explain why the letters brought by the postman at six ten were not taken to Prentice at once and Stephen answered that the rule was for him to examine the post first and to leave the evening letters until after dinner unless there was something urgent. He also explained that Prentice never wrote letters by hand, so that the one written and burnt after Brade left the room must have been of special importance. I've been writing this while Hines fetched the car, and here he is, so it must go. Stephen still in the stand. I think the jury's wanting to see Chen is in Tom's favour. They are evidently impressed by the mystery of his presence in the room.

J. J.

Mullie, arriving at the door with the tea-tray, stopped to speak to someone in the hall below. "No, I don't know where he is," she said, "and ye'd better go and look for him yourself, and my Miss Tassy with a fever on her!"

"Mullie, can't they find Chen?"

"Now don't ye fret yourself," Mullie pleaded. "What they want the dog for I don't know, and him dumb and unable to tell them what they'd like to hear."

"They want to see him, and Hines must find him!" Tassy cried. Her face flushed in her anxiety. Chen was Tom's witness. He must be found.

"Oh, Mullie, he must have got out and taken himself for a walk. I've heard Uncle Selford say that if he was neglected and no one took him at the usual time he would go alone. Make Hines find him."

"Now, don't you fret, I'll tell him." Mullie went and Tassy heard the car move off.

Useless to say not to fret when to Tassy's fevered imagination everything might depend on Chen's evidence. "He is quite big for a cairn, and such a bright colour," thought Tassy. "If the jury see him they'll know he couldn't have slipped through the house without being noticed. Rachel may try to make them believe he came in through the studio window. She wants to think Tom did it. Oh, if I could only get up and look for him myself!"

But though she tried to get out of bed she was forced to sink back into the pillows before she had put her foot to the floor. "I can't, I can't," she sobbed.

Nothing happened. The room darkened and Mullie moved from window to window, drawing gay curtains over black casements, turning on lights, making up the fire. "They'll never find Chen now," fumed Tassy. "Oh, Mullie, can't you do something?"

But no one could do anything, it seemed, and Tassy had to wait, listening, thinking, trying to see by sheer force of will what was happening in the Mayor's parlour of the Medbury Town Hall, and seeing in a grotesque nightmare Tom, helpless and alone, accused of a crime so vile that it seemed impossible to believe in at all.

If Tassy had only known it, Chen was in the witness-stand long before Hines returned to say that the dog could not be found.

Since returning to the Grange, he had attached himself to Tom, and as he liked driving in a car and saw Tom's car waiting at the door, he had jumped into it and curled up unnoticed on the rug on the back seat. Here he was found by the garage man at the Blue Boar Inn, who knew that Hines had gone to look for him and brought him to the Town Hall.

Braythorpe carried him to the improvised witness-box and held him up to face the jury.

Chen struggled, his paws in the air. Braythorpe eased him against the stand, and Chen, fighting for a comfortable position, found a rest for his forefeet on the thin black testament used for swearing in witnesses. Then, comfortable and confident, he eyed the jury with some curiosity and more disdain.

The Coroner coughed.

"Are you satisfied?" he asked the foreman of the jury, who had suggested that they would like to have a look at the little dog.

"Yes, sir," the man said slowly. "He isn't a dog you'd be likely to miss seeing. That's what we wanted to know."

Half an hour later Jerrold stopped at the Blue Boar Inn and telephoned to the Grange.

"Tell Miss Tassy that the jury has brought in the verdict. Murder. By person or persons unknown."

CHAPTER 20

MAURICE insisted on carrying out his election eve program. Even his agent tried to persuade him to cancel the engagements. "There's no one more conservative than the working man when it comes to respect for the dead," he urged. "They won't like it if you appear before your father's funeral."

Election eve in Medbury was riotous. The chair-factories were staffed with Bramshire men, and Bramshire was a county which, until recently, had been notorious for its unruly population. A tributary of the river Med had been turned into a canal which ran along one of the streets and the houses overlooking it were held in bad repute. Trouble, if it came, would start here, and any excuse was seized on by the dark-faced men and slatternly women who resented their condition and took any means of expressing this underlying sense of injustice and inferiority. Perhaps this discontent was the finest thing about them, the one touch of fire in bleak lives, and the stupidity of their use of it a fault of others, more privileged. At any rate, the Bramshire police understood well the meaning of uncouth groups gathered in doorways of the Duke's Head Inn, and prepared for disorder.

It was in one of these houses that Bernice Langrove lived when she was not in service, and it was here she came on the evening before the inquest, her tin box, tied up with string, accompanying her. Her mother looked at the box and Bernice and sighed. Her life was far too hopeless for the relief of tears. Her father looked at Bernice and shot at her a spate of questions, his bloodshot eyes unresting and his thin hands shaking. He was not hopeless. He was on fire with faith and felt the conditions surrounding him far less acutely than the lurid splendour of a revenge on the social order. He saw great houses in flames, streams of blood reddening the canal at his door, gentlemen in tail coats shrieking for mercy, and ladies in velvet offering their diamonds and pearls in exchange for loaves of bread. He was slightly mad, but he was a skilled artisan and, in spite of his lurid speech, managed to keep his family alive and himself well fortified with bad whisky. There was a poetic fervour in his madness, not to be despised. He was afraid of no one and would have denied his creed for no man. England was perhaps the only country where he would have remained at large. Certainly in Russia he would have been suppressed for his objections to the mildness of the punishment inflicted on many persons guilty of having been born to wealth and honour. It was horrible to him to observe the meekness of the Labour party, and the ordered processions of the Communists on May Day. He wanted the Revolution now and here and he wanted it violent, merciless, and without pause. It was the Revolution itself he wanted, not the new world to follow. He was glad that Selford Prentice was dead, and said so. Any man who could persuade the workers to wait one moment for their revenge was a traitor and better dead.

Some of the young men listened to him and were moved, not by his reasoning, for he did not reason, but by his passion. On election eve they gathered around him. The Conservative candidate could not make himself heard when he tried to address the crowd from the roof of his car. A stone was thrown, but before the body of protestants could be scattered by the local police, it had divided itself according to plan, to unite elsewhere.

The office of the *Active Sentinel* was modestly tucked away in a narrow Street next to a yard littered with abandoned bodies of derelict motor cars, wheels without carts, and twisted frames that might once have been bicycles; on its other side a Methodist mission house stood square to the pavement, empty and respectable. A light was burning in the office, behind unshaded greasy windows, and a group of men gathered outside, cheering. That day the Active Sentinel had come out with a leader headed "No Sanctions," calling on the workers to refuse their votes to the Labour candidate, who supported a capitalistic government and a policy that would lead to war. "Vote for Labour and you vote for Baldwin and slavery," it assured them.

Rachel and Maurice, driving from a meeting at Agminton to Medbury, where Maurice was due to speak, had ten minutes of dark solitude, the wind in their faces. Rachel said: "What are you about, Maurice? I'd better know."

"I must do my father's business, Rachel. His spirit is moving me. Suddenly I see that he was right. He need not have died. I would not have betrayed him. I've turned the corner. I know now what I'm here for. Last night I dreamed of my father. He was there, I'm sure of it. He said: 'You are living in a world of fools with a few wise men among them. Order will come out of chaos when the few rule the many and never otherwise. Stand with the leaders or fall with the mob.' I've chosen. I shall never look back."

"I think you're mad. Your speech at Agminton was just so much flapping of red rags in the faces of—sheep."

"You can scatter sheep with red rags."

"Is that what you want—just a riot?"

"Confusion spells opportunity."

"You and the *Sentinel* are singing in tune. And the object—to weaken the pressure on the government to force sanctions? Is that it, Maurice? Are you playing the Fascist game?"

"I'm playing my own. You don't know me. I know myself at last."

"The British dictator, Maurice?"

He did not reply to that, and Rachel was silent. They were nearing Medbury, driving downhill so fast that the gears strained with an ugly sound.

As they turned into the crowded High Street, Rachel said: "If you take that tone in Medbury I shall interrupt you. I give you fair warning."

The street was a seething mass of men and women whom half a dozen mounted policemen tried vainly to disperse. There was no open violence as yet, but the voice of the mob was gathering volume, and the note of hysteria creeping in here and there. Langrove himself was silent, but he was there and the number of his followers grew swiftly. Someone had obtained a poster picture of the National candidate, decorated with horns and a pointed beard, and carried it as a banner on a broomstick. A red flag waved under a lamp-post. A chant started up: "We want Peace." The isolated catcalls, even the singing of the *Red Flag* and the demand for the shilling rise in wages which was an issue in the local factories, merged in the chant: "We want Peace." Many did not know what they meant. Langrove certainly did not want peace, politically speaking or otherwise. But the chant served.

Maurice Prentice stepped up on the seat inside the windshield. His supporters saw him and cheered. They surged around the car, cheering. He put up his hand for silence. Then he spoke.

He was one of those speakers who succeed, not because of what they say, but because they say it. His voice carried conviction and roused emotion. Less than ever tonight did he choose his words. In this he resembled Langrove himself. As he went on he repeated again and again: "I," "I," "I," "I," "I will give you justice," "I promise you," "A seat in Parliament is nothing—I do not intend to stop there," "I will lead you on the way you have chosen," "I know what you want. Give me power and I will give you fair play." "Wait —temporize—compromise— apologize—I will have none of them. I will not wait! I have left the side of my dead father to tell you so. I am here to promise you victory."

Enthusiasm mounted high, individual passions merged in it. The man with a scolding wife joined his shout of resentment with that of the man who had been sacked for insolence and the decent workman crushed by economic conditions he did not understand. The woman who had brought eight sickly children into an overcrowded world and lost hope meanwhile, screamed louder than any and felt better for it. For one who had any idea of mending injustice by political reform, twenty shouted and clamoured and pushed as a protest against life itself as they found it.

Rachel sat so still that she was unnoticed until suddenly she rose and cried in her clear voice, that rang above Maurice's: "Men and women of Medbury, I speak for a man who was ready to die in your service. You have nothing to gain by revolt and everything to lose. In this country the public voice prevails. We are not like the Russians, a huge mass of illiterate children, only to be saved by strong discipline from above. Your homes, your welfare, your livelihood, and that of your children depend on the steady pressure of reasoned and enlightened legislation. You have your Labour party. Return it to power. The fight is against Fascism and loss of liberty. Break the Labour party and you break your own hope. Shatter the support of the League of Nations and you vote for war. War breeds Fascism, not freedom. Women of Medbury, do you want war, or do you want a world policed against the criminals who make it, as our country today is policed against the robber barons who made serfs of such as you? Once they built fortress castles against their neighbours. Now our country is a fortress, and other countries are our enemy neighbours, fortified too. One day we shall smile at all that as we smile at the derelict castles of other days now. Only the submission of all nations in collective agreement can bring the happy Day."

Some of her words were heard. But Langrove was shouting and Maurice was speaking, and the few who caught the drift of what she said were past thinking.

In the midst of the confusion the car of the Conservative candidate came down the street, flaunting its blue ribbons. Here was a common enemy. The hundreds of voices became one, in a howl of rage.

Without warning the street lights went out, and the headlights of the cars streamed in spreading tracks, showing massed faces, waving arms. The police were helpless. Some of the men had armed themselves with sticks and clods. They rushed the car occupied by the Conservative candidate. By now there were enough supporters of the government present to push their way to his side. The street was a mass of men and women struggling before a stampede of horses' hoofs as the police came charging in. Suddenly a cry went up: "Fire!"

The supporters of Labour had collected before the Sentinel office, hooting, hissing, throwing stones and bricks. When the lights went out, a smashing of window glass was heard above the noise. Some of the young men had entered the building and were wrecking the premises, lighted in their efforts by friends who struck matches as they stormed through the building. Someone was inspired to set alight a bundle of sheets lately brought from the printer's office and these kindled and blew about the room, spreading the flames to a mass of stacked paper in a corner. A blaze sprang up so fierce that it lighted the room and drove back the rioters. Soon reams and reams of wrappers, unused paper, printed sheets, and envelopes were in flames and the room was on fire.

The mob before the burning building retreated, blocking the way of those who were running toward them, and at the corner where Maurice's car stood, the police and their supporters met the fugitives. Light from the fire was obscured by smoke. Many were trying to get to safety. Maurice's car was overrun by a streaming mass of men. Rachel, crushed and defenceless, was thrust against the open door and fell, saving herself by a hand on the arm of her seat. But she was in darkness, and men were fighting above her. She could not keep her feet. Something struck her and she fell while the crowd surged past.

"Rachel, where are you?" shouted Maurice, fighting his way across the car, reaching out with his hands for her. Whistles were blowing. A body of men had gathered behind the police, who charged the crowd. The street lights sprang out and showed the street blotted at its narrow end with the rioters who had not been able to escape in the darkness. Women had fainted—men had been injured. Maurice was kneeling at Rachel's side, and the group from the car of his opponent had joined him.

Maurice, looking up, saw Jerrold. "Thank God," he sobbed, pushing away the group gathering around Rachel's body. "Thank God, you're here."

Jerrold knelt and picked up Rachel's arm, felt the wrist, thrust his hand inside the tweed coat, looked at the dark hair matted and warm with flowing blood. "She's dead," he said brusquely. "Stand away. Is Brade here?"

Simon Brade came forward. For a second he paused, wavered. Then he stepped to Jerrold's side. The light shone in his face and his eyes glittered.

"Did anyone here see what happened?" he asked quietly. "Did you?" he asked Maurice. A policeman pushed his way to Brade's side, dragging Bernice Langrove by the arm. The girl's face was yellow. Her hat had fallen off, and she was struggling to free herself. "I ain't got nothing to do with it," she screamed. "Let go. I'll have the law on ye. I ain't seen nothing. Let go, I say." She set her teeth on the hand that encircled her arm.

"Ye would, would ye? Tell us why ye were hiding then. We found her flattened out against the wall inside that archway. She knows something."

"I don't. I don't. I was only trying to keep out of the way. The crowd was like to kill me. It was dark. I seen a man climb over the car before the lights went out, that's all I know. I swear to God. Leave me go, I say."

A man stepped forward. He lived in the rooms above the jeweller's shop opposite.

"I was looking out the window," he said. "All I could see was the crowd. The car was full of people trying to get out of the rush. Just for a few moments everyone was struggling and pushing around it. I've never seen such a sight. If the lady fell she was certain to be killed. It's those that started the riot you'll have to hold responsible."

"We'd better take the poor lady to the Blue Boar, sir," said the constable. Men had bared their heads. Maurice still knelt beside Rachel. Now he raised himself and spoke to the people.

"She is a martyr," he said in his deep and majestic voice. "Don't forget that. She cared for the liberation of the oppressed more than for her safety or her happiness." His face was lit by a radiance inspired by his words. "I told her there might be danger in Medbury tonight, she knew that she ran a risk, but she came to help and encourage me. She was a great soul and we must fight better for her sake."

They laid her on a litter, covered her face, and carried her into the inn, between lines of spectators, awed and silenced.

The *Active Sentinel* burned. Unsold copies, stacked on racks, curled up at the edges and, burning, illumined the violent printed words of their headlines. "Destroy the Newspaper!" screamed out a line of print and then the flames licked up the words, greedily, and they were gone. "Pacifists Beware" vanished slowly, letter by letter, in the caprices of the spreading fire. "Europe in Flames" was destroyed. "Peace is our Banner" was gone before it showed, and the blank papers in their brown wrappers ready for the copy, burning gaily elsewhere, smoked sullenly for a few moments before they, too, yielded and shot up a lovely glow, red, blue, green, and gold, into the deserted room, while the fire-bells clanged down the emptying streets.

CHAPTER 21

BRADE clambered up the steps of the air liner bound for Frankfurt on a dark and windy morning.

It was his first flight, and he showed his interest, approving of the comfortable chair in which the steward settled him, looking with a good deal of suspicion at the adjustable strap, and then settling down to study a recent book on Chinese art, which he pencilled freely as he read, making deprecating "Tut, tut" sounds when he came on errors or mis-statements.

The starting of the plane jostled him out of his occupation. "Dear me," he murmured, "this is very disturbing. Well, upon my word, we're off the ground. Most efficient!"

He looked curiously at the receding land. "Impossible to take the world seriously when all you've got to do is to jump off it and turn to blobs of colour and blots of smoke like that. I suppose that's the sea." He caught sight of a dim grey blankness almost below. "Well, well! So that's all!" he remarked. Then the clouds intervened. There was nothing to look at at all. The passengers, varying between nonchalance, genuine or assumed, and the frank interest of the adventurous novice, were settling down to the four-hour journey, and Brade returned to his book. He read steadily, refusing lunch, roused only when the sun came out and the plane mounted over Switzerland. His head began to swim and he shut his eyes.

"Quite comfortable, sir?" the steward asked, still fatherly.

"Just a little—er—uplifted," Brade replied with closed eyes. "No, I don't think I want a drink, thanks very much. It might be a waste of money." He opened an eye long enough to see a lady wasting her lunch money on the opposite side of the plane and closed it again quickly. The steward passed on. Brade slept, and when he woke, the liner was circling over the aerodrome.

"Too quick for me," he decided as the earth came back, a rushing spectacle of alarming solidity. "I shall enjoy that train."

The nursing home for which he was bound was situated not far from the Austrian frontier, among snowy peaks and pine-covered slopes, with a chilly lake neatly arranged below. It was a white building, once the summer residence of a nobleman, and even the immense stoves fitted in all the rooms failed to cheer its immaculate spaces. The room where he was invited to wait was furnished with essentials taken over from the former owner, but all the comforts regarded as a useless expense had been removed, so that a stiff Italian chair, with painted leather seat and back, a massive walnut table, and a cabinet filled with paper-backed novels, periodicals, and medical-looking pamphlets were stationed austerely as far apart as they could get from each other. The carpet was a newcomer, Brade decided, and disagreed with everything else, but he hoped that no one used the room very much and supposed he could bear it for live minutes. He sat down, his toes stretched out to reach the floor, and finished the book. Then he waited, in growing discomfort, until a nurse appeared in the doorway and said smoothly in German: "The Princess— that is, Mrs. Prentice—is not feeling equal to visitors. I am sorry."

"Then," said Brade, "I shall have to wait. And, frankly, nurse, I'm very bad at waiting. I shall cause a good deal of trouble. I can only get really interested in Patience when I've got something else to do."

The nurse stared at him, baffled.

"There's an inn at the village. It is quite comfortable," she suggested.

"Yes, but, you see, Mrs. Prentice might find herself equal to seeing me, and if I weren't on the spot I might lose the chance. Unfortunately, I can't return to England without an interview. It is a great pity, and very annoying for you. But you know the English police. It would be as much as my life is worth. Can I have some tea—and a blanket? This room is cold. And you haven't a telegraph form handy, I suppose? I'd like to send for some books. I didn't really expect to settle down here for a long stay."

"I'll speak to the nurse in charge." The woman withdrew in apparent despair of dealing with her visitor. She returned accompanied by an older and severer person, who frowned on Brade confidently.

"If you will leave an address we will notify you when the patient can see you," she told him. "The tragedy in England has been a shock to her nerves, you will understand. Quiet is necessary."

Brade looked at the landscape. "How marvellous for her!" he commented in his most friendly tones. "She must get such a lot of it here! The worst of it is, madam, quiet is awfully bad for me. If I take it in gulps, as I'm doing now, it has an alarming effect. I can't answer for the consequences. Does anyone play Chinese bezique? That sometimes gets me through. Perhaps you can spare one of the younger and less professional nurses. I could teach her."

"I have said we will notify you when the patient's condition is more satisfactory."

"Are you going to turn me out? I don't know what the British Consul will say, I'm sure. The truth is, madam, I dare not leave until I have seen Mrs. Prentice. My directions were definite. Five minutes' interview with your patient, and you are rid of me for ever."

It was a bribe worth considering and even the head nurse showed signs of indecision.

"Do I understand that you will be satisfied with five minutes' conversation?"

"Certainly. I have three questions to ask, and Mrs. Prentice can answer them with a yes or no. If she likes, that is. Of course, if she's a talkative lady—"

The two nurses withdrew. There was a clock on the mantelpiece. It ticked. Half an hour passed. Then the head nurse reappeared.

"Please follow me," she directed him, and Brade obeyed meekly. She took him up in an elevator and led him along a bleak passage to a door where she stopped. "Five minutes," she reminded him threateningly, glancing at her watch.

The woman who turned her face toward him was fully dressed in a gorgeous negligee of green velvet, girdled with gold. Gold slippers were on her feet. She was a handsome creature, hard-boned and muscular, with restless eyes.

"Sit down, Mr. Brade." She spoke English with a faint accent. "They say you insist on seeing me. This tragedy has postponed my recovery and I am feeling very ill. But as you have come so far to see me, I will make a great effort."

"Mrs. Prentice, I've promised to ask you three questions only. Have you seen your husband since you parted thirty years ago?"

"Can you suggest anything that might help in the investigation?"

"No." Even these short replies seemed to leave her breathless and shivering.

"Did you know that Nurse Jonsen is under serious suspicion of murdering your husband?"

She never answered that question. She started from her chair and then fell back, her hands over her face. They were strong, bony hands with wide nails, filed short. She stood there shaking when the nurse came in again.

"The five minutes is up," she said.

Brade glanced around the room. There were a few photographs, a few books, some roses in a vase. He went to the side of the bed, took up a Bible lying there, and carried it across the room to the woman.

"Will you swear on this that you know nothing to account for the death of your husband?" he asked.

"Yes." She laid a hand on the book. "Yes, I swear."

Brade carefully replaced the volume. "Thank you," he said cheerfully. "That is what I came for."

CHAPTER 22

SIMON BRADE bent over a page of typescript. He was reading aloud, sentence by sentence, dwelling on each word as he read it, and Tassy Litton was sitting opposite, listening. He came to the last word and looked up. "Now, Tassy, what was it? What was it in that interview your sister wanted us to forget? And why?"

Tassy stirred for the first time since he had begun to read. "I can't imagine," she said slowly.

"Yet she tore those pages out of Jerrold's book and she did it for a reason. What is wrong with me that I can't see it?"

Tassy got up and went to the window. They were in the drawing-room at Hartover House, the room with the ruby-red curtains, Rachel's favourite colour, the pale-green walls, and the sparse, comfortable furniture she liked.

"Mr. Brade, won't Dr. Jerrold tell you why he has never allowed anyone to read his book of notes?"

"No. Jerry is extraordinary. I'm afraid— Well, I'm afraid, that's all. Afraid to the bottom of my soul—if I've got a soul and it's got a bottom, which seems unlikely. No, I think a soul must be rather like the high point of light shining on a porcelain vase. Something not of it, yet making it what it is, and it wouldn't have a bottom or feel afraid either, would it? Metaphysics are a difficult subject," he sighed, "and metaphors are worse!"

Tassy was not to be won to a smile. She had grown fond of Brade during the last tragic fortnight. His frivolous nonsense no longer irritated her. Of all the people who had tried to console and support her, he had succeeded best. He had a touch at times that turned solid things into transparent films. Once or twice when with him she had seen through her horror and agony of mind, into a play-world of his habitation as if that were real and the suffering a shadow of no substance. She had seen him shaken and quivering with dread and rebellion against the tragedy of Rachel's death. When he said he was afraid, she knew he meant it, and she knew why. Though Rachel's death was a horrible accident, Brade believed that an evil force was at work among them, like a deadly germ, all the more terrible because they did not know where to search for it or how to protect themselves against it, that Rachel had died of it and others might die too.

When she had told Dr. Jerrold this, expecting to be reassured, he had at first said nothing.

"Dr. Jerrold, I'm not a baby. I must know the truth. You are afraid too. Why?"

"If I am afraid I don't think you need be, Tassy."

"Why not?"

"Because you know nothing of all this morbid business, and your mind is a clear and direct instrument, not likely to take infection from it. Tom is like you. He is not in danger, either."

"But he is."

"There's no doubt that Stair believes he killed his uncle and that the facts tell against him, and if Pennleaf weren't so determined to make a case against Langrove, he might be arrested. But even if he should be, even if the worst happened, he's not exposed to the danger that threatens Brade and Maurice and even me. Perhaps others. You and Tom are the strongest of us all just now."

"Dr. Jerrold, you don't think someone killed Rachel because she knew?"

"No, no, Tassy," he said quickly, "don't think that. I don't. But she did know something—and was her fear her enemy, when the critical second came? Did she think: 'This is the end'? Was her instinct for self-preservation damaged? I tell you this because I want you to get out of this house. Go home, or go away. You are strong and sure and sunny by nature. Get away from this place."

"And leave Tom alone?" thought Tassy. "Not I."

Nevertheless she had gone home, for Mullie needed her. The old woman, stricken by the loss of her nursling, collapsed, and Tassy, who often in illness had lain obedient under those strong hands, put her to bed and tended her night and day. Mullie was restless if Tassy were out of call. Stephen, too, came to Hartover to live, partly to reassure Mullie, partly because Maurice said he would prefer it. He went to the Grange to work by day and kept Tassy company by night, and Tassy was glad to have him there. She thought now that Langrove had killed Selford Prentice, and he was safe in jail, having been arrested on charges connected with the riot of election eve.

Now Tassy watched Simon Brade for a moment as he went through the motions of rolling a cigarette.

"Do you think that Dr. Jerrold knows something we don't and is afraid to tell us because it would put us in danger, too?" she demanded.

"Jerry knows too much. I think he's afraid that if he tells me, I'll make a mistake. He thinks I've too much imagination, Jerry does. Well, if Jerry knows something and won't tell me, it's because he's afraid I'll be clever and build up a case whether it's true or not. Jerry overrates my intelligence. A great mistake."

"But Dr. Jerrold doesn't want you to drop the case."

"No. He wants me to find out, unbiased by what he knows. Then he'll be sure I haven't been influenced by it. Oh, Tassy, how I wish that red-eyed little man in Medbury jail had done it! He'd positively enjoy being hanged, so long as they'd let him talk on the scaffold. But he didn't, he didn't, and I've got to find out who did. I've got to find out —I've got to. And there is a clue in these sheets somewhere—I know it. Your sister knew it too."

"But," Tassy said, as she had said before, "if Rachel had known who killed Uncle Selford she would never have shielded him."

"But perhaps she didn't. She only thought it pointed to someone she believed innocent. Suppose, for instance, there had been something there that might involve you. She'd have wished to destroy it—to save you from even a passing suspicion. Or herself. She knew she did not do it. Why give anyone the chance to think she did? And then gradually the true meaning may have dawned on her. She may have resisted the suspicion and yet—we don't know what happened. Perhaps she let the murderer know she had the information that would lead us to him, and in some way he showed her his guilt. Even then she may not have been sure enough to speak. She may have been hesitating— Oh, Tassy, forgive me." For Tassy had thrown herself on the chair Rachel had used and she was shaking with sobs.

"I'll go away," Brade said. "I can do that. I wish somebody would just dump me down a drain or something. It would be suitable and tidy and I'd come out in the sea somewhere and I can't swim."

Tassy shook her head and sat up. "But I made you promise to talk to me," she said vigorously. "I didn't mean to cry. I've got to think about it all. I've got to help Tom. I'm in love with him." She added the last words almost absentmindedly.

"Yes," Brade agreed in a matter-of-fact voice, "so you are. Why don't you tell him so?"

"I can't do that."

"Well, then, how is he to know? And I do think it's nice to know things like that."

"But don't you see? He'd be grateful."

Brade considered the matter, his head on one side. "But, just at first (I'm not a psychologist like Jerry), if I were in love with a girl and she said she was in love with me, I wouldn't be grateful a bit. I might be surprised. In fact I should be—if it happened to me." He put his head on one side and considered the matter. "Very surprised! But I don't think Tom will be as surprised as all that, because girls do like him and he's used to it. I think he'd say: 'Then that's all right, Tass,' and probably kiss you." Brade seemed delighted with this bit of guess-work.

"But I don't know if Tom is in love with me. I don't think he is, Mr. Brade. He was in love with Nurse Jonsen three weeks ago."

"Now come, Tassy, she had red hair and a taking way with her, and Tom noticed it. Do you call that love? Might as well call soapstone porcelain and be done with it."

Tassy laughed, not out loud it's true, but still she laughed.

"Even if he wasn't in love with her, he's not with me. I haven't red hair or a taking way."

"Hm." Brade made an inspection through his eyeglass as if to verify this statement. "No," he admitted, "it's not red. It's the brown of a robin's wing. And I haven't noticed a manner. But there's a kind of do-you-mean-what-you-say-then-I-think-we'll-get-on air about you that's not exactly repellent, and I should think if anyone acquired a taste for your company, the appeal of somebody else's manner would wear off in time. Of course I'm no judge. But it does occur to me that Tom seems remarkably pleased to have you about the place."

"That's what he says," remarked Tassy, coldly.

Brade danced a step or two in distress. "I never could say the right thing to a lady. I do wish Jerry were here. Tact is Jerry's hall-mark. 'Made in the Hall of a Thousand Compliments,' that's Jerry. But there's one sure thing: if Tom adored you he'd never say so now, and it must be painful to be thinking a thing for twenty-four hours a day and not to be able to say it even once, and have half the county believing you've murdered your uncle besides. No wonder Tom is grumpy."

"Do you mean Tom wouldn't tell me because people are saying he killed Uncle Selford?"

Tassy opened her brown eyes wide and then screwed them up again in thought.

"Well, what do you think? Could he? If, for instance, he had marriage in view? People do think of marriage when they fall in love, though I've never been able to understand why unless it's because it's the shortest way out of a painful condition."

"Of course, if people fall in love they get married."

"I've always said I don't understand the human mind," sighed Brade. "Sometimes I'm glad and sometimes I'm sorry, but there it is. Consider the great lovers of history and fable. Did Aucassin marry Nicolette? Or Tristan Iseult? Mary Stuart married Bothwell, but look what came of it! Titania married Oberon, and they remain the prototype of marriage to this day. Divorce not being a feature of fairyland, they go on squabbling through the ages until she even blames him for the weather! Luckily human life isn't as long as that. I've heard of a good many complaints of husbands and wives, but it takes several centuries of vituperation to get to that, Tassy. Blaming another for the weather, I mean. It's well we are assured that there's neither marriage nor giving in marriage in heaven."

"Were you ever married, Mr. Brade?"

Simon paled visibly. "I dreamed I was, once," he whispered. "Somebody had fed me on lobster, strawberry ice, and champagne."

Tassy laughed again, and Brade himself smiled with the delight of a child who did not mean to be funny but is. Then he looked down at the typed pages lying on the table. "Come here, Tassy; let us go over this again!

"There are a few words before the interview with your sister began. Those were torn out with the rest, as they were on the same page, but they can't be what she wanted. Let's begin with her first words to us—all about Langrove and the anonymous letters. Is there anything there?"

"I shouldn't think so. Unless—well, yes. She says Langrove could not have got in. Afterwards—the next morning —she tried to make out that he might have come in the studio window. Did she want you to forget that she had said he couldn't?"

Brade shook his head. "Not very probable. Well, go on. You can skip the part about me. Jerry always makes me out sillier than I am. We'll go on to the note from Mr. Prentice to her. Is there anything there?"

"She says: 'He did not want even Stephen to know how urgent it was. You see he refers to a letter he wanted me to post for him. Perhaps that was the secret.'" Tassy paused. "Was she afraid of throwing suspicion on Stephen?"

"That had occurred to me. There's certainly nothing in what follows immediately. More of my silliness. I wish Jerry wouldn't write down things like that. If my relations wanted to get me certified it might be used against me. Now go on. The disposal of the persons concerned at the time of the tragedy. Read that."

Tassy read: "'Maurice, Lady Charlotte, and Nurse Jonsen were in the studio all that time. Tom and my brother were not there after six.' Then, after Dr. Jerrold's question: 'Lady Charlotte went outside for a moment to look at a clematis. . . . Nurse Jonsen went out twice, the first time to get a bandage for Maurice's hand—the second time to rearrange some flowers. . . . The first time was soon after we came in—and she was only away two or three minutes. The second time was later and she was away from five to ten minutes. But the postman came just after she returned, and that was six ten, so she was in the room for that last fifteen minutes.' Then comes what she said about Chen barking, timing the accident about six twenty-five, and her description of where everyone was sitting. She says they could all see each other, even Maurice, who was writing at the window. She says she got up once to speak to him and to feel her skirt, which was drying on a chair by the radiator. Then there's all that bit about Tom when I was talking. Rachel said nothing more until Dr. Jerrold asked her if everyone loved Uncle Selford and she spoke of his wife. All that you would have found out anyway. Then she explained about the fortune Uncle Selford inherited from his mother and why Tom's father left his half in trust. She says: 'The friction had increased very much lately,' and you go on to speak about the letter to the lawyer. There doesn't seem to be anything more till she explained why Uncle Selford sometimes came to her with things he didn't want to discuss with Maurice, and all she says about the difference between Maurice and his father. There's a bit about his book, and then she speaks of Stephen again and says he was under a cloud when Uncle Selford took him. Did she want you to forget that?"

"Perhaps."

Simon was reading the typescript over Tassy's shoulder as she ran through it, slipping a finger along the page.

"Then about Nurse," and Tassy went on: "She suggested that Nurse was attracted by Uncle Selford and told you about Tom's infatuation and agreed with Dr. Jerrold about her being a good nurse and says she noticed how clever Nurse was at bandaging Maurice's hand and thinks Uncle Selford liked her because she was so skilful and a trained masseuse. Then she lost her temper with you because of what you said about Nurse liking pretty things, and that's all."

Brade put his finger on the lines where Rachel said: "I got up once to speak to Maurice."

"What did she say to Maurice?" he asked. "Did she take out those pages because she didn't want us to ask? And there's that bit about Nurse Jonsen. Did she think she had been unjust—had suggested that Nurse was trying to persuade Mr. Prentice to divorce his wife and marry her, for instance, because he was rich? Did she think that reflected on Mr. Prentice's character and want to suppress it? Or is it something different? If I could remember one thing I should know. While she was talking that night, I was seeing the room. I could see it plainly. Then for a second there was a blur, as if she had described something I couldn't see or said something I couldn't understand. But I can't remember when I felt it. If I could— Tassy, read it all to me again, every word!"

He sat down and shut his eyes. Tassy read. Once his eyelids flickered, but he did not move until she had finished. Then he sat still for a moment longer.

"What is it, Mr. Brade?" she asked. "You've seen something. You look—frightened."

He put out his hand for the pages. "Give them to me," he said. "I'm sorry I ever let you see them. Don't tell anyone you've read them. Not anyone, Tassy. Promise me that."

"But why?"

"You must promise."

"Why?"

"Because of Tom," said Brade, taking the papers. He folded them, enclosed them in an envelope, and put them in his pocket.

"Very well, I'll promise. But I wish you'd tell me what it is you've guessed."

"I hope I'll never have to tell anyone," he answered, and then he went away.

CHAPTER 23

MULLIE had taken a turn for the worse in the last few days. Her old heart beat on steadily enough, but her mind seemed to dwell in the past, and she forgot for hours all that had happened in the last few weeks. Sometimes she talked to Tassy as Rachel, and sometimes she thought that Rachel, Tassy, and Stephen were all in the nursery again, and that Tassy, sitting beside her, was their mother.

Usually she was calm and happy, but on the evening following Brade's visit Tassy, coming in from exercising the horses, found her restless. She looked at Tassy with questioning eyes, their blue dimmed, and then at the changing pattern of firelight on the walls. There she seemed to see shapes of presences that spoke to her, for she answered them in eager whispers, forgetting Tassy.

Hadley stood there, and Tassy asked if Dr. Garnet had called.

"Yes, miss. He said she's in no danger, but she'll be like this perhaps for months and months. It's a great trouble to you, miss."

"I don't mind so long as she's happy. I'll sit here awhile, Hadley. You can go."

It occurred to her as Hadley went away that in the last weeks since Rachel died she had taken her place as mistress of the house without noticing the change. Yet it was a great change. There was no one to think for her now, no one to impose a stronger will on hers. She was completely independent and utterly lonely. Stephen was no support; in fact, he had become her responsibility. She was alone.

At first her grief for Rachel had been childlike, desperate, filling the world. Only the spur of Tom's danger shocked her into seeing that she was needed for something besides rebellious sorrow. She stood above it now, but the mighty passion of desolation was there, ready to overwhelm her in moments like these. The torment that embittered the loss of her sister was the memory of their quarrel, and the worst of it all was her doubt of Rachel. If she had lost not only her sister and best friend, but the memory of her in her lovely pride and perfection too, her whole life seemed like a wound she could not bear to look at.

Mullie's hands, blue-veined and pale, moved along the shadows of the white quilt. She was looking at Tassy now and speaking to her. "Ye will not marry him, Miss Rachel. I promised your mother ye should not. No, listen to your Mullie speakin'. I said I would not tell—not unless I had to, fer ye're only boy and girl and naught may come of it. Mr. Selford himself would not have it, but I've lain thinking here, and I've a fear in my heart ye might do it without telling your Mullie before—"

Tassy laid her hand on the bony, restless fingers. It was torture to hear herself called Rachel. "Hush, Mullie, do hush. I can't bear it."

"Nay, ye must hear," Mullie tried to raise herself. "The time's come I must tell ye. The good God give me strength! It was years and years ago it happened, before Mr. Maurice was born, or you either, my pretty, and Mr. Stephen but a babe in arms, and a sweeter one never lived. My dear lady was the only one to know the truth, for she'd been friends with Mr. Selford and sometimes I used to think that if she'd known him before your father she'd have been his wife. He went away to travel and there he met the foreign lady. Not even French or German, wasn't she, but from a wild country of the South where the men wear daggers in their belts, so I've heard, and clothes like actors on the stage and no Christian. And she was beautiful, that lady, big and strong and grand to look at, and of noble birth, but she was promised to a nobleman of her own people, and she hated him, so she told Mr. Selford, and he being young and loving her for her beauty, took her away in secret and married her."

Tassy was listening in spite of herself now. Mullie's voice came clear and musical—her fairy-tale voice, they had called it. She knew she must not interrupt. The room grew dimmer. Only the fire blazed out, throwing a glow over the bed.

"At first he was happy, it may be, but not for long. Her father found them out and told him the truth. For there was a taint in the blood and her mother had been such another. Beautiful as the first flowery morning of spring, and with a mind for sweet things, but there would be times when if she was denied her wishes, or life went on with one day like another and the sun rising and setting the same and no change or happenings coming to please her, then she would go wild, and if there was wine to be had, she would drink herself crazy, and then she was cruel and stopped at no crime, and clever too in her cruelty, so that only those who knew would suspect her. The mother died at last, a prisoner in her own home, and the daughter was like her, and this was the woman Mr. Selford had taken to be his wife.

"At first he would not believe it was so, but at last he knew. For she had not married him because she loved him, but to get away from her father and brothers, who knew the truth and kept always with her to guard and care for her. Anyone who did that, she hated with deadly hate. So at last she came to hate her husband. It was power and admiration and the love of men she wanted and must have, and money to spend on her silks and satins and jewels, and when he tried to reason, she sat there with the wineglass in her pretty fingers and drank and drank and grew lovelier and calmer and cleverer as she drank, and with every glass rules and reason got dimmer and dimmer and her own will grew stronger and stronger till one day, when he had taken her to a lonely place in his fear and love, she bent her mind to murder. There was a road winding along and the edge of it dropped away to the cliff and the sea below. She went there with him, kind and repentant and loving, she seemed, and then, Miss Rachel, she thrust him over the edge, for she was strong as a man and he was unprepared. But God in His mercy saved him to be a cripple for his whole life. They sent for her brothers and they took her home. And there she lives to this day and is gay and beautiful and clever, and only a few know the truth. But sometimes she is too clever for them and gets away, and she is not mad, Miss Rachel, only when she can get the liquor to drown her conscience. Only then. But she hates Mr. Selford, because she thinks she could marry someone else and be free, but he will not let her go to spoil the life of another and will not say the truth, for he promised her father he would not, and for Mr. Maurice's sake. And that is why Mr. Maurice cannot marry, Miss Rachel my lamb, for his child might be like her. Promise me you will not, for I have told you at last and your mother told me all before she died, for she feared that you loved him."

"Mullie, is this true?"

"True, true, true." Mullie turned her head restlessly. Then her eyes widened and took fire. "Is Mr. Selford dead?" she asked in a whisper. "Did she kill him, Miss Rachel? Did she kill him at last?"

Tassy leaned over the bed, quieting the old woman, whose bewildered mind could travel across the years and set her moving through scenes of today and those of long ago in the same swift moment. But Mullie was exhausted by her effort, and relieved too, for she had unburdened a secret of the years.

"Why did you never tell me before, Mullie?" asked Tassy gently. For she believed the story. Had Rachel known?

"Nay, I promised, Miss Tassy," Mullie said quietly, "and Miss Rachel fell in love with another man, so there was no need. But lately I've wondered if perhaps she might think of him again. Is she safe, Miss Tassy? Is Miss Rachel safe and well?"

"Yes, Mullie dear."

"She's gone to one of her meetings. Will you look and see if the fire's alight in her room? Those maids forget more than they remember. And her dress put out, the red tea-gown she'll like tonight, for it's cold and she'll be tired. You'll see to that, Miss Tassy, my lamb, for there's something wrong with my legs tonight and I'm maybe sickening for a chill. I'll just sleep awhile and be well in the morning, my dear, if ye'll see to Miss Rachel's fire."

"Yes, Mullie. Go to sleep. I'll go now."

Indeed, she had to go. She could bear it no longer. Mullie's head was quiet on the pillow. The fire dropped lower. The room was still. Even the shadows rested from their dance. Tassy went away.

Stephen was in the drawing-room when she went downstairs. He looked up as she came in, and swept some papers out of sight. "They're recovering from the election," he remarked, "but luckily they've decided Langrove is guilty, so it's not a particularly exciting murder, and Europe takes up a lot of room. Where are you going, Tass?"

"I'm going to the Grange. I've something to tell Mr. Brade."

"But it's dinner-time," Stephen protested.

Tassy laughed. That was so like Stephen.

CHAPTER 24

TASSY rang the bell.

There were no shutters at the Grange and she could see thinks of light between the curtains. Every light in the house seemed to be turned on.

She rang again. No one answered. She pressed her finger on the button and kept it there. The cherry trees chattered behind her, and the ends of the climbing roses waved against the sky. A thousand minute voices sang with the wind on a rising note of panic. The garden talked, whispered, called, hissed its secrets in a language she did not understand. Would no one let her in?

Running steps shook the door she touched. A catch was pressed back and Braythorpe stood there in the lighted hall, is hair more erect than ever and his face whiter. She came n with a rush of wind and he shut the door and shot a bolt.

"What is the matter?" she demanded.

"It's that fish, Miss Tassy," he said. "It's been found and everybody's upstairs and there's the devil to pay, begging your pardon, miss, and I'm sure it's not my fault, and Mrs. Myster's in such a state and accusing everybody of everything, and what this house is coming to I don't know. If it wasn't for Mr. Maurice and Mr. Tom I'd leave tomorrow wages or no wages. When luck's gone from a house, there's no telling what'll happen. You can come and see for yourself, miss."

Tassy was already half-way down the passage. She ran up the stairs and down the long corridor to the end where everyone in the household seemed to be gathered.

Brade, the centre of the group, held the porcelain fish in his arms. He stood there in silence, dignified and absurd at once. His face was masked in despair. There were two large tears, already dry, on his pale cheeks. So real was his distress that the group surrounding him seemed to concentrate as one man on defending itself from some guilt.

"And I'm sure I do look after the house when I'm not too busy, and what more can be expected with all this delay in the autumn planting?" Lady Charlotte was tearful.

"Naturally, as no one knew its value—" Maurice, for once, was rather like a small boy caught near a broken window with a cricket bat in his hand.

"It's an awful pity," Tom muttered with an air of having said the same thing before, "but I don't see—"

Mrs. Myster stood, arms crossed, challenging everyone and accusing some, and the new housemaid, terrified and quaking, sheltered as far as possible from her indignant eye, while Lily, the kitchen-maid, and Phelps, the odd man, looked on hopefully, with evident conviction of innocence.

Seeing Tassy, everyone except Brade started to explain, but it was Maurice who eventually cleared the confusion in her mind by saying: "The jug has been broken and mended and replaced in the cabinet by someone. Carter, the new housemaid, says it has been there ever since she came. It is quite possible. It was standing at the back, with a vase before it, and no one would have noticed it, unless looking particularly at the china."

Brade held it out to her with a gesture of resignation in a sorrow too deep for words. She took it from him and looked at the ugly thing for the first time. Then she handed it to Maurice.

"I can't see the break."

"And it's beautifully mended, Mr. Brade, and you might have overlooked the crack."

Brade turned on Lady Charlotte a cold scrutiny which silenced her.

Unnoticed, Chen had followed Tassy upstairs and now caught sight of his enemy. He began to bark, shrilly, frantically, his legs braced, his coat stiff, his eyes reddened with fury. He leapt at the hated creature grinning down at him, struck it from Maurice's hands. It fell, hit the brass leg of the cabinet, and broke, lying in scattered fragments of colour on the carpet. Chen barked. He moved forward step by step, sniffed at the bits of green and brown for a second, then lay down placidly and began to lick his paw.

"I'm awfully sorry." Maurice was shocked by the accident.

Brade waved a hand.

"It's better so," he said. "Yes, it's quite right," he added in a voice unlike his own. "Maurice couldn't hold it safe!" He leaned over and picked up one fine and fragile fragment, looking at it thoughtfully. "May I keep this?" he asked Maurice. "You can sweep up the rest and bury it." Then he looked at Chen. "I've heard that dog bark three times before. The first time was at my fish, the second time you all remember. The third—" His eyes lighted. He stood stiffly as Chen himself had stood a moment ago. Then he stalked away toward the stairs.

Tassy ran after him. "I want to see you, Mr. Brade. I've something to tell you," she said as she seized his arm.

"Then you can come with me. There's no time to lose."

"Where are you going?"

"To Medbury."

"I'll drive you there."

Lady Charlotte and Tom were picking up the broken china. Maurice was looking after Brade, and Mrs. Myster was hurling questions at the frightened housemaid. Tassy and Brade went downstairs.

"Aren't you going to put on a coat and hat?" asked Tassy.

Brade appeared to be in a trance.

"Coat and hat? Why, yes, I suppose I am." He stopped helplessly. Tassy found the garments hanging inside the front door and helped him into them. When they were seated in the car, she began to tell him what Mullie had said.

"You aren't listening, Mr. Brade."

"Yes, I am. That's the trouble." He covered his ears. "I'm listening to the voices of a million troubled souls. The San Ts'ai is broken, Tassy. Every hand that touched it is stirring star-dust. The hands that gathered the clay, the hands that plucked the dye from the earth, the hands that fired and glazed it. Above all, the strange pale hands that obeyed the master brain of a potter long, long ago. I can hear them. The fate of hundreds was woven together in that shape, and now it is shattered, a chain is broken, and spirits have escaped. They are speaking to me and I'm listening to them. Your voice is only one. Speak louder and perhaps I shall hear."

She tried to tell him.

He turned toward her. "Say it all again. I can hear you now."

When she had finished, he said:

"Yes, they are there—those other voices. They're not disentangled yet. Not quite. And we can wait for them. We shall find out the truth now, my dear. Quite soon. There's something of all of us in that broken jewel. Something of you and me. The other time I heard Chen bark was when I came out of Selford Prentice's room half an hour after he died. He was barking at the San Ts'ai."

They were winding down the hill that overlooked Medbury, and the lights of the town were spread out like a child's drawings of a star.

"Where are we going, Mr. Brade?"

He directed her toward the canal and asked her to stop opposite a narrow bridge that led to a track running along the face of half a dozen mean cottages.

"Come with me, Tassy. I shall want someone to hear what they say."

She parked the car in a widened space farther on, under the shadow of a factory, and followed him. He knocked at one of the cottage doors. A woman, so small and thin that the lamplight seemed to shine through her, let them in.

There was a hot fire in the open range, a wooden high-back chair drawn near it, the cushions flattened and soiled by use. A sofa, with a mahogany frame and rolling head-rest, leaned tipsily on three legs and displayed the white stuffing under its horsehair covers. A table was spread with a red table-cloth and furnished with half a loaf of bread on a plate, and what was left of a pound of very yellow butter. Curtains which did not fit hung from a string over the window, where a geranium flowered without enthusiasm, and another curtain covered a doorway at the back. Everything in the room touched its neighbour, and the fire heated the farthest wall.

"Bernie, 'ere's Mr. Brade and a young lady," called the woman. "Please to sit down, miss. Bernie, ye'd better come and speak to Mr. Brade." Her voice took on a sharp and threatening note. "Washing her finery, she is. We 'ad a bathtub put in by the Council in the scullery, and now I got no place to put anything down. I've tried boards across, but they slip and break the crockery. Bernie! I'm sure, sir, we're grateful to you, and Bernie is too. We ain't 'ad meat twice a week before since Langrove took to politics, and the butcher polite as a pedlar, and I told Langrove as much and hope it'll do 'im good, though I doubts it. Bernie!"

Bernie appeared. Tassy, who had seen her at the Grange, was surprised to see her now. She was wearing a pink blouse, and her hair was curled into a friz. Lipstick had been applied to the thin line of her lips, and her cheeks had been treated with a rouge suitable to blondes. Bernie was not a blonde.

She came in, shoulders lifted, wary-eyed, but civil, with a mixture of defiance and assumed refinement not altogether pleasing.

"Very kind of you to call, I'm sure," she said. "Good evening, Miss Tassy."

Brade, seated on the edge of a chair, rose and shook hands with her hurriedly.

"Did you want to see me special?" asked Bernie, "because I was going out."

"I did, rather, Bernie. I wanted to ask you who broke my San Ts'ai—the porcelain fish, you know."

"Why do you want to know?" she asked, sullenly, poised ready for flight.

"It interests me," murmured Brade, "quite a lot. A girl that can mend china like that might get a well-paid job in a shop I know. Why, even Braythorpe didn't notice the crack."

Bernie grinned suddenly, but she still hesitated.

"Now, Bernie—"

"You keep quiet, Ma. Suppose I tell you all I know— everything. Will you believe me?"

"I think I'll know the truth when I hear it. I don't seem to have heard it for a long time."

"And no wonder. A pack of liars they all are—all except Mr. Tom, and he's too stupid. And Dad didn't have anything to do with the way Mr. Prentice died. I know that—and I know they're saying he did." Bernie flung down her coat. "Will you get me a job in London if I tell you, honest to God?"

"Now, Bernie—"

"You be quiet, Ma. I've got wits, I have, and I'm going to London to try 'em out. If Mr. Brade'll swear he'll help me I'll tell 'im everything. I don't 'ave to, but I will."

"Well it all depends on how that water-pourer was broken. I'd never trust you with so much as a soapstone if you just dropped it, and that's the truth."

"But I didn't. It was a queer one—that fish. I was afraid of it. How was I to know what was in that basket? That night, when everyone rushed to Mr. Prentice's room, I wanted to know what was going on. Who wouldn't? But Braythorpe told Mrs. Myster to keep us away. Molly Hegan and the others got behind a curtain, but they wouldn't let Lily and me come, so Lily, she went out and looked in at the window, and I went upstairs and leaned over the banisters. It was dark and I never see the basket on the table and I rested my arm on it to see better and the basket rolled off and the cover flew open and the fish rolled out and come a crack against the stair and broke in two, with 'is face leerin' at me and 'is tail sticking up in a corner. Well, I couldn't leave it there. Somebody was coming, so I shut the basket and put it back and fastened it and I took the fish under my apron. I was sort of sorry it was broken. I don't know why. It was ugly as anything, but it was queer too—made me want to know what it meant. Made me want to laugh too, sort of deep inside me, and not tell anybody I was laughin'. I declare, it made me feel funny all over, as if, now it was broke, something had been spilt out of it. I took it and hid it under my new aprons in a drawer ever so careful and all the time I kept thinkin' about it, like. And next morning nobody was watching me, with Mr. Pennleaf and Mr. Brade asking questions, so I got it out and took it to the carpenter's shop that Mr. Tom's got fitted up in the little room next his bedroom. You have to go through Mr. Tom's room to get to it, but Molly Hegan, she sent me up there to dust. And I found some glue and I mended that fish ever so careful, laughing, like, inside all the time, and it was laughin' too, and just as I was coming out with it hid in a duster, somebody opened the door of Mr. Tom's room and come in. The door opened away from me, so I had time to go back, but I could see through a chink. It was Mrs. Norbury. She went up to Mr. Tom's dressing-table, and then I could see her go behind the mirror and throw something out of the window.

"I waited till she went away. Then I took the fish and stood him in the glass case behind the other things. I didn't think anybody'd notice the crack, he looked so good, and he grinned at me till I wondered if it was a put-up job and he knew everything, and I had a funny feeling he wanted me to find out what Mrs. Norbury threw away. So I went out into the garden and I found that key. But when I got back Mrs. Myster saw me and you know what happened. I knew they were saying Mr. Tom had gone

and done for Mr. Prentice and I didn't believe it and I like
Mr. Tom and it seemed to me if that key was in the
garden they'd think somebody else could 'ave got in and
Mr. Tom would get off. I thought that was why Mrs.
Norbury did it. So I wasn't going to say anything. But at
the Coroner's 'quest they made it look as if Mr. Tom had
thrown it out there 'imself and I know 'e didn't—and that
fish knows it too."

"Rachel!" Tassy exclaimed.

Simon Brade jumped up, seized Bernie's hands, and
shook them. "I might have known!" he cried. "There is
fate in my San Ts'ai, and fate in porcelain breaks it at
last. Bernie, you're a genius. You and Chen are the only
two who understand. You shall—" he paused solemnly—
"you shall come and dust my collection. I'll teach you. You
shall be my pupil. You have caned chair-seats for the last
time. Here's some money. It's all I've got at the moment.
You shall take your mother to London and she shall walk
all day in patent-leather shoes."

"Oh, I wouldn't care to do that, sir," protested Mrs.
Langrove, glancing down at her heelless slippers. "They
look fine, but they aren't easy on my corns, and that's a
fact."

"You shall visit a chiropodist." Brade waved a hand.
"You shall—" He viewed Mrs. Langrove intelligently
through his eye-glass. "You shall sit down frequently
and—er—study the shoe catalogues," he promised.

Mrs. Langrove's petulance yielded to bewilderment,
not without reason. She looked at Tassy, then at Brade,
then at Bernie. Then, giving way to the habit of thirty
years, she sighed heavily. Brade might be mad, but
Bernie's hand was closing on two authentic-looking green
notes, and that young woman, who, though certainly
perverse, was intelligent, seemed pleased.

"Only," added Brade, his eye-glass still in play, "I'm
not fond of that shade of pink." Whether he was referring
to the blouse or the rouge, no one knew. "Or kinks," added

Brade decisively. "Wait till you've looked at my stem cups, Bernie. Then you'll understand."

"My eye," Bernie remarked feelingly, gazing at the money in her hand, "you're a funny gentleman!" Then she turned to Tassy. "Does 'e mean it?" she asked.

"I think so, Bernie."

"Well, if 'e does, I'm game. I can dust china if that's all 'e wants." She picked up her coat and hat. "And if 'e's got some more jugs like that fish, I won't break 'em either." She went to the cracked mirror on the wall, adjusted her hat with care, and turned toward the door.

There she paused and faced them. "You all think you're so clever," she said. "Well, I'll tell you one thing, the servants in a house see more in five minutes than all the superintendents and inspectors in Bramshire together. Any one of us could tell you that Mr. Tom didn't do in Mr. Prentice, nor my dad either, for all his talk. And I can make a pretty good guess who did. Mr. Tom wasn't the only one who had words with Mr. Prentice that morning. Mr. Maurice came out of his father's room afterwards and his face was black as a window-pane on a dark night. And you ask Braythorpe about the letters in the green envelopes. That's all I got to say."

On their way back to the Grange, Tassy asked. "What did Bernie mean?"

Brade sighed. "I thought I was so bright," he said, "but Bernie guessed before I did why Mrs. Norbury stole those pages out of Jerry's book."

"I can't imagine how Maurice could have had anything to do with it, unless he—is that it? Do you think he gave his key to someone else?"

"But if we begin to believe in an accomplice in the house, Bernie herself comes under suspicion, and I couldn't bear that, Tassy. Not after the way she talked about my San Ts'ai." Brade laughed suddenly, uncontrollably. His shoulders shook, his whole body shook. In spite of the sinister mystery so personal to her in her loneliness and sorrow, Tassy heard his laughter without anger or resentment. "Three hundred years ago that grin was moulded by a master, and it convulses us today. It made Bernie laugh deep inside, so nobody could see,'" he quoted. "Bernie is cursed with a dose of the cosmic soul, my dear." Brade sobered as suddenly as he had yielded to his mirth, and his voice in the darkness was deep with sadness. "Perhaps you don't know what Bayard Taylor says the Chinese told him about the fish that holds up the earth. When he is angry he convulses it with volcanoes and earthquakes. The Chinese told him it was a fish. Some call it a dragon. Anyway, it is a god who assumes different shapes, and he is angry. His wrath is convulsing the world today. I wonder—"

"What do you wonder?" asked Tassy.

"I wonder if Mr. Prentice would be alive today if he had not tried to sell me the San Ts'ai."

This seemed so fanciful an idea that Tassy ignored it. She asked: "Shall I take you back to the Grange?"

"Yes. I want to see Lady Charlotte. We've neglected her, rather, you know, and it's not quite polite. If only one could tell whether she's talking about people or insects. The other day she said quite suddenly: 'I know who did it!' We thought she meant who murdered her brother-in-law, but it was only the grub that had spoilt her new lily, a very special sort of caterpillar. Confusing. And she has one or two excellent pieces of furniture. I'll say that for her. That transition chair, now—interesting. Would you believe, she told me it was Chippendale? Did you ever see that massive naturalistic carving in Chippendale? The combination of masks and the eagles' heads on the arms? I mean to say, a schoolboy could tell you—" He continued in this vein as they mounted the last hill before arriving at the Grange.

"You won't come in?"

"No, I must go back to Mullie. I'm going to hunt tomorrow. I've booked Jennifer J. for the ladies' point-to-point at Weleven in April and I have to ride in a side-saddle. She's never been hunted in a side-saddle yet, so I've got to begin."

"A side-saddle? Miss Tassy, will you come back to the Grange for tea? Will you promise to come?"

"Why?"

"I want you. I do want you. There's no telling what may happen before that. Will you come?"

"Why, yes, if Mullie's all right and it's important."

"When I want something," Brade remarked with dignity, "it's always important. Please come."

"All right, I will." Tassy drew up the car, and Brade scrambled out. "Good night, Mr. Brade."

He laid his hand on the door before he shut it for her.

"And be careful, Tassy. Ride alone tomorrow unless— Yes, I will. Tom offered me a mount. I'll come out myself to look after you."

Tassy laughed. "Why, I'm as good in a side-saddle as out of it, and Jennifer J. can keep on her feet, trust her! You needn't worry about me. We know the Yale of the Med better than the alphabet, Mr. Brade."

She could see his face grave and colourless in the lights of the car.

"You haven't hunted for three weeks. The Vale of the Med may have changed since then," was all he said.

CHAPTER 25

"WILL YOU mount me today, Tom?"

Nurse Jonsen waylaid Tom as he came downstairs to breakfast. He scowled, although she was looking handsome enough to ask favours with confidence from any man disposed to admire her. The truth was, Tom no longer admired her.

"How do I know you'd stick on?" he fenced sulkily.

"That's my risk."

"No, it isn't. It's mine. I'm thinking of the horse. Can't afford to have a mount laid up at the beginning of the season."

"Your mount will be all right. I promise. I'm a good horsewoman, though I haven't hunted for years. After all, I deserve a little pleasure, Tom. I've been shut up in this house since June. 1 can't stand it much longer."

He could understand that. Anyone would want a day with hounds after all she'd been through. "I'll see what I can do," he said, ungraciously. "There's Blackfriar, but he' not had much work. Still, you managed all right the day we hacked to Agminton." He stopped, confused, for that ride had marked the peak of his infatuation.

"Tom," she said, "is Mr. Brade doing anything? He never seems to. He wanders about asking a question now and then, and that's all. Do you know what he thinks about the case or whom he suspects?"

Tom shook his head.

She passed him and went on up the stairs. At the landing she stopped short. The telephone bell was ringing. She stood listening, while Tom went on into the dining-room. Braythorpe was coming to answer the phone. Nurse Jonsen ran down and took up the receiver.

"I'll inquire. Hold the line." She turned to Braythorpe. "Ask her ladyship if it will be convenient today for them to return the furniture borrowed for the exhibition."

But when Braythorpe had taken the message and answered it, he said to Mrs. Myster: "That nurse is queer today. Answered the phone, and no business of hers, either, and she was breathing as if something had hit her."

Stephen Litton, for once, was up early. He walked to the cross-roads below the Grange and caught the nine-o'clock bus to Medbury. It was the first time he had ever travelled this journey by bus and he fretted at its deliberate pace and long pauses. Yet when he reached Medbury market he seemed to be in no hurry. He loitered, bought a morning paper and a packet of cigarettes, and then with sudden haste crossed the street to the new temporary offices of the *Active Sentinel*.

When he came out, his hesitation seemed to be over.

He found Dr. Jerrold and Simon Brade in the parlour of the Blue Boar Inn, both in hunting kit. They looked up in surprise as the landlady showed him in.

They offered him a cup of coffee, which he refused, and whisky and soda, which he accepted. He sat there drinking and allowing their surprise to deepen. Finally he looked up, without his usual suavity, and said in a rush:

"I've come about a letter I've had from a friend in the Diplomatic. The fact is I've made an ass of myself. You know I persuaded Mr. Prentice to take Nurse Jonsen, and you know why. I felt sorry for his wife. Well, I didn't know she had a finger in politics. You'd better see this letter." He took an envelope from his pocket. "No—I'll read it to you. The first part is personal. This is it.

"'You ask about the lady your boss married. She goes by her maiden name out in these parts, I believe, Princess Elena Velbesco. You know the family is connected with most of the royalties in the Near East. I only learned by accident that this lady is Mrs. Prentice. Ware riot, my boy! They tell me she's financed by a party in her country that's just now out to back Italy, and it is whispered that an underground movement, going by the name of the

New Order, is financing her. Don't know if you have heard of the N. O. When you do, someone will tell you, probably, that it's just a bogy to frighten the ladies with, like the Jewish conspiracy, but I believe there's more truth in it than people think. Only the inner circle know the plan, but hundreds of discontented factions have been drawn in to work for it for their own ends, a powerful body of royalists in France, a section of patriots in Croatia, an anti-Teutonic group in Greece, the Carlists in Spain, and so on. The idea is that at some favourable moment, when Hitler dies, for instance, or Mussolini is assassinated, a chain of dictators will be set up in as many countries as possible, under the leadership of one man, whose name I won't mention. It is well known in financial circles. The final aim is to create a Federation in Europe and abolish sovereignty, though half its adherents don't know this. Of course, this may all be just one of those stories that do get themselves spread over Europe these days. Don't ask me. Anyway, your lady is supposed to be mixed up in it. She can't do much out here, she's too well known. But she may try her hand in England. If you hear she's moving in political circles, you'll smell a rat!'"

Stephen folded the letter and replaced it. "Well, putting two and two together, you get Nurse Jonsen sent to the Grange by Mrs. Prentice and making a dead set at Uncle Selford. And about the same time you get the *Active Sentinel* launched out of a blue sky."

"What does an *Active Sentinel* do?" asked Brade, innocently.

"It tried to split the Socialist party on sanctions and swing them away from the League. It's the outcry from the Left that's stiffening the government, and if that weakened they'd come to terms with Italy. You'll see, there'll be peace proposals before long and the Cabinet would like to get peace at almost any price. I know something about what's going on. There's too much trouble brewing everywhere for them to concentrate against Italy. It's the howl that'll go up from the Left if they play France's game that scares them. It's a shrewd stroke to try to play on the Socialist division between pacifism and support of collective order. There's money behind this new paper. Where does it come from, and who's directing it?"

"Well, who is?"

"Someone who's paid for it, mark my words. And I'm not sure you won't find him at the Grange."

Dr. Jerrold looked quickly at Stephen. Brade shook his head. "You'll have to be very plain with me if you want me to understand politics," he apologized meekly.

"I've no business to talk—and I wouldn't if it didn't have some bearing on the case you're trying to solve, Mr. Brade. I've told you about Selford Prentice's wife. If Nurse Jonsen is the agent of a foreign country and her business at the Grange was political and not personal, it seems to me to open up a considerable field we haven't explored. And there's one more thing. My sister Rachel worshipped Prentice. Suppose she suspected, or was told, that he had betrayed his cause. She wouldn't believe it herself and she'd have died rather than allow such a slur to be cast on his memory. She would have thought it might undo all the fine work he had done and negative the effect of the book he had just finished. It might explain all she did that seems strange now." He looked from Jerrold to Brade and back again. "Anyway, I've got that off my chest." He rose. "I know I was an ass to meddle with Uncle Selford's affairs. I swear I thought he'd be happier, too, to do the right thing by his wife. It seemed so rotten to keep a woman tied to him and never see her, and of course she couldn't move without an annulment. But if she sent Nurse here for the other reason, I've been running pretty close to the wind just as there's a chance of my getting back into the Diplomatic, too. I can't believe that Uncle Selford, or Maurice either, would have taken cash from a foreign power, but there've been things in the Sentinel that have made me think—a sort of twisted paraphrase of some of Uncle Selford's favourite sayings. Well, I'll go back. I had to come by bus. All the cars were wanted for the meet, and I don't care about running into any of the others just now."

He took his leave abruptly and went out.

"What is the position of a man who is bribed by a foreign government, Jerry?"

"He's liable to be charged with treason, I believe."

"But a man might think himself justified—in a cause?"

"He might, I suppose. Mussolini has been accused of doing it in his early days."

"But in England, if he should be found out?"

"I should think that would finish him. I don't know what the penalty for such an offence is."

"Why did Mussolini do it—if he did?"

"His enemies say because he had to have money before he could have power. And a newspaper of his own was a big step to power. He certainly switched from pacifism to war propaganda on the side of the Allies almost overnight. But I'm no authority on the facts. I'm bound to say I admire him."

"Because he succeeded—swung it—isn't that the phrase? But suppose he hadn't."

Jerrold shrugged his shoulders.

"He'd have bolted to America or somewhere. It might be amusing to speculate. The point is—if he did it—it served its purpose."

Brade looked thoughtfully out of the square-paned window into the market place, still quiet and empty.

"How many budding Mussolinis are there in the world today, I wonder," he mused. "Even here in England. How many egoists dreaming of power? And where will it take them?" He stiffened abruptly and faced Jerrold. "Don't you think you'd better tell me all about it, Jerry?"

"All about what?"

"The conversation you had with Prentice that night—just before he died."

"It has nothing to do with the case."

"Sure?"

"If you must know, Simon, I swore on my word of honour—my professional honour—never to tell, unless—"

"Unless what?"

"Unless someone else found it out."

"Then tell me, my boy. I've found out."

"You can't know."

"Can't I? He wanted to ask you if, in view of the family history, he was right in trying to prevent his son's marriage."

"You're guessing, Brade."

"Oh, no. I never guess. Mullie told us, you must remember. The queer strain in the family. When they wanted to do something really naughty, they had only to drink enough and it no longer seemed naughty but only inevitable. Even if Maurice had escaped this blight, his children might inherit it. Take the facts, Jerry. Prentice knows you specialize in such things. He has such a problem. You are friends. He is closeted with you for forty-five minutes, and you, in writing your notes, keep all of that conversation secret. We know from Mrs. Norbury that he had some special and private problem on his mind. Those two things alone would have been enough to give away the truth. But when Maurice told us that he was engaged to be married, the matter was settled."

"He said his father did not know that he was engaged."

"Perhaps Maurice thought he had kept his secret— just as you thought you had kept yours. And you were not content to keep the conversation back, but you typed all your notes over again for fear you had dropped a hint, although you are on holiday and typing half the night is not the sort of work to rest the weary brain-slogger! Well, Jerry, what have you to say?"

"Only that I'm going back to London tonight. Elena Prentice is doing a rest-cure in Austria. Maurice was in the studio and never left it that evening until after the tragedy. They'll never get enough evidence to arrest Tom Prentice. We'll have to leave it at that."

"We shan't be allowed to leave it like that. There'll be other tragedies if we don't solve this one."

"Do you really believe that, Brade?" Jerrold moved restlessly. "Or are you just saying it to make me speak?"

"I believe it. And what's more, I believe you and I actually hastened if we didn't cause Prentice's death."

"What do you mean by that? You carry your jokes too far!"

"Do I look like joking?" Brade did not.

"Then what do you mean?"

"I mean that your reputation and mine preceded us and roused the suspicion of the criminal. He guessed that Prentice meant to confide in one of us—to get advice. It did not matter to him which of us it was. It told him that Prentice knew the secret he had to conceal, and the message to Mrs. Norbury confirmed this guess. Prentice knew this might happen, and that is why he used the San Ts'ai as a blind. Did he caution you not to give away the real reason for wanting to see you? I thought so! But the ruse failed. Now do you understand?"

Jerrold was silent.

"And, Jerry, there's no doubt whatever that Prentice suspected Maurice of something."

"Why do you say that?"

"There are several reasons, but the principal one is what Braythorpe told me. Bernie Langrove gave me the hint. She told me to ask Braythorpe about 'those green envelopes' and I did. It appears that at one time Prentice gave Braythorpe orders to take to Maurice all the letters written to him by his wife. The letters distressed him, and Maurice offered to deal with them. But for the last three months he altered this rule. The letters, which always came in green envelopes, were brought first to him, steamed open, read, resealed, and handed on to Maurice apparently untouched as if they had arrived by a later post. Prentice had read them and Maurice did not know it."

There was fitful sunshine in the market place. It illumined the façade of the Queen Anne Town Hall and the hurdles for penning cattle and the town cross. It made the windows of the cramped little shops blink and glitter and picked out puddles left by last night's storm. A groom riding one horse and leading another passed the window.

"Well," said Jerrold at last, "if I hadn't been convinced that Maurice could not have been in his father's room at all after you left him, I'd have told you long ago. Mr. Prentice did know of his son's engagement and was determined to prevent his marriage. For all I know, the burned letter may have been written to Maurice's fiancée, telling her all the facts."

"And that is all he knew?"

"I believe he connected Maurice with something that came out in the Sentinel, but I'm not sure—"

"That's all?"

"Yes, definitely, Simon—that is all he told me. He wanted to consult me in the matter of heredity. When I had given my opinion we talked of other things."

Brade looked out of the window, where horses, riders, cars, and pedestrians were gathering in the square.

"Come, Jerry, let's see if the boots has done justice to our mahogany tops. The hunt is up," he said.

CHAPTER 26

THE DRAW

Tassy moved as far from the main body of the hunting field and as near to the covert as she could, listening to the rustling in the underbrush and watching Tom as he stood or moved forward, following the progress of the pack. She turned with a frown on two riders who were talking behind her.

Then she forgot them, for Haphazard was speaking. She knew his voice. She had walked him as a puppy, and he was the best of his year's entry. Harpsicord, his twin, was efficient and painstaking enough, but Haphazard had more confidence. Nothing distracted him, and no one could persuade him to doubt, once he had settled the matter in his own mind. He had an ugly streak in his make-up and had attacked a new kennel man once, in a difference of opinion about his bed.

Miracle acknowledged Haphazard's challenge. Sobriety took it up. The covert rang and vibrated with the music. The field master spoke sharply to some stragglers, and a whipper-in rode round the covert at a gallop to Tom's side.

It was a disciplined field. Even the thrusters rode well away, afraid of spoiling sport. Tom went ahead. Jennifer J. shivered with excitement. She did not think of the saddle now. She knew that in a moment she would be free to go, and Tassy's light hand would tell her the moment when she might fly to escape the crowding flanks of horses making for the first fence. She knew, and Tassy knew, that to be held up now would be disastrous. Those first few fences left behind, the field would be weeded down to a third of the three hundred, and there would be no more infuriating interference. Another half-hour and

Jennifer J. would be flying straight over the firm soft turf in the company of her peers.

"Gone away, Gone away, Gone away," sang Tom's horn from the other side of the covert, and most of the three hundred plunged forward while the echo lingered in their ears.

There were hounds, the beauties, streaming down a slope, Haphazard and Sobriety nearing the first hedge, and there was Tom riding away on their flank. The day had begun.

THE RUN

The sky was already gathering into grey folds in the west, and the sheet of blue overhead slid into them.

Golden stubble, bordered by hedges still patchy with brown leaves, a triangle of plough-land with hounds working over it more slowly now, and waving blackthorn boughs ahead, then grass as far as Tassy could see, bending down to the willows on the bank of the stream, and the rosy roofs of Saul's farm, two miles away.

She had no eye for the horses and riders she passed, one by one. She marked a place in the first obstacle and rode for it, straight over the stubble, settling her weight on her right leg, feeling Jenn's mouth with her left hand, her crop ready for signals on the bare off-side. There would be a ditch beyond the hedge, but Jenn gave herself room to spare as she landed, feeling for safety with her clever hind feet. All well and on, down one furrow, up another, making for a thin place in the blackthorn, down-wind. The storm was behind them, riders of the sky following the hunt.

Tom had jumped through the blackthorn, the hunt servants after him. Tassy left the half-dozen riders who chose to wait their turn at the gap made by the last man through, and chose her own spot. She collected Jenn and rode for it, sheltering her face with her arms as Jenn rose. All right that time and only a stinging scratch on her neck which she hardly noticed in the perfection of the landing. She looked to see who had survived, and marked Maurice and the Pirate well up, with Blackfriar just behind. "Why, I believe that's Nurse Jonsen! I never saw her at the meet," she thought. "She looks all right." The black coat and buff breeches were travelling at an even pace close to the Pirate's near flank.

Jennifer J. had her chance now and took it. No one could pass her on the turf. She and Tassy overhauled and left behind the three or four riders ahead and were first after Tom over the rails at the bottom of the field. The river was before them, a winding branch of the Med. Tassy could have laughed in her confidence and delight, but she spared no pains studying the bank of the stream as she neared it, choosing a firm place near a willow, collecting Jenn until the moment came to let her gallop at it as fast as she liked, for speed was safety here. For moments, it seemed, she and Jenn were flying with nothing below but clear running water and then came a clutching of the mossy bank beyond, a faltering second as the hold slipped under settling hoofs, a lengthening of the slender chestnut neck with lowered head, freed by Tassy's hand, a swift recovery, and on.

"Good work, Jenn. That was twenty feet and not too good a landing. Good girl!"

Hounds had filtered through some palings into an orchard that spread precisely on two sides of the farmhouse.

"Our fox will have fouled the scent in the farm yard. There'll be a check," thought Tassy. "And then, Franklin's or the Spinneys, and either way we'll want all our wind, Jenn, my girl, so ease up, little lady. There's more to come."

MAURICE

No man in the hunting field likes being taken on as pilot by a lady. Maurice did not like it when he realized that Nurse Jonsen was riding in his pocket.

He enjoyed the sport. Tassy was wrong when she suspected him of hunting for the exercise or because his smart friends rode to hounds or for any reason except his own pleasure. He would have liked to command a stable full of thoroughbred hunters in the shires. Some day, perhaps, he could, if he had time.

When hounds checked at Saul's farm, he hoped to shake off his lady follower.

"Will it be Franklin's?"

Maurice decided for the Spinneys. The wind was wrong for Franklin's, though it offered the hunted fox a nearer shelter. He edged away from the group cf horses and riders, gradually augmented by a few of the second flight. Another larger company could be seen surmounting the brow of the hill, where they waited to judge which way hounds would turn.

Maurice rode round the farm garden to the other side of the orchard, where he had no business to be. As he opened the farmyard gate he saw Blackfriar making for it, and kept the gate hanging on his crop handle to admit Nurse Jonsen. They crossed the farmyard together and emerged out of view of the rest of the field in the shelter of the trees. Here they would have an advantage if the fox decided on the Spinneys, though they might have to retrace their steps if Franklin's was his objective.

She rode to his side and said: "Well, Mr. Prentice?"

Maurice said: "Brade is coming through the farmyard." They were silent as Brade, mounted on his hireling, jogged up beside them.

"I don't think he'll travel up-wind long, do you?" asked Brade, scanning the hillside. "We'll get a good start if he does the right thing. And we shall want it." He tapped his mount's neck. "We do our best, but we have our limitations. A miracle we escaped a bath just now, though we picked a narrow place for our effort. He's no refuser, I'll say that for him. He seems to think the sooner it's over, the sooner to sleep, which is all very well as armchair philosophy, but unsuitable to the hunting field."

Miracle was speaking. On the slope above them a labourer stood, his hat raised at arm's length. Hounds were hunting out of the orchard. The horn sounded. The leading hounds increased their pace. Haphazard's voice came with an exultant peal.

"It's the Spinneys," said Maurice as Pirate quivered, sprang forward, set his breast to the slope, with hounds working upwards toward the chalk hills, and the storm clouds nearly overhead.

CHEN

For weeks Chen had been dreaming dreams that were better than his waking hours. He no longer waited for the regular walks he had been taught to expect. Instead he went by himself. At first he trotted along the footpaths and lanes, looking for amusement. Then his searching, pointed muzzle led him into the beech woods above Hartover, and when he came back Mrs. Myster shut the door on him because he reeked of fox-scent.

He was not unhappy, but he grew thin with excitement. Even in his dreams he did not rest. Sometimes he hunted, sometimes, deeper in the darkness, he padded away from mysterious enemies. When he woke, the warm house stifled him, and he watched the doors until someone let him out. For longer and longer times he was absent, slipping in at the studio window afterwards and lying full-length on the rug, indifferent to the meal which Braythorpe never forgot to place for him at six o'clock on the pantry floor.

One night he did not return at all, but in the morning Lady Charlotte found him asleep in the summer house and nearly unrecognizable for blood and dirt. She picked him up and took him in, bathed him, and dressed his wounds.

"It's the vixens he's after," Braythorpe declared. "Mr. Prentice used to say he'd get killed some day by a dog-fox if we let him go free in the woods. He's going wild, my lady, I shouldn't wonder."

On the morning of the meet at Medbury, Chen jumped into Tom's car waiting at the door, and settled himself unnoticed in the rug on the seat. Tom drove off to join hounds who had gone by motor as far as the outskirts of the town, and by the time he saw Chen it was too late to turn back. "He'll be all right in the car. I'll tell Higgins to look out for him," thought Tom.

Higgins did look out for him at the meet, but after hounds had moved off he followed on, hoping to see a bit of the hunt before he turned in at the Royal George according to orders. A good deal could be seen from the road and there was no harm in looking.

When the hunt left Saul's farm, making for the Spinneys, Higgins was too interested to give up the chase. He knew better than to take the car across the line the fox might choose, but a lane led away at right angles and from the rise at the top he could catch glimpses of the run while hounds circled the Vale.

Here he forgot Chen.

The Spinneys, so called, consisted of a series of wooded depressions hollowed out of a hillside, where wild things were at home. Many a vixen made use of it for her nursery. The earths were never stopped. If they were, rabbits and badgers and foxes made others in no time and the chalky ground was tunnelled with old burrows. Chen, jumping out of the car, sniffed the wind and trotted straight for it.

A few moments later a slim young vixen came out at an easy pace and Chen, his coat foxy with earth and scent, followed her. She led him back down the field, for she meant to shake him off, cross the lane, lead her pursuer on until he was outdistanced, and return home. Her yellow eyes were alert, and below, running along in the shelter of the hedge, she saw the hunted fox, and he saw her. He was not bent on love-making, only on saving the handsome brush, growing heavier now, though still held out of the mud. He saw her cross the field and saw a small yellow shape follow. He considered the pair, stopped to listen, then left his shelter, made straight across the field, with a sidelong glance at the road, saw with satisfaction that a thick clump of beeches stood between him and the rise where enemies were stationed, made use of his best pace, and crossed the trail of the two animals just where the soft grass was firmest, mixing his failing scent with theirs. Then he bolted for the hedge, crawled into the dry drain beside it, and waited, the red rag of his tongue hanging out. Hounds were straining over the field behind and men were riding close to them, scanning the slope that led to the Spinneys.

Chen was breathing hard and the vixen was drawing away from him. She was twice his size and had no fear. She crossed the lane and then, for the fun of the thing, led on, toward a wooded park. Chen followed.

THE KILL

Something had gone wrong. Haphazard and Miracle, leading the pack, checked. Feathering their sterns, they seemed to be going round in circles, whimpering, Miracle plaintive, Haphazard spiteful, Harpsicord evidently at a loss and looking to his bolder companions in his difficulty.

"Some cur dog or other!" growled Tom. "Hark to Miracle." For the bitch, less keen for blood than the more savage Haphazard and more anxious to please, had taken up the line of the vixen, and was travelling, muzzle down, across the road.

"Headed!" grunted Tom. "Hark to Miracle. Hark on, my beauties." Tom waved the sceptics forward.

"We'll never kill in Blachett's," complained someone. It was rarely that a hunted fox took this line. The village, the railway, and a park preserved for pheasants lay on the other side of the lane.

Hounds and field obeyed the master. For once Tom was in error. Miracle was his favourite hound and he trusted her. Only Haphazard, unnoticed, worried over the patch of turf where the tangle of mixed scents had not been sorted to his satisfaction.

Tassy watched him, and Harpsicord, the faithful, padded along at his side.

So it happened that the hunted fox, believing the way clear, hearing the horn fainter in the distance, ventured out, and Tassy viewed him as he trotted toward the slope leading to the Spinneys. She put her hands to her lips and sent the view halloo ringing, hoping to reach Tom. Haphazard raised his head at her call and saw his prey escaping over a rise, with half a mile still to travel to safety. The race began. No need to study the scent now. Haphazard's head went up. He raced for it.

Tassy found Maurice and Nurse Jonsen at her side. The three followed, Jennifer J. keeping well ahead of her stable-mates.

It was a question of speed, but the fox was rested and refreshed. He looked back once. Only two hounds, and they had the hardest part of the hill to travel. But the distance between them and his brush diminished with every stride. If the worst came to the worst he would turn and make them remember him before he died. Almost he was ready to try it. But prudence prevailed. He laboured on. He would take the first earth that came and trust to its depth and security.

The vixen, followed by Chen, had thought better of her plan when she heard Miracle's voice and knew that she was being hunted. She doubled back toward the Spinneys, and Chen saw her as she crossed a ride and turned back too, close to her again.

He was lying panting at the mouth of the earth and seeing the points of fire which were the eyes of the young vixen glaring at him from the darkness, when the hunted fox reached it, with Haphazard and Harpsicord close behind. There was no time to bolt. The fox had strength to punish this enemy at least, and with a yap of rage, thwarted of his safe refuge, he fastened his teeth in the small dog's shoulder before Haphazard, aiming true, caught at his loins. The jaws of the fox loosened and Chen turned on his assailant, his own blood flowing.

Tassy leapt down. "Chen!" she cried. Ignoring her own danger, she lifted the little dog, now so weak that he could not resist. "Maurice, your handkerchief. Chen—oh, Chen!"

In that moment, his earthy eyes dim, Chen understood his dreams.

Maurice helped Tassy to remount. Then he gave the little dog to her and she rolled him in her skirt.

"I'll take him to Harridge, the vet in Medbury. He'll save him if he can. Don't come with me. I can carry him like this." Tassy rode away. She knew the shortest way, through the field below, to the lane, past Saul's farm, and on to the highroad. Chen understood and lay still, wrapped in her skirt, and Jenn, puzzled and frightened at first by the smell of blood, quieted down and trotted steadily under Tassy's warning hand.

"Poor Chen, not you too! Oh, not you! Quiet, old boy. Keep still." Saving Chen seemed the most important thing in the world. "Please God, let Harridge be in!" prayed Tassy with conviction.

He was in and did not stop to ask questions, but took the dog from her and carried him into the surgery. Tassy waited, people looking at her curiously as she passed. In five minutes a boy came out to say: "Mr. Harridge says he thinks he can save the little feller. He's lost a lot of blood. Will you just leave 'im, miss. How did it happen?"

"It was the hunted fox. He attacked Chen. Ask Mr. Harridge to phone the Grange later and tell us how he is. Can you wash my skirt?" She looked at the stained cloth and felt faint, suddenly.

The boy brought out a bucket of steaming water and a sponge and was engaged in scrubbing the stiff material when a small open car swerved round the corner at unusual speed, slowed down abruptly, and stopped a few yards beyond them.

Captain Stair jumped out.

"We want the hunt, Tassy," he said abruptly.

She told them what she knew.

Stair hesitated.

"Tassy, if you can find Brade, will you give him a message? It is urgent." He tore a leaf from his note-book, wrote something on it, folded it, and gave it to her. "Don't show it to anyone, but ride your best and get it to him if you can. A lot may depend on it. We'll take the car to Medwick. They may cross the bridge there. Can I depend on you?"

"Can't you tell me, Captain Stair?"

"No time. Only do what I say." He joined the Inspector, who was waiting stolidly in the car, took the wheel, and drove away.

Tassy tucked the note into her pocket, gathered up the reins, and followed. She left the road at a farmyard gate just beyond the turn and made for the Marsh, thinking in terms of the hunt map. Hounds would be on the opposite side of the river hunting down toward it probably. That meant she would have to cross the stream at the only negotiable place between here and Medwick. The Marsh was treacherous ground, planted with osier-beds.

She had to ride through the hamlet of Brackdown on her way. In the yard of the inn she noticed a car with a low racing body. She thought it an odd place for such a car and then forgot it as she opened the gate and galloped downhill, in a diagonal line, to meet the Med where it flowed through a field, reclaimed from the Marsh. The river made a boundary-line between a big farm and the osier-beds.

Captain Stair had passed on his excitement to her. He had said that the message was urgent. She did not doubt that it was, nor that something had happened that might clear up the mystery darkening their lives.

She listened for the horn or for the voices of hounds, but heard only the smooth thud of her horse's feet under her, and the sighing of the falling wind. Far distant, a train was puffing out of the station at Medwick. She was alone, and some of the spring had gone from Jenn's gallop, but she went on steadily and jumped a flight of rails with precision and a flick of her tail. You could not beat Jenn's pride.

A mist from the river crept forward to meet the mare and her rider. If hounds ran into the osiers, Tom would stop them. She pulled Jenn up and stood, her face to the wind, listening. Yes, it came again, sweetened by distance, hardly more than a thin quaver carried on a passing breeze, hounds acknowledging the scent. Tassy rode toward the signal, and presently she heard the horn. They were coming her way. She pressed Jenn on, over a staked and bound fence, into the field that sloped down to the river.

"Now, Jenn." She concentrated, thinking the mare's thoughts as she rode. The going was heavier than she had expected. She was asking a great deal of her mount at the end of a long day.

Cattle had fouled the bank since Tassy had ridden that way last. She moved along slowly, looking for a better take off. As she turned she saw a rider making toward her or the opposite side. It was Maurice. She recognized the Pirate's shape and action. He was on the right side of the stream and could take the message to Brade, and it would save Jenn a leap Tassy would rather not give her tonight, tired as she was. Besides, if she fell, there would be a delay in getting the message to Brade.

She put her hands to her lips and called: "Maurice!" He seemed to be heading for the lane which would take him round to Brackdown. Why, she wondered suddenly. I was not his way home.

He heard her, hesitated, and then turned the Pirate's head her way. They faced each other on opposite sides of the stream.

"I've a message from Captain Stair for Mr. Brade," Tassy said. "Can you find him?"

"What is the message?"

"It's written down. I haven't read it. I'm not keen to put Jenn across the stream here. The take-off's bad and the landing worse; she may give herself a fall. Will you take it?"

"Is it so important? The hunt will be over in half an hour and you can pick them up at Medwick."

"It is urgent. Captain Stair must have wanted Mr. Brade to have it before the field breaks up. If you won't do it, I must."

"Ride up to the foot bridge and I'll take it."

They cantered along until they reached a plank bridge thrown over the marsh and water wide enough for pedestrians but not for horsemen. Here Maurice dismounted, tied the Pirate to a tree, and crossed the stream. Tassy handed him the note.

He unfolded and read it. Then he looked up. He glanced backward over his shoulder and then up toward Brackdown.

"Get down," he said to Tassy.

"Why?"

"Get down."

He meant it. He had a hand on Jenn's bridle and another on Tassy's arm. The branches of the tree seemed webbed with rising mist as if a net were closing in on them. There was not a sound. Even the wind was silent. The stream flowed slow and deep.

Maurice's hand went from Tassy's arm to her waist and swung round so that her knees were forced out of the pommels and she slid off into his arms as Jenn veered nervously away. He flung Tassy aside, seized the mare's neck, and scrambled into the saddle. Before Tassy could find her feet he was galloping away, bending low to avoid the branches, and was gone.

"Maurice," she called, "Maurice, Maurice!" There was no answer. But she could hear hounds now, perhaps a mile away, racing down toward Medwick. Was Maurice mad? Brade would never get that message now.

Was Maurice mad, mad, mad? Red-hot suspicion flared in Tassy's mind. She gathered up her skirt, ran across the foot bridge and unloosened the Pirate, mounted him, and galloped upstream. She had to get him over and follow Maurice. "You can do it if you like," she told the horse, her teeth set. Her skirt was rolled on the saddle in front of her. She did not stop to shorten the stirrups. She found a place which seemed to offer a chance of success, gave the Pirate room, and rode for it, crouching forward in the saddle.

It was not the Pirate who made that leap, but the fierce will that fired his rider. Down the two lines of leather to the corners of his mouth the message travelled. His sides were caught in a hold that kept him straight. He never thought of refusing. Into his single brain darted just one idea—the far side of that water which he must reach or die. He was a powerful beast, lacking only the extra brilliance of the thoroughbred and he excelled himself under Tassy's hand. They were over, and on in Jenn's track, so close that Tassy could see Maurice riding at a fence, a grotesque figure astride the side-saddle. "He'll be off," thought Tassy, but though he lost his balance as Jenn landed he regained his seat and rode on, while Tassy—the stirrups flying out of reach—followed him over the knots and tangles of the barrier. He was riding almost exactly as she had come and they would reach Brackdown in five minutes. She thought of the car she had seen there. Was that what he wanted? She must stop him somehow. She had never trusted Maurice and now he was trying to get away.

Already the horizon was moving up closer. Night was coming, the early night of winter. Tassy did not ask herself how she, single-handed, was to deal with Maurice. She rode on. Firmer going now. "Good horse," she whispered in the Pirate's twitching ear. "Good horse. We'll never catch Jenn, but we're moving. He'll have trouble with that gate. My God, he's going to jump it, and Jenn just about done."

The Pirate, fired by excitement, laid himself down to the turf in strong strides. Tassy could see Jenn rise at the five-barred gate, clear it, swerve, and gallop on, her reins trailing. She had unseated her unwelcome rider at last. She made for home.

Maurice picked himself up and ran, his short legs and long body taking the pace awkwardly. But the yard of the Cock and Spur was near now, and the headlights of the racer sprang out. The car moved to meet him as he turned the corner and the Pirate came through the gate behind.

He tore open the door of the car.

"Drive like hell," he shouted to the person at the wheel as he jumped on to the step. The car made a dash at the corner just as Tassy reached it. The Pirate crouched. The car stopped to avoid the horse. "Drive on, damn you!" cried Maurice, half in the car, half out.

"No! On second thoughts I think we won't," said Simon Brade. "Tassy, if you'll just go in and phone to Medwick, I believe Captain Stair and the Inspector will join us here. It's quite all right. Maurice won't leave me. You see, he wasn't expecting me to be here. He expected someone else and I didn't think he'd like it, so I borrowed the Inspector's gun."

CHAPTER 27

MAURICE, in an armchair by the fire in the studio, sat shapelessly, his face blank of expression. Every now and again his long, helpless hand went out, folded around the glass on the table beside him, and brought it to his lips. Nurse Jonsen watched him.

"And no one will tell me what's happened or what it's all about, and I had such a good day in the garden, and everyone hunting just as usual and all the Weleven furniture back again, though there is a scratch on the Chippendale chair," Lady Charlotte complained.

Tassy and Tom stood side by side. Tom's face was wooden over his bewilderment. Tassy was waiting, braced for what was coming. Stephen walked up and down. "How long do they mean to keep us waiting?" he demanded, looking at his watch.

Jerrold came into the room.

"Maurice," he said abruptly, "would you like to talk to me alone before Stair and the Inspector see you?" Maurice looked at him without replying.

"I think you ought to be warned that you will have to answer a grave charge."

"What is it?"

"Shall I tell you now, with everyone here?"

"Why not?"

Tom stepped forward. "You'd better tell us. The thing is preposterous. No one here will believe anything against Maurice, and one of us may be able to prove that we are right."

"Murder is preposterous, Tom. I must ask you to listen without interruption. Litton, sit down, over there. I am speaking as a friend of the family, and I've guaranteed that no one will leave the house for the present. In any case it is watched." He glanced at the dark window. "Maurice, you knew I was with your father for nearly an hour on the evening he died. He asked me to promise to keep the subject of our conversation secret unless the facts should come out in some other way. In that case I was to use my own judgment. I was so careful to keep my promise that I typed over all the notes I made on the case, for fear that some chance word might give Brade the clue. This led, indirectly, to helping him in his investigation, for Rachel destroyed part of my note-book, not knowing that I had kept a copy of the interview we had with her. It was obvious that she had done so to conceal evidence, and eventually Brade found out what it was."

"Will you tell me what they have against me?" asked Maurice, scarcely moving, his voice inert as his body.

"There was a case against you from the first. You wished to marry. Your father opposed it. More than that, he could stop it, by telling Miss Lofield the facts about the taint in your mother's family. Your father told me this, asked me if he was right, and I said he was."

"He didn't know of my engagement."

"On the contrary, he did. The servants knew, and something Braythorpe said made him suspicious. It was not difficult to find out then."

"Is that all?"

"No. You were responsible for launching the *Active Sentinel* and worked against your father's policy in secret. You had been paid to do this, and he knew that too."

"Is that the story? I have another to tell."

"Brade told me you'd say that. Don't tell us now. You must get advice before you speak. But Brade has a theory that you saw Rachel on the night of the murder, transferred your own treachery to your father, and warned her that if you were forced into a defensive position you would make your accusations public. He thinks that explains her attitude and that she was shielding you, for the time being, to protect your father's reputation."

Maurice asked: "Why did Stair send that message to Brade today?"

"Because he had found out that you meant to leave the country by air tonight. Now I've told you everything, I have promised to send for the others."

"I can prove that it was my father who was mixed up with intrigue against the League. I hold letters that will make it clear," Maurice muttered.

"You had better not rely on that, Maurice. Those letters were addressed to your father. They were actually intended for you. Long ago he had told Braythorpe to take to you the letters your mother wrote to him, to save him the distress of dealing with them. You made use of this arrangement to carry on a correspondence with those you served abroad. It put you in a strong position, since you would always hold apparent proof of his guilt. But you did not know that he became so suspicious that he examined these letters before you handled them and had collected the details of the scheme to pass on to our secret service. He would have given Rachel the material that evening if he had not died."

Tom broke the uncomprehending silence. "You're implying that Maurice had a hand in his father's death. It is outrageous. Mother—Nurse—you saw Maurice in the studio there at that writing-table all the time! You know he wasn't out of the room. Why don't you say so?"

"Well," said Simon Brade, getting up from the table and walking toward them, "I know I'm smaller than Maurice, but no one saw me, and I've been sitting here for five minutes."

Tom stared. They all stared. Tom stuttered: "Tass, why did you hang your skirt over that chair!" Tassy's riding skirt was spread out across the back of the great armchair. Stiff as boards, it stretched to either side of the carved back, making a perfect screen.

"Mr. Brade told me to," Tassy answered. "You see, Tom, Rachel hung her skirt there to dry that night. It is such a big chair and the skirt is so stiff it screens the writing-table."

"It was all there in Jerry's notes," Brade remarked. "Mrs. Norbury said: 'I got up once to speak to Maurice and to feel of my skirt, drying on a chair by the radiator.' It's a little thing and no one seems to have noticed it."

"But," Tom stammered, "Mother—Nurse—"

Nurse Jonsen spoke up. "Of course, I remember now. Mrs. Norbury must have moved the chair when she got up to speak to Maurice. He was visible before, but after that he might have been screened. We were having an argument, and I don't suppose anyone looked around after that started. He could have gone out and come in by the window without being seen if he had stooped."

"And he didn't like the drift of the conversation at all," Brade added. "It was the first he had heard of Mr. Prentice being so anxious to talk to Mrs. Norbury that night, though he knew he had asked her to come and see him. She stressed the fact that he wanted to see her about something of more than usual importance and he guessed it was the very thing he could not afford to have her know."

For the first time Maurice roused. He got up, stared at the great chair. "Rachel's skirt. I never thought of that," he said. Stair and Pennleaf came in at the window.

"Are you satisfied, Captain Stair?" asked Brade.

"I am. I didn't believe you, but I do now. If you could come in by that window and sit there at the table for five minutes unnoticed, Maurice Prentice could have gone out and come in again without being seen."

Pennleaf, red and embarrassed, stepped forward.

"Wait a minute." Brade raised his hand. "There was something else in the notes Mrs. Norbury destroyed. In fact, there are two things, and I don't believe Mrs. Norbury herself realized that they were of any importance. I think she tore them out with the rest because she wanted to destroy the record of the whole interview, to lessen the chance of our remembering the detail she had to suppress." He turned to Stair.

"Before you accuse Maurice of being in the room when his father died you must remember that when Chen began to bark Maurice Prentice had been here with the others for several minutes at least. Why?"

"That's a minor problem, I should say."

"You've got to account for it somehow. The theory is that Maurice left this room, let himself in by the front door with his latch-key, went to his father, and left his father's room by the garden door, afraid of meeting someone in the hall or passage—that he let Chen in as he went out, not seeing the dog, perhaps, or not being quick enough to shut him out. Chen barked—either at the fire, which must have started already, as it had spread so far when we got there, or at the body, or to give warning of danger. He would not have waited five minutes in a burning room before giving the alarm. Why did he?"

"Nurse," said Jerrold quietly, "are you certain he was not barking when you opened the door?"

Jerrold was standing behind the sofa where Nurse Jon-. sen was seated. She turned to him. "Why—yes—" she began. Then she stopped, her lips drawn into an ugly grin. Standing in the doorway was a tall woman, handsome and haggard, who said:

"You sent for me, Mr. Brade?"

"Yes," said Brade. "Will you please tell these gentlemen who you are?"

"My name is Selma Jonsen. I am Swedish by birth and a nurse and masseuse by profession."

"Can you identify this lady?" Brade walked to the sofa and laid a hand on the shoulder of the tall woman with the convulsed face and flaming hair.

"That," said the stranger, "is the Princess Velbesco—Mrs. Selford Prentice. She paid me to take her place in the nursing home. I had done the same thing for her before. I was sorry for her and it was the only way she found to have a few weeks' freedom. In the home they knew me as the Princess, and her as the nurse. She had nursed for two years during the war and was able to play the part."

Maurice stared. Elena Prentice had drawn composure about her once more, and now she laughed. "Your mother, Maurice. You did not know that. It's a pity our plan to fly away together miscarried. I would have told you then."

They stared at each other.

"My mother!" Maurice said, stupidly. "A spy!"

"A Princess of a royal house," she corrected him, "bent on restoring her own. Why not?"

"My God!" Stephen Litton crumpled up before them. "I might have guessed."

Lady Charlotte spoke for the first time. "It can't be Elena," she said reasonably. "Selford must have known her —even after thirty years."

Stair said: "Of course he must. It is absurd."

"Of course," Brade agreed, "but then, I expect he did know. Didn't he, Mrs. Prentice?"

She stood looking at Brade, her eyes narrowed, and answered him. There was no sign of fear in her manner or her voice. Her confidence was unexpected, disconcerting.

"He did not know me at first. Thirty years is a long time —the thirty years between seventeen and forty-seven. But at last he guessed. I meant to tell him in any case, as soon as I had won his affection. He let me stay on. We were both Catholics and I persuaded him to believe that I was a penitent. I begged to be allowed to prove it and then, perhaps, when I had, remain here with my husband and son where I belonged. He said he would give me the chance. My husband was in love with me still. That is why he would never trust himself to see me."

"You used your opportunity to corrupt his son and yours?" Jerrold asked.

"Do you call it corrupting him? If my family should be restored to power, Maurice is the only one of his generation descended in direct line from the last reigning Prince. I wished him to work with us. There are other mothers today with the same secret hope. You do not think it unnatural?"

Brade turned to Stair.

"Which of these two killed Mr. Prentice?" he asked. "They had the same reason. He had discovered their plot. The burned letter was an exposure of it. He meant to trust it to Mrs. Norbury. There would have been arrests all over Europe, and Mrs. Prentice would have gone to prison. She tried to kill her husband once thirty years ago. Did she do it on Friday, November 9th? Or did Maurice do it? Which?"

"Tom did it," Maurice said desperately. "I swear before God I've believed all along he did."

"But you didn't want anyone else to think so. If he had been tried, other disclosures would have been inevitable. Was that it, Maurice?" Jerrold asked.

Stair, the confident, was angry in his confusion. Pennleaf waited. "Which are you going to arrest? And in either case how do you account for Chen barking when he did?" Brade insisted. "What are you going to do?"

Elena Prentice turned to Tom. "Confess," she said. "Why do you wish to delay the inevitable? Tell us the truth, or let me tell it for you." She faced the others. "There is only one reasonable explanation, and Maurice knows what that is. Tom upstairs, prepared for his bath and then full of his own grievance, went to his uncle's room. They quarrelled. Tom burned the letters. Selford tried to save them and then he struggled to reach the bell in Tom's hand to call for help. Tom pushed him, not meaning to injure him, expecting him to fall back into his chair. Instead of that he fell against the fender with great force. The newspapers on the floor were alight. Tom realized his own position and did not dare to call for help. Then he remembered Chen. He let him in, knowing he would give the alarm and trusting for a moment's delay, long enough to get up the stairs and appear to be on his way to his bath. Remember—Tom did not answer when

Molly Hegan knocked on his door at six twenty. Chen was not barking then! Tom was in his uncle's room."

"There is just one thing wrong with that theory, Mrs. Prentice," Brade remarked.

"What is that?"

"Your own testimony. You were halfway down the passage when you heard Chen bark. At that moment Tom, having let Chen in, would be crossing the hall or letting himself out of his uncle's room. You would have seen him."

"I did see him," Elena Prentice said. "My reasons for keeping this a secret were those Dr. Jerrold ascribed to Maurice a moment ago."

"I always thought Tom did it," Captain Stair exclaimed. "And Mrs. Prentice's theory accounts for the dog."

"Does it?" Brade asked. "I've got quite good eyesight, and I was walking along the passage above at the same moment she was coming down the one below. I arrived on the upper landing when she called for help. If she had seen Tom in the hall I should have seen him on the stairs. As it was, I saw him come out of his bedroom door."

"You are lying, Mr. Brade."

CHAPTER 28

"'WELL, Brade, we are waiting," Jerrold said.

Captain Stair sat moodily at the desk in the library, Jerrold opposite him, and Pennleaf, observant, on a stiff chair by the typewriter. Brade stood by the mantelpiece, rolling cigarettes.

"It's there in your notes at that interview, Jerry. You can read the truth for yourself."

"I wish you'd be less mysterious, Mr. Brade," Stair protested angrily. "I'm tired of it. We've three suspects and the case against each one of them seems to be weakened by the timing of the dog's bark— How did you find out Mrs. Prentice's identity, by the way?"

"Quite simple. The rosary in her room suggested the idea first. It wasn't in character. Swedish nurses are seldom Roman Catholics. If they are, they are converted ones, or so I'm told, and we should all have known it. When we found out that she was in the house through a sort of plot to act for Mrs. Selford Prentice, I thought it worth while having a look at the patient in Austria. A Swedish nurse with a rosary—a Near Eastern R. C. Princess with a Protestant Bible, the short nails of a nurse, and a strong objection to hearing that Nurse Jonsen might be accused of murder, tended to make me think my guess was a good one. When I was sure, I wrote to her and told her to come to England and gave her my reasons. Have a cigarette?"

"Well, Brade, we're still waiting."

"Don't you see I want the Captain to find out for himself! He's read those notes. So has Pennleaf, so have you."

"I can't see anything to account for Chen not barking at once, or any clue to the criminal except the part about the chair. That I give you credit for," Stair admitted.

"Then"—Brade shrugged his shoulders—"read this." He took up the typed sheets, marked a paragraph, and handed it to Stair. It read:

"But she seems to be a good nurse."
"Yes. She seemed to be. She is very strong. . . . She has good hands too. I noticed how quickly and cleverly she bandaged Maurice's hand. . . ."

"But what in the name of all common sense has that got to do with Chen?"

"Tell them, Jerry."

"Brade, I simply don't know. I'm sure that woman is guilty, but I don't understand what you mean."

"You've forgotten the handkerchief," said Brade, wearily. "I always told you that we'd never know the truth till we'd explained that—why it was lying where it was and what it had been used for."

"You mean—"

Pennleaf almost shouted: "She tied up the dog's head in it. He couldn't bark till he worked it off!"

Brade said reproachfully: "Oh, Jerry!"

Jerrold nodded slowly. "I see. But couldn't Tom or Maurice have done the same?"

"I don't think so. Maurice was too clumsy and his own hand was out of action. It had to be done quickly and efficiently. Mrs. Prentice was the only one who knew just how to go about it. She did it so well that it took the dog at least ten minutes to get it off. And there's one more thing. It was she who picked up the handkerchief from the floor and smoothed it out. If I hadn't been there, who would have thought of noticing it? There's a regrettable indifference to little things in this world."

"And why couldn't Tom have done it?" asked Stair. "He was used to handling animals. He had good hands."

Brade sighed. "Either Mrs. Prentice spoke the truth and is innocent or she's lying and guilty," he said with forced patience. "If she spoke the truth, she saw Tom in

the hall at the moment Chen began to bark. Now, he had
to let Chen in, shut the door, draw the curtains, and leave
the room, and Chen would have been barking then. But
her story is that she saw Tom and heard the dog at the
same moment. Impossible. The other alternative is that
Tom muzzled the dog. If he had done that a moment
before, Chen would not have worked it off so soon. And, in
any case, if she spoke the truth I should have seen Tom
on the stairs and not coming out of his own room. I set a
trap for her when I suggested that she would have seen
Tom if her theory was right. She fell into it, as you heard.
Do have a cigarette!"

"Well, Jerry," said Brade when Stair and Pennleaf
had gone, "I hope you haven't missed the point."

"There seem to be a good many points. I might have
missed one or two."

Brade stood white and silent, his tobacco-pouch
squeezed in his hand.

"The real point is my San Ts'ai," he said slowly. "But
for that porcelain fish I should never have been in the
house on Friday 9th. You brought me. My coming
alarmed Mrs. Prentice. It was the first definite hint that
her husband suspected her of other motives than she had
disclosed to him in entering his house by strategy. You
see, Lady Charlotte talked about the case of Came, and
Mrs. Prentice took alarm, thinking Prentice had sent for
us because he had detected her real business in the
house. Because she was alarmed she went to his room to
find out what he meant to tell Mrs. Norbury. She saw the
written exposure of the plot and killed him. But for that
bit of porcelain the tragedy might never have happened
and but for it I should not have been here to find Out the
truth. Yet you laugh at me when I say that there is fate
in porcelain. Chen knew."

CHAPTER 29

THE court-room at the Old Bailey was filled with silent people. Rows of barristers, their wigs moving this way and that on heads of varying shapes and sizes, their black robes quenching the light, made a barricade against the hysterical attention of the spectators behind them. In the dock, vast and unsuitable, more like the architecture of a massive organ-loft than anything Tassy could think of, Elena Prentice sat, impassive, and the jury below on her left lifted ordinary faces toward the Judge, dominating the court opposite the prisoner.

"Why doesn't he sit in the big chair in the middle?" The question repeated itself stupidly in Tassy's head as the trial went on.

"Will you make the experiment, Mr. Brade?"

Braythorpe was coming in, carrying Chen. Tassy could see the faces behind the dock lean nearer. All the witnesses who had given their testimony were there, Molly Hegan dressed in an incredible shade of blue, Bernie Langrove looking like a thin, sharpened, unmanicured, lesser Greta Garbo—a resemblance no one had ever seemed to remark. Maurice was not there. Who was the dark man, so respectable, in the new suit? The postman, of course.

Braythorpe, directed by Brade, placed Chen on a huge table below the jury box. Papers were cleared to make room for the dog. Now Brade was opening a handkerchief. He spoke to Chen, patted him. Then he said to the jury: "I have tried this experiment before. First I wrapped the handkerchief, folded, around the dog's muzzle, like this," he showed them what he meant and Chen with one shake of his head and a push with his paws removed it. He wriggled around Brade's hand, seeming to regard the proceedings with interest. "After many attempts it occurred to me to try another method." Brade swiftly covered the little dog's whole head with the opened handkerchief and deftly folded the edges round the collar, tucking them in securely. Then he took his hands away.

Chen stood there, his head swathed in the linen. He seemed to be waiting for Brade to remove the handkerchief. When no help came, he shook his head impatiently without effect. He waited again. The complete silence, with all these people breathing into it, was new to Chen. He crouched and tried to work off the linen muzzle with his paws, but the twisted edges held. Then he started down the table rubbing his head against the wood. The clerks and reporters hurriedly made a path for him, and Braythorpe put out a hand to catch him if he fell. "Cruel, I call it," murmured someone behind Tassy. But Tassy knew that Chen was not anxious or distressed. He liked Brade. He knew that Braythorpe was there. He seemed to understand the part he had to play.

In the oppressive silence he worked back and forth along the table, first rubbing his muzzle on it, then using his paws. The Judge was studying his watch. Once or twice Chen rested, seeming to ask if the game was not over. Then he began to work again. He had loosened the folds, but it seemed he would never rid himself of the envelope shutting him in. Now, however, he found more purchase for his paws in the slightly bagging pouch over his nose. He was angry, growling softly for the first time. One paw over the other he worked at the linen. The twisted ends tightened around the collar as he pulled at them. Would he never free himself? It seemed to Tassy hours since that ghastly silence fell on the crowded, overheated room.

Suddenly from the chair in the dock came a strangled sound of laughter. The Princess was laughing. A wardress stepped to her side with a glass of water. Chen stopped, rigid. A strangled sound came from his throat. He began to fight the stout linen. He pushed, laying his head on one side, flat on the table, pushed and pushed with one paw. The white folds moved, an end was free.

Chen worked at it, growling and whining. It gave. He shook his head free. Then he ran three or four stiff dancing steps forward, looking up at the prisoner in the dock, treading on the linen as he went, and barked frantically like a dog gone mad.

The Judge laid down his watch. "Twelve minutes," he said, unheard, as Braythorpe took Chen in his arms and carried him away.

Maurice Prentice, himself under the shadow of trial for a political offence, heard the verdict of his mother's guilt with indifference. It was chiefly through the testimony of Jerrold and Brade that he had escaped being tried as an accomplice in the murder of his father. He knew this.

He was glad that he was innocent, but not proud of it. Secretly he knew he would never be guilty of such a crime. Secretly he admired his mother because she was. His egoistic and stupid optimism was reasserting itself. He went back to the book he was reading. He read: "Morality is a menagerie; it assumes that iron bars may be more useful than freedom. . . . The moral man is not a better man; he is rather a weaker member of the species."

"Guilty."

Jerrold said the word, laying a hand on Brade's shoulder. Brade himself had left the court while the jury was considering the verdict.

"But insane?" pleaded Brade.

"No, Simon, she wasn't insane. She used drugs and drink for her purpose, to blunt her sensibilities and strengthen her fiendish will. I could have got the verdict you wanted—if I had lied in the witness-stand. "Well, I didn't. If ever a woman deserved to suffer the full penalty, she is the one."

Brade, shaken and sick, shivered. "Jerry, I gave her my best stem vase and she keeps it where she can look at it all the time."

"You're a fool," Jerrold said gently. "I suppose I shall laugh at you again some day, but just now I don't feel like laughing. You're coming home with me tonight."

Tom and Tassy drove home together. They did not talk very much. Spring was hesitating on the hillsides, putting a tentative footstep here and there, but they did not see her as she passed.

Braythorpe said as he took Tom's coat: "Her ladyship's in the garden. I shouldn't disturb her, sir."

Tassy and Tom looked at each other, hesitating.

"Somehow, there doesn't seem to be anything to do," remarked Tom. "Funny, isn't it, Tass, when there's really such a lot?" He looked so helpless and lost that she rallied. "I'm going to have a boiling hot bath and go to sleep. You can turn on the tap for me, Tom."

He brightened. "All right, I will."

She went to the room at the top of the stairs and found a dressing-gown, shaking off her clothes. Tired. So tired that the light hurt. All these weeks she had worked to help Lady Charlotte and Tom, acting for them. Answering questions, interviewing solicitors, managing servants, writing letters, and bracing Tom to keep up his work with hounds. In these months Simon Brade had been her friend. It was he who took on his own shoulders the duty of visiting Elena Prentice.

"How can you!" cried Tassy.

Brade answered the question with a troubled smile.

"Because I'm sorry for her," he apologized. "It seems to me very sad to start out to be a superman and end by becoming a prisoner. Considerably worse than dying. I like my San Ts'ai better smashed than cracked."

"What do you talk about?"

"Well, I'm educating her." Brade waved a hand. "Really she has a very good memory, and she likes beautiful things."

Tassy thought of all this as she undressed. That woman shut up, thinking! There would be an appeal from the sentence. Mrs. Prentice's lawyers would try to get her off on the grounds of insanity, but Tassy hoped they would not succeed.

Tom knocked on the door. "Look out for the water, Tass. It's boiling hot," he said. There was a pause; then she heard his voice again. "By George, Tass, that's what Molly Hegan said to me that day, when she knocked on the door."

"Oh, Tom, what?"

"She said: 'Look out for the water, sir, it's boiling.' If I'd remembered that sooner it would have proved I was in my room—but it doesn't matter now."

"Oh, Tom, how exactly like you—to do everything too late!" She was smiling.

While she was gathering together her towels and sponges he came to the door again and called.

"Tass."

"Yes?"

"I've thought of something else. I don't want to leave everything till too late."

"What is it, Tom? I want my bath."

"Well, it's only—do you think you could marry me?" Tassy laid her cheek against the door, in silence. "Tass, is it too late?"

She shook her head, forgetting that he could not see her. "Tass, what are you doing?"

"I'm—crying," said Tassy with dignity.

"Because you can't marry me, now? Don't cry, Tass. I say, open the door."

"Do go away, Tom."

"But will you?"

"You're in an awful hurry all of a sudden. I'm going to have my bath. I'm too—tired—to marry anybody till I've had a good sleep."

"Well," said Tom, "I'll wait till you wake up." And he did.

Resurrected Press books in A. E. Fielding's
***The Chief Inspector Pointer Mystery* Series**

RESURRECTED PRESS BOOKS IN ELAINE HAMILTON'S *INSPECTOR REYNOLDS OF SCOTLAND YARD* SERIES

The Casino Mystery (1936)
Murder Before Tuesday   (1937)

MYSTERIES FROM THE JAMES "BONNIE" DUNDEE
MYSTERY SERIES BY ANNE AUSTIN

The Black Pigeon
The Avenging Parrot
Murder Backstairs
Murder at Bridge
One Drop of Blood
Murdered, But Not Dead

**Like us on Facebook to stay up-to-date on
all of our latest releases:
http://www.facebook.com/ResurrectedPress**

AVAILABLE FROM RESURRECTED PRESS!

BRITISH WOMEN OF MYSTERY
Three Novels Penned by
Women of the Golden Age of Mysteries

Three Full Length Novels in One!

- **Whose Body by Dorothy L. Sayers**
- **The Westminster Mystery by Elaine Hamilton**
- **The Clifford Affair by A. E. Fielding**

Prior to World War I, detective fiction in Britain was largely a male preserve, but in the period between the wars—an era that has been called the Golden Age of British Mysteries—women authors in Britain not only embraced the genre, but came to dominate it. Authors such as Sayers, Allingham, Marsh not to mention the great Agatha Christie topped the best sellers lists, but there were numerous other women writers working to satisfy the public's demand for mystery fiction. Unfortunately, many of these authors are virtually unknown today. This volume brings together the first mystery novel of one of the best known of these writers, Dorothy L. Sayers' Whose Body?, along with novels by two of the lesser known women of the period, Elaine Hamilton's The Westminster Mystery and A. E. Fielding's The Clifford Affair, in the hopes that it will serve as an introduction to the British Women of Mystery.

- The Conundrum of the Golf Links by Percy James Brebner
- The Silkworms of Florence by Clifford Ashdown
- The Gateway of the Monster by William Hope Hodgson
- The Affair at the Semiramis Hotel by A. E. W. Mason
- The Affair of the Avalanche Bicycle & Tyre Co., LTD by Arthur Morrison

RESURRECTED PRESS CLASSIC MYSTERY CATALOGUE

Journeys into Mystery
Travel and Mystery in a More Elegant Time

The Edwardian Detectives
Literary Sleuths of the Edwardian Era

Gems of Mystery
Lost Jewels from a More Elegant Age

E. C. Bentley
Trent's Last Case: The Woman in Black

Ernest Bramah
Max Carrados Resurrected:
The Detective Stories of Max Carrados

Agatha Christie
The Secret Adversary
The Mysterious Affair at Styles

Octavus Roy Cohen
Midnight

Freeman Wills Croft
The Ponson Case
The Pit Prop Syndicate

J. S. Fletcher
The Herapath Property
The Rayner-Slade Amalgamation
The Chestermarke Instinct
The Paradise Mystery
Dead Men's Money

The Middle of Things
Ravensdene Court
Scarhaven Keep
The Orange-Yellow Diamond
The Middle Temple Murder
The Tallyrand Maxim
The Borough Treasurer
In the Mayor's Parlour
The Saftey Pin

R. Austin Freeman
*The Mystery of 31 New Inn from the Dr. Thorndyke
Series*
*John Thorndyke's Cases from the Dr. Thorndyke
Series*
The Red Thumb Mark from The Dr. Thorndyke Series
The Eye of Osiris from The Dr. Thorndyke Series
A Silent Witness from the Dr. John Thorndyke Series
The Cat's Eye from the Dr. John Thorndyke Series
*Helen Vardon's Confession: A Dr. John Thorndyke
Story*
As a Thief in the Night: A Dr. John Thorndyke Story
*Mr. Pottermack's Oversight: A Dr. John Thorndyke
Story*
*Dr. Thorndyke Intervenes: A Dr. John Thorndyke
Story*
The Singing Bone: The Adventures of Dr. Thorndyke
The Stoneware Monkey: A Dr. John Thorndyke Story
*The Great Portrait Mystery, and Other Stories: A
Collection of Dr. John Thorndyke and Other Stories*
The Penrose Mystery: A Dr. John Thorndyke Story
The Uttermost Farthing: A Savant's Vendetta

Arthur Griffiths
The Passenger From Calais
The Rome Express

Fergus Hume
The Mystery of a Hansom Cab
The Green Mummy
The Silent House
The Secret Passage

Edgar Jepson
The Loudwater Mystery

A. E. W. Mason
At the Villa Rose

A. A. Milne
The Red House Mystery
Baroness Emma Orczy
The Old Man in the Corner

Edgar Allan Poe
The Detective Stories of Edgar Allan Poe

Arthur J. Rees
The Hampstead Mystery
The Shrieking Pit
The Hand In The Dark
The Moon Rock
The Mystery of the Downs

Mary Roberts Rinehart
Sight Unseen and The Confession

Dorothy L. Sayers
Whose Body?

Sir William Magnay
The Hunt Ball Mystery

Mabel and Paul Thorne
The Sheridan Road Mystery

Louis Tracy
The Strange Case of Mortimer Fenley
The Albert Gate Mystery
The Bartlett Mystery
The Postmaster's Daughter
The House of Peril
The Sandling Case: What Would You Have Done?
Charles Edmonds Walk
The Paternoster Ruby

John R. Watson
The Mystery of the Downs
The Hampstead Mystery

Edgar Wallace
The Daffodil Mystery
The Crimson Circle

Carolyn Wells
Vicky Van
The Man Who Fell Through the Earth
In the Onyx Lobby
Raspberry Jam
The Clue
The Room with the Tassels
The Vanishing of Betty Varian
The Mystery Girl
The White Alley
The Curved Blades
Anybody but Anne
The Bride of a Moment
Faulkner's Folly
The Diamond Pin
The Gold Bag
The Mystery of the Sycamore
The Come Back

Raoul Whitfield
Death in a Bowl

And much more!
Visit ResurrectedPress.com
for our complete catalogue

About Resurrected Press

A division of Intrepid Ink, LLC, Resurrected Press is dedicated to bringing high quality, vintage books back into publication. See our entire catalogue and find out more at www.ResurrectedPress.com.

About Intrepid Ink, LLC

Intrepid Ink, LLC provides full publishing services to authors of fiction and non-fiction books, eBooks and websites. From editing to formatting, from publishing to marketing, Intrepid Ink gets your creative works into the hands of the people who want to read them. Find out more at www.IntrepidInk.com.